The Bridge

The Bridge

SM TOVEY

Matador
9 Priory Business Park,
Wistow Road, Kibworth Beauchamp,
Leicestershire. LE8 0RX
Tel: 0116 279 2299
Email: books@troubador.co.uk
Web: www.troubador.co.uk/matador
Twitter: @matadorbooks

ISBN 978 1800462 892

British Library Cataloguing in Publication Data.
A catalogue record for this book is available from the British Library.

Printed and bound in Great Britain by 4edge Limited
Typeset in 11pt Minion Pro by Troubador Publishing Ltd, Leicester, UK

Matador is an imprint of Troubador Publishing Ltd

Thank you to family and friends, past and present, for sharing part of your life with me, creating memories that still mean something to me, no matter how long or brief our time together.

PART ONE

PROLOGUE

Dear Michele,

People keep telling me to write you a letter, it's in all the advice literature, although who writes letters these days, surely they should update it to 'write an email'?

Anyway, here goes...

If I close my eyes I can go back to the moment I met you, during our first week at secondary school. I actually heard you before seeing you – I'll never forget that sound – and I looked round for the source and found you lying in the middle of the school field, headphones on, blissfully singing along at the top of your voice to 'The Whole of the Moon' by The Waterboys. You loved that song. I can still smell the freshly cut grass, hear the chatter and laughter as friendships were forged around me, recall how awkward I felt, standing there alone. Not you though, I watched as you gave it your everything, singing the way people did when they thought they were alone, oblivious to the groups of kids around you.

I find myself staying in that memory for hours, at the beginning.

It's comforting, thinking we've got twenty-one years ahead of us. It seemed like a lifetime, yet it passed so quickly.

I've often pondered the path never taken, the alternate life I could be living if I'd made a different choice. If my parents hadn't forced me to sit that stupid exam – which I thoroughly resented at the time. I just wanted to go to the high school up the road like everyone else – I would never have met you, and my life would have been incredibly lonely. I see that now.

You epitomised fun, brightened my world on a daily basis with your outbursts of emotion. It came so easily to you. It was freeing to be around. You offered me refuge at your house when mine was toxic during my parent's divorce, allowed me to express emotions I wasn't allowed to at home, to scream and cry, admit my relief. You were always there for me, even during those heartbreaking eighteen months after your dad was diagnosed, as we watched that once strong, vivacious man, who'd never missed a day of work in his life, slowly fade away in front of us until he was unrecognisable. Although for me, it was more heartbreaking watching how it gradually etched away at you, especially when you moved in with me and Mum towards the end. I never told you, but I heard you, you know, sobbing into your pillow each night, knowing what was coming but powerless to stop it – I'll never forget that sound either. It was during those years that our friendship evolved; we fused through the pain and became sisters, family, women. We were inseparable, always there for each other. I guess that's what makes this even harder.

If we weren't together, we were on the phone, mystifying our parents with how we could possibly have anything left to talk

4

about and why it couldn't wait. We were teenagers, nothing could wait. We had such a sense of urgency back then, didn't we, in a rush to get on and live our lives? Yet now I find myself wishing I could rewind time.

Remember when we watched Superman with Adam, that scene where he flies around the world spinning it backwards, turning back time? You can't imagine how many times I've wished I could do that, go back to that Thursday evening. Maybe if I'd stayed, if I was there, I could have saved you.

Was that truly the last time, that sunny Thursday evening in July? If only I'd known that as we walked down your hall to your front door, as we quickly thought of things we'd forgotten to tell each other, like we always did even though we'd been chatting for hours, as we giggled and waved goodbye. I play it over and over in my mind in slow motion, me closing your gate, you standing in the doorway, I look up, we both smile, still giggling from our conversation, 'Drive safe,' you say – you always said it – I wave as I say that one tiny word, 'Bye.' I climb into my car, turning and waving as you close the front door. It was something we'd done a thousand times, how could we have ever predicted it would be our final goodbye? I replay our conversation, desperately clinging onto every word spoken, wondering what I should have told you, what I would have told you if I'd known it was the last time I would ever speak to you. You knew what was coming with your dad, had a chance to say what you needed to, a chance to say goodbye, to hold him, to let him know he was loved. I hope you knew, Michele, I hope you knew how much you were loved, are still loved, how that day in July has changed our lives forever. I miss you so much. This pain you've left is overwhelming. Is this how you felt back then? This deep, gut-wrenching, physical pain that leaves you in a

5

constant state of nausea. I've never experienced anything like this. I thought I knew hurt, but that was timid compared to this. This feels like I'm being stabbed repeatedly, the sharp blade being twisted inside me, dipped in salt to burn, to take my breath away. There's a hollowness too, a void that runs from my constricted throat to the pit of my stomach. Is this how you felt when your dad died?

I spend my days closing my eyes and picturing you, to feel close to you, to pretend you're still here. My brain thinks you're away on holiday and due back any day now. It can't compute the truth. My world will never be the same without you in it, it's a very different place without you, a sad and lonely place. A place I don't recognise.

I'm going to stop now as I am once again in pieces. I've never cried so much in my life. The world's become a blur. I can see you wagging your finger at me, reprimanding me for being sad – you still have the power to make me smile through my tears. Oh, I miss you. We all miss you. I'll take care of Adam for you, that's something I never needed to say to you out loud, I know you know I'll always be there for him. I'll make sure he lives a full life, that he finds happiness, that this doesn't define him, just like losing a parent so young didn't define you.

Even though we can't see you or hold you, you'll be with us every day. You'll never be far.

Goodbye, Michele. Thank you for filling my life with laughter, for always being there for me, for being the sister I never had, and always had. You made my world better every day.

I'll never forget you, I promise.

Alex x

1

SUNDAY

'You're not going to jump, are you?'

The English voice jolted me from my thoughts. Was he asking me?

I glanced to my right to see who the voice belonged to. He was standing a few metres away, casually leaning against the bridge and watching me, concern on his face.

'No,' I answered, distracted, as I rested my arms on the ledge of this beautiful Roman stone bridge, almost a thousand miles away from home. 'Life's too much of a gift,' I muttered, looking down, my head so full and pounding it felt like it'd explode at any moment.

I'd been a mixture of sadness and anger all day. Well, since it happened if I'm being honest. I wasn't sure at any given moment which one was going to win out. In this moment, it was sadness.

I took a deep breath and looked around at the mismatched buildings, yellows, pinks and creams sliced up by the river I was standing over. Nothing here was new. Verona was an old city, filled with history; some of it Michele's. I pictured her in the photograph, standing in this very spot, laughing and carefree, unaware of what fate had in store for her only three years later. I placed my palm against the stone, closing my eyes and imagining myself covering her handprint, desperate to feel close to her again. But the warmth of my hand against the coldness of the stone only brought back the memory of the last time I had touched her hand, the final time I would ever touch her hand or indeed ever see Michele again; cold, stiff and lifeless. My pulse quickened as the familiar soaring pain struck inside and tears rushed to the backs of my eyes, threatening to burst the dam I now spent my days rebuilding. It was exhausting. I closed my eyes tighter, trying to erase that memory of her that haunted my dreams every night, and resurfaced every day, creeping up on me when I least expected it, making me retreat to the nearest place I could find to be alone.

I jolted back to the present as he appeared beside me, his arm delicately pressed up against mine, his touch warm. He mimicked my stance, looking down at the water rushing below. Then I felt his eyes on me and glanced across, meeting his gaze as he removed his 1950s sunglasses to reveal intense brown eyes.

'I'm Max,' he said, offering me his right hand to shake.

As he smiled, his eyes sparkled, his face softened and the lines on his forehead were replaced by laughter lines that ran from the sides of his nose to the edge of his lips.

'I'm Alexandra, but everyone calls me Alex.' I put my hand out, my English cordiality taking over.

'Everyone except your mum, I'm guessing.'

I nodded. How did he know? Do all mothers refuse to shorten their children's names? I pictured my mum years ago answering the phone to a boy I'd liked who'd asked for Alex. She'd told him no one of that name lived there and hung up. I'd been devastated. He'd assumed I'd given him the wrong number. I never saw him again.

I don't know if it was the familiarity of another English person in this foreign place, or the way Max gently squeezed my hand, lingering a little too long for a handshake. Or the way his eyes smiled and held mine like they could somehow see inside my mind. But something about him calmed me and made me feel at ease for the first time since the news had hit me all those weeks ago.

We both leant against the bridge, looking out at the view. It really was magnificent. I could see why it had captivated Michele.

'You want to talk about it?' Max asked.

Talk about it? How did he know? Of course, I could never hide when I'd been crying, had always envied people who could. I actually welcomed sudden amnesia. Having no memory would mean having no pain. But that would also mean having no memory of Michele. I couldn't imagine my future without her, but at least I had my memories of the last twenty-one years, even if they were painful right now.

Did I want to talk about it? Or did I want to run away and hide? That had always appealed to me. I remember being on holiday years ago, driving around France with my then-boyfriend. We were visiting a small village when I suddenly had this urge to disappear, to start again. There was nothing wrong, being there simply made me crave a new life. I didn't of course, I went back to his little blue Peugeot, somehow read the map wrong and got us completely lost, but since that day I've often wondered what it would be like to start again, disappear to a completely different

9

place and reinvent myself where no one knows me. I remember reading about the guitarist of a famous band who had mysteriously disappeared. He was presumed dead but they never found his body. I always thought he was still alive somewhere, starting over, living a new life. I don't know why I found it so attractive. That ship sailed for me long ago though. A distant fantasy, now I'm in my early thirties with a career, a mortgage, and Adam of course. There's no way I could disappear from his life too, not now.

I could feel Max searching my face, waiting patiently for a response. I kept my eyes fixed ahead as I began to speak.

'I needed to escape, be somewhere peaceful for a while. It's been a...'

I paused, focusing on the view before me, shaking my head free of flashbacks as I tried to come up with a suitable word to describe this shitty, fucking awful, heart-wrenching, tragic–

'... tough day.'

It was all I could manage out loud if I was to remain composed and halt the eruption of tears that was still threatening. How were there any tears left? How hadn't the river below me washed them all away?

As I turned and met Max's gaze, I noticed sadness in his eyes. It was as if he had studied me and somehow recognised exactly what I was feeling, my loss reflecting back at me.

He turned away, breaking eye contact, staring out at the piece of Verona before us, his mind travelling elsewhere, momentarily leaving a vacant body beside me. I couldn't help but see myself in his distracted state as I wondered where exactly he had gone.

After a few moments he broke the silence, gesturing out at the view as he spoke.

'It is lovely here, you've picked a nice spot, but it doesn't come close to my favourite place.'

I noticed that he pronounced a slight 'sh' sound in his esses, like Sean Connery, and it made me smile, catching myself in the moment and struggling to remember the last time I had smiled, naturally anyway. There'd been a lot of fake smiling and 'putting on a brave face' these past weeks. It still amazed me how through all of this torture, both Adam and I had managed to shake people's hands and smile as each one told us how very sorry they were, like they were somehow responsible for Michele's death, when all we really wanted to do was curl up in a ball and cry.

'Would you like me to take you?' Max asked, turning, his eyes meeting mine. 'It's the most tranquil place in all of Verona.'

His eyebrows were raised and those creases appeared at the sides of his mouth again as he smiled, making his eyes sparkle. He had the kindest smile I had ever seen.

'Yes.' I found myself nodding, captivated by his hypnotic eyes that seemed to know exactly what I needed, and desperately wanting to remain in the moment, the ease it brought. The idea of wandering around a foreign city with the handsome stranger standing before me suddenly felt like the most natural thing in the world. In some crazy way, it felt as if Michele were here watching. Like she had followed me out of the restaurant to check I was all right and seeing that I wasn't, had sent him to me, my guardian angel. Not that I believed in all that.

We wandered through a maze of ancient, narrow streets in silence but I didn't feel any pressure to fill it. It was an easy silence. The kind you have with someone you've known for years. Like when Michele and I used to go on our weekend hikes. Well, sometimes we were quiet because we couldn't climb uphill, breathe and chat

11

at the same time, but mostly we were simply enjoying the beauty around us. Then there it was again, boom, that unbearable punch in the gut. You don't realise how many times a person pops into your thoughts each day, how often you actually think about them, until they're gone. Then the regrets begin, and the guilt for every moment you could have spent with them but for one reason or another chose not to, because you stupidly assumed there would always be a tomorrow. I couldn't help but remember all the times I'd made excuses or been too tired to join her at whatever class was her flavour of the month. Right now, I would have given anything to be in a Pilates class next to her. Anything.

'You can talk about it if you want to. Or not,' Max offered, as if sensing my pain.

I knew by the way he said it that if I chose not to, he wouldn't press me, which somehow made me want to tell him. It felt easy talking to him, a stranger.

I closed my eyes, thinking back to earlier, then began.

'The bridge where we were, I scattered my best friend's ashes off it earlier. Although best friend doesn't begin to describe... we were more like sisters.' I paused to steady my breathing; I didn't want to fall apart.

'She came here a few years ago on holiday, fell in love with the place. She always used to say if she died she wanted her ashes scattering off that bridge, that she'd finally get some bloody peace and quiet.'

The last part made me smile as her voice replayed in my mind as clearly as if she were standing there, telling us herself.

'It always made me laugh when she used to say it, "some bloody peace and quiet." Thing is, you never actually think you'll ever have to do it.'

My smile faded as the reality of the situation hit me again.

I was suddenly back at Michele's house. The memory as vivid as yesterday. She had returned from a weekend break in Verona and was showing me the photographs from her trip over a bottle of red wine. The guy she was dating had taken her for her birthday. I remember teasing her because she sounded more in love with Verona than with him. Turns out she was; they broke up a few months later. When she got to the zillion pictures she'd taken of the antique stone bridge and the view from every angle possible, she gushed about how beautiful it was, how it had survived centuries despite so much change in the world around it, and the feeling of calm that had washed over her while standing there. It had quite an effect on her. That's when she said it. She took my wine glass out of my hand and placed it on the wooden coffee table. I remember how she looked at me so seriously I thought she was going to share some terrible news. She simply made me promise that if she died before me, I would take her ashes and scatter them off that bridge. Both imagining ourselves as grey old ladies with Zimmer frames. Then she added the line that always cracked me up, 'I'll finally get some bloody peace and quiet.' I promised. We laughed. Never for one second imagining it could become our reality so soon.

It still didn't seem real. Even on the flight over, yesterday evening. Even as I'd met her mum and the others who'd travelled to honour Michele's final wishes and pay their last respects – I hated this recent terminology, *last*, *final*, each one delivering a soaring ache. Even as I'd watched her ashes float away earlier.

We had the funeral ten days after it happened, which I was told would bring me closure. It hadn't. This though had required more organisation and had been looming over me, filling me with dread. The final act. It was strange flying abroad but not feeling excited, not looking forward to the final destination. People were either flying home tomorrow or moving on to another destination in Italy, but I wanted to get to know this place that had captured my friend's heart, that she had chosen as her 'final' resting place. I'd booked to stay the week, planning on walking, reading and drinking lots of wine. I was hoping being here would somehow make me feel close to her again or offer this 'closure' I'd heard so much about.

I'd made sure to stay in a different hotel to everyone else though, knowing I would crave space. I'd always felt comfortable being alone, easily filling my days, never getting bored, but this was different, this was a *need* to be alone. The only person I could bear was Adam. Every time I looked at him I saw Michele, in his eyes, the same nose, her thin top lip, which she had always hated on herself and used lip liner to make look bigger, but it suited Adam. He didn't want to come and I fought on his behalf as relatives said he would regret it. We knew better because we knew all his mum would care about was that he was all right, that he knew how much she adored and loved him, which Michele showed him every day she was alive. He was in no doubt about that.

'Were you alone when you scattered them?' Max asked, pulling me from my thoughts as we walked.

To be honest, that would've made the whole thing easier. I could have let myself surrender to the surge of emotions inside. Instead, as those around me sobbed, I stood, stoic, a single tear escaping down my left cheek, hidden by my oversized sunglasses.

'No. Lots of people came. Friends from the school where she

14

taught, some family, and her mum. The most heartbreaking was her mum.'

The pain inside intensified as I remembered watching a mother say goodbye to her only child. Grabbing onto me as she sobbed that it was the wrong order.

'She kept on saying that the parent is supposed to die first. She's right. As much as we try not to think about it, at some point in our lives we'll lose our parents. But that's the natural order of things. The way it's meant to be. Not this. This is wrong.'

I had desperately tried to offer strength to the woman who had bandaged my eleven year-old hand after a fall. Who had listened to my teenage ramblings when I'd phoned upset after a break-up and Michele hadn't been home. Who had held my hair as I threw up on my twenty-first birthday. Easing my embarrassment by telling me a story that she had once been eating grapes and cheese and drank too much red wine and as she was violently sick a whole grape had popped out of her nose. To this day I don't know if it had actually happened or if she'd made it up to make me feel better. I desperately wanted to make her feel better but it was an impossible task. How could a world without Michele ever feel better?

I gave the tears building in my eyes time to clear, focusing on the trees lining the road, allowing their gentle rustling to calm me before recounting this awful day out loud.

'Afterwards, we all went to a restaurant, though no one was hungry. There were photographs of Michele all around and I sat there watching people reminisce and laugh and I know Michele would like that people were sharing happy memories and not sitting around crying but it felt off to me, like we were all gathered there for her birthday or something, but she wasn't there. I found

15

myself looking around for her, searching the room, expecting to see her, the centre of attention, talking and laughing. That's when it hit me. She's really gone. Gone. I'm never going to see her ever again. That's it for her. Time has stopped. She'll stay thirty-two forever. It's really over. There's only a past. No present. No future. She'll never create any new memories. She's had the rest of her life taken from her. But why? Why did *she* have a heart attack? She wasn't even ill. It makes no sense. Everything's so empty without her. She's always been there. I'm lost without her. I miss her so much. It makes no sense. Why her? Why?'

My thoughts were spilling out of my mouth as my pace quickened, my body mimicking how it had felt earlier in the restaurant: my breathing heavy, my eyes filling with tears and my heart pounding. My voice verged on shouting as my brain replayed people's faces appearing in front of me, offering their sound-bites of wisdom.

'And why do people insist on saying stupid clichés that don't help. *It was god's plan.* What god would take a mother from her teenage son? She's been robbed of a future. Her son has to grow up without his mother. He has to face every birthday, every Christmas, every milestone without her. She'll never get to see him finish school or go off to university, or graduate or fall in love. Every time I picture him waking up without her... we just want her back.'

I stopped walking and realised tears were streaming down my face. I was struggling to breathe, sobbing, gasping for air. I closed my eyes and hid behind my hands as I tried to catch my breath and halt the pain. I felt Max wrap his arms around me and hold me. His touch took me by surprise at first but my body instinctively relaxed in his embrace and my breathing slowed.

I wouldn't have blamed him for running away, but instead this complete stranger, who I had just broken down in front of, offered me comfort. Then he started to speak the most sense of anyone I had spoken to since it happened.

'They tell you it helps to talk about her, to keep her memory alive, but she's very much alive in your head, you can't get through five minutes without a million thoughts of her, each one bringing with it a pain like being stabbed in the heart over and over. They tell you it'll get better in time, a pointless thing to say, it hurts like hell and you can't ever imagine it getting better, how can it, you're alone, you miss her, how can that ever feel better? You've been robbed of this incredible person that you love, who had the rest of her life ahead of her, her plans, her dreams. *Your* dreams. It is unfair and of course you feel angry. What makes it worse is that no logical explanation exists. Nothing anyone can ever say will let it make sense, so people offer clichés instead, crap like "God needed another angel in Heaven," or "she lived a full life." The only comfort *that* could possibly offer is if you were allowed to punch the person saying it in the face.'

The last part almost made me smile. It was refreshing to hear such honesty.

Max released his hold and put his hands on my shoulders. Offering a hopeful smile that I noticed didn't reach his eyes, he bluntly told me what my future held.

'It will always hurt, but you somehow learn to live with the pain so it doesn't consume you as much.'

With that, he wrapped his arms around me and held me again. This time I held him back, his words sinking in, loss evident in his voice. He must have lost someone to know this. Who? Just as he had allowed me to share in my own time, I resolved to offer him the same courtesy.

2

SUNDAY

As we released each other, I began to wipe my tear-stained cheeks and apologise, but Max stopped me.

'Don't ever apologise for feeling. You don't have to hide it.'

It was as if I were standing in fog for a moment, unable to see my surroundings. My entire focus was on Max and his compassion towards me, his words sinking in. 'I don't have to hide it.' That was all I'd ever done, my entire life. My parents had rarely shown emotion, always remaining composed in front of others. I'd occasionally heard my mother cry when she thought she was alone. They'd frowned on what they referred to as 'airing your dirty laundry in public' and viewed it as a sign of weakness. Michele was the only person I'd ever been vulnerable in front of, we'd been through so much together. When she died, I naturally fell into the role of being the strong one for Adam and her mum; someone had to be. But standing there, in that moment, it felt freeing to finally allow myself to feel, to let it out, to be the recipient of comfort for a change.

Max searched my face, checking I was all right to carry on before offering a reassuring smile as he took my hand in his and we walked on. I felt calm again and somehow lighter, like some of the load had been lifted. Maybe there was something to the 'problem shared, problem halved' cliché after all. Or maybe it was simply refreshing being with someone who got it, someone I didn't have to fake being strong around.

I felt like I'd been leading a double life these past weeks. Initially it was the shock that had allowed me to hold it together, to be strong for Adam. Then I had to refocus as it was left to me to inform Michele's mother and Ben, then all her friends and work colleagues. An endless list. If only it were somehow permissible to inform everyone by sending a group text, or a Tweet or Facebook status update. That would have saved me having to repeat the words 'Michele is dead,' over and over until they were engraved into my heart, tearing at the muscle and ripping open the arteries, the ache inside overwhelming. It didn't stop there. I'd needed more strength when Michele's mother had begged me to officially identify the body. Me. She couldn't face it. Each night when she closed her eyes she saw Michele's father, but it was always how he'd looked in those final days, that haunting image eroding and replacing how she wanted to remember him. She couldn't face remembering her daughter that way too. She needed to remember Michele joyful and full of life. How could I say no to her, even though internally my entire being was screaming it? Even though as I tried to walk into the morgue, my body fought itself, making moving impossible. The man had to pry my hand from the doorframe it was clinging to and lead me inside to where her body lay. Oh, how I had wanted to turn and run. More strength still as funeral plans were discussed and made. Even more strength each time I saw Adam. To everyone else I was the strong one because they didn't know the truth, I'd kept that hidden; only allowing myself to cry when I was alone, when no one else was privy to it. That's why I was astonished that I had allowed myself to break down in front of this complete stranger. What was it about him that made me feel comfortable enough to do that? What was it about him that calmed me?

I didn't need to understand it, it felt good so I resolved to simply go with it.

I returned to the present, remembering the task at hand. We'd been walking uphill for some time.

'Where exactly are we going?' I asked, turning and looking at Max.

He started to grin and his smiling eyes returned.

'Okay,' he said, playful but serious, 'where I'm taking you isn't exactly open to the public.' Seeing my confused look, he continued, 'Let's just say it's not in the guidebooks.'

We stopped and he gestured towards a gap in an old grey stone wall. I moved closer and looked inside. Ahead of me were gardens with clothes flapping on washing lines and chickens roaming freely. To the right, ancient houses of mismatched grey stones with small shuttered windows and terracotta tiled roofs. I felt like I had stepped back in time. Max gently put his hand on my side and manoeuvred me out of the opening and towards the wall so our bodies were hidden from view. Just two peeking heads that could quickly duck out of sight if anyone appeared. Even though he had removed his hand from my side I could still feel his imprint.

He pointed and lowered his voice. 'We're going to creep through the gardens, climb over that wall at the end and we're there.'

We're going to what? I looked down at my just above the knee, belted black dress and sandals. An outfit I had packed for ash scattering, not scaling walls.

'So just a bit of trespassing and climbing then? You are aware I'm wearing a dress,' I said, sarcastically.

Max smirked and looked me up and down. I caught the way he looked at me. I hadn't been looked at like that in a long time, not since James. I felt a shift in our mood and was unexpectedly filled with a sense of excitement. I recognised myself feeling it and was amazed how this stranger had the capacity to do that on a day like today.

Max took my hand in his, met my eyes and whispered, 'You'll be fine, and I promise it'll be worth it.'

Just like that, I completely believed and trusted him, allowing him to lead me through the gardens. I felt exhilarated by this crazy, spontaneous adventure. It was definitely a welcome distraction from this day. *He* was a welcome distraction. I was very aware of my hand in his.

We were about three-quarters of the way to the wall when a loud squeak and clatter made our heads snap to the right as a wooden door swung open. Max yanked me back into a narrow opening between two of the houses. We stood, squashed into the gap, indents from the mismatched stones in my back and Max facing me, my hand still in his, his other hand resting on my shoulder. I couldn't remember the last time I'd stood this close to a man. I breathed in his scent: coconut and caramel, a heady combination. As I looked up to speak, he moved his forefinger to my lips and I was rooted to the spot, as if an electrical current were holding me in place. My body didn't feel like my own anymore. Max smiled his reassuring smile and I allowed myself to search his face. His deep brown eyes that glistened when he smiled, framed with long eyelashes. His thick eyebrows and short brown hair swept back. He had that 'just got out of bed' look. A small scar next to his eyebrow. His crooked nose that sloped to the right. Those creases that were now running from the sides of his nose and around his smiling lips. The dimple in his chin that became more prominent when he smiled. I felt an urge to trace his face with my fingers, to touch his full lips. I looked up and met his now serious eyes. Burning into mine. My breathing grew shallow and my heart felt like it was going to burst out of my chest as we stood paralysed in the moment.

We were suddenly cast into darkness, causing us to quickly turn our heads. The moment lost.

My eyes adjusted to find the back of a short, plump woman scattering what must have been feed on the ground as chickens came to life around her. Then she was gone and the sunlight once again stretched through the narrow gap that was acting as our hiding place. We heard the clatter and squeak of the door closing and both let out a sigh of relief at not being caught.

'Come on,' Max breathed, his whispered breath dancing on my neck, making my entire body tingle.

He led me back into the gardens, stopping to check the coast was clear before running the rest of the way to the wall.

'Just copy what I do, it's easy,' he prompted, standing on one of the wooden chicken coops and pulling himself up using the top of the wall.

As he reached up, his teeshirt lifted and I found my eyes drawn to the line of flesh above his belted waistband. He sat straddling the wall and reached down to help me up. He had strong arms, defined biceps. I sat on the wall and carefully swung both my legs over, keeping my knees together, trying to maintain my dignity. There was a raised bed on the other side between the trees, which had been cleared. Max jumped first then turned and held out his hands to steady me as I landed, taking my hand in his – which now felt strangely natural – and leading me down to ground level before stopping and standing in front of me, facing me.

'Okay, close your eyes. I promise, nothing bad's going to happen. I just want it to be a surprise.'

I focused on his smiling eyes, offering me reassurance, then closed mine. I felt him cover them with his hand to ensure no peeping. His other hand guided me forwards, then to the right, then back. I felt something touch the back of my legs.

'Can you feel the bench?' he asked, offering me a reassuring hold as I felt the bench with my hand and sat. Max sat beside me. A moment later he took his hand from in front of my eyes and declared, 'Okay, open your eyes.'

I blinked a few times and there it was. *Wow.* He was right. It was magnificent. Well worth the trespassing and climbing. We had a bird's eye view of the entire city. Looking down on terracotta rooftops, splatters of pink, yellow and cream buildings dotted between green trees. The blue river that mirrored the sky, carved up by infinite bridges. It was breathtaking, immediately giving me that sense of perspective and calm I always got when I was somewhere truly beautiful. I sat, breathing it in, peaceful except for the soothing sounds of rustling leaves and birdsong. I was suddenly aware of the tension in my forehead but only because it was falling away. Yes, this was exactly what I went looking for when I left the restaurant earlier. Instead, I'd found myself drawn back to the bridge, to the very spot where Michele had stood, where she still stands in the photograph, where I scattered her ashes.

I looked out at the incredible view before me, certain Michele would love it, and wrapped my arms around myself in an attempt to soothe the pain that thinking about her brought. Max was watching me, reading my reaction.

'Thank you.' I turned to look at him. 'I needed this.'

He gave me a satisfied smile and looked out at the view.

'I've never brought anyone here before. You're the only other person in the world who knows about it.'

'How do you know no one else comes here?' I questioned.

He met my confused gaze. 'Oh, I come here a lot. I'd know. This bench wasn't here,' he said, patting the horizontal plank of wood with tree trunks for legs. 'I made it.' He looked very proud.

'How did you find this place?' I found myself wanting to know more about the extraordinary man sitting beside me.

Max stood and pointed below. In the distance I could just make out a road, mostly hidden by trees and foliage.

'I was down there walking, looked up and thought how peaceful it must be up here. I became fixated on finding it, wandering up different roads and paths until I eventually figured out it had to be over that wall, hidden at the end of those gardens. One day I went for it, snuck in, climbed the wall and found this.' He spread out his arms to reveal the incredible view.

'When was that?' I asked, as we sat back down.

'Six years ago,' he answered. I noticed his expression change and sadness appear in his eyes as they remained focused on the view.

It was clear from his demeanour that he didn't want to be questioned further. I'd sensed earlier that he too had experienced loss. I understood craving somewhere peaceful, the need to be alone. I felt honoured that he would share his intimate place with me, a stranger. Although, oddly, we no longer felt like strangers.

I joined him in looking out at the breathtaking view, soaking it in and enjoying the peace and respite it offered from this chaotic day, and I realised he must live in Verona.

'She would love it here,' I sighed, breaking the silence. 'We used to hike to the tops of hills and sit, looking out for miles, listening to her favourite song. It would put whatever problem we were having into perspective. Make us feel like tiny dots in a universe filled with struggles way bigger than ours. It always worked.' I stopped and shook my head. 'I wish it would now.'

I felt Max cover my hand with his and give it a gentle squeeze, leaving it there holding mine.

'What was the song?' he asked.

For a moment I didn't understand his question I was so caught up in my pain, unsure if I was even speaking out loud.

"Come Home' by One Republic,' I eventually answered. I smiled as I pictured Michele singing her favourite part, the lyrics reminding us to open our eyes to the beauty all around us, and for just that moment, the ugliness in the world would disappear. I looked from the view to Max's eyes. 'I'm guessing you've never heard of it?'

Max grinned as he began to recite the exact lyrics I'd just played in my mind. I was astounded he knew it. I also couldn't ignore the way he looked at me or the way I felt as he brushed his thumb across my hand when he recited the word 'beauty,' as if he were somehow talking about me rather than the view. Even with my tear-stained face and puffy eyes, the way he looked at me made me feel beautiful.

He reached inside his pocket and pulled out a retro iPod, just like mine, sharing his earphones. I secured the bud in my ear and there it was, that melody, that soothing piano, Michele's favourite ballad filling my ear. Max patted his shoulder. I smiled, then accepted his invitation, closing my eyes and resting my head against him, his hand still on mine, enjoying the closeness as One Republic eased my pain, instantly making me feel close to her, like she was somehow there with us, watching over me.

When I opened my eyes, pink and peach streaks had appeared in the sky. I had no idea what time it was. I pictured my watch on the bedside table in the hotel room where I'd left it. What I did know was that I wanted to remember this moment forever.

'I wish I had a camera.' I hadn't packed one because I didn't see this as a holiday.

'What about your phone?'

'Didn't bring it.' I wanted to be cut off from the world. Adam was with Ben, and Michele's mum would be home tomorrow so I knew he was safe. Plus, there was the hotel phone for emergencies.

Max smirked.

'What?' I wasn't sure if he was teasing me.

'It's nice to meet someone else who can live without a mobile phone.'

'Someone else? Why, where's yours?'

'I don't own one.'

'You don't own a mobile phone?'

He shook his head. 'Nope. I don't want to be contactable twenty-four hours a day. Well, people say *contactable*, I say *disturbed*. I don't do all that Social Media rubbish either.'

I couldn't help but giggle. 'You do know you sound ancient.'

Max laughed as he contemplated it. 'Yeah, I guess I do don't I? But anyway, you don't need one.' He leant across and framed the view in front of my eyes with his fingers.

I copied him, looking at the framed image of Verona and closing my eyes to picture it, then looking again until I had it memorised. I turned to Max and framed his gorgeous face, my action making him laugh, his eyes sparkling as they laughed too. He had the most beautiful smile I had ever seen, it was contagious. I wanted to remember him forever, this stranger in a foreign land who had made me feel comforted and safe on this awful day I had been dreading.

As I sat next to Max, watching the colours fade and the sun dip down behind the horizon, I became aware of a sense of dread stirring inside because my time with him was coming to an end. I couldn't help but think how sitting here with him should feel awkward – I hardly knew him after all – but it didn't. There was a connection between us that felt somehow innate. Like he was an old friend I had shared part of my life with, who knew my ways. I found myself not wanting to say goodbye to him. He made me feel contented, something I hadn't felt in quite some time.

I had expected to spend this evening the same way I'd chosen to spend most others since Michele's death – alone. I'd spent numerous evenings at the cinema, using whatever film was playing to escape my reality for a few hours. It was something I'd often done alone, even when I was in a relationship, as it allowed me to fully immerse myself without being disturbed by someone talking in my ear or munching popcorn; I'd never understood why they sold food in cinemas. I was able to cry at the sad parts without having to concern myself with someone else's reaction to my display of emotion. I'd never given going alone a second thought until two women noticed me and asked if I'd like to join them. I knew they were only being kind but their action made me feel uncomfortable and the solitude I enjoyed suddenly feel unnatural, wrong even. Friends had been constantly checking on me and trying to keep me occupied but the few times I had ventured out I'd quickly come up with an excuse to leave early. I had come to realise that I felt more alone *with* people, even with wonderful friends, than when I was actually alone. I'd spent countless hours analysing and wondering if I'd always feel that way, if the void Michele had left would feed my solitude for the rest of my life. I also never knew when the pain was going to strike, so it was safer being alone; I could let myself succumb to it. That was why I was finding this incredibly confusing, why I didn't feel like I had to hide my pain from Max. I had broken down and allowed myself to be vulnerable in front of him. Maybe it was because there were no expectations; he was here today, gone tomorrow. Maybe that was why I'd let him see the real me. There was something more though, an ease between us, being with him was effortless. I was savouring his company.

'So what do you do when you want to forget, not think for a while?' Max asked, breaking my thoughts. 'Besides hiking to find amazing views of course, we've done that.'

His use of 'we' made me smile. I thought for a second but it wasn't a difficult question to answer.

'Music,' I replied. 'Go see a band I love and get lost in every song. Dance and sing along until I lose my voice.'

I thought back to the last time I had felt that way, watching Kodaline. Listening to their first album on repeat for months hadn't prepared me for how incredible they were going to be live. I was mesmerised, dancing and singing along to every song. I had a constant smile on my face throughout the whole gig. Really good gigs have the power to do that, they fill you with a mixture of blissful happiness and satisfaction, allow you to forget there's a world beyond that room, allow you to forget your problems. You could be there alone but never feel lonely, singing in unison with hundreds, sometimes thousands of others just like you as you become part of something bigger, the energy in the room merging into a force so powerful it could lift anyone's spirit. I'd always wanted to bottle that feeling so I could take a sip whenever I needed it. Being here with Max was like taking a sip. Maybe that was why I didn't want our time to end. I wanted an encore.

Max suddenly turned to face me and fired a question at me. 'Name five bands you love that you've seen live. Go.'

My mind raced as I thought back to past gigs. 'Erm, okay, not in chronological order. Kodaline, Imagine Dragons, Muse, R.E.M., Kings of Leon, James, The Stone Roses, The Killers, The Chameleons, Damien Rice but he's not a band.'

'That's ten,' he interrupted, a huge smile spreading across his face.

'There are too many to choose from,' I explained, laughing, before being distracted by the view, which now looked like it had been scattered with fairy lights.

We both looked out at the magical land before us, then back into each other's eyes, now lit by the moonlight.

'Do you need to be anywhere?' Max asked.

I shook my head. 'Not until Friday.'

He stood and held out his hand. 'Then I've got just the place.'

I placed my hand in his, allowing this stranger to lead me off into the night, with no idea where he was taking me

3

SUNDAY

The rumbling of car tyres on cobbled streets accompanied us as we walked down narrow pavements, between romantic shuttered buildings, some grand, others more rustic, the peeling paint only adding to the charm. Ornamental streetlights lit our way, accentuating colourful flowers that draped down from balconies above our heads, their fragrant perfume mixing with wafts of coffee and garlic. I breathed the city in as I walked, about to ask Max where he was taking me when he stopped outside a charming wooden doorway, an oval sign above it reading 'Vita Musicale.' I followed Max as we passed a door on the left and went downstairs towards the thumping bass sound and through some double doors. I stopped to take it in. He was right again, it was the perfect place. We were standing in a basement club, dark enough to blend in on the dance floor. I instantly felt the music take hold, closing my eyes and getting lost in the chorus. I had to stop myself running straight onto the dance floor. This was music from home, music I loved, that I danced nights away to. It was my medicine. It was exactly what I needed. I felt a calmness wash over me, it was like taking a deep breath. This day had taken an entirely unexpected turn. I would never have found such a place if I hadn't met Max.

* * *

I was sixteen when I went to my first nightclub. It was with new friends I'd met at my first job. They were older than me so I had no problem getting in, even though I was underage. That was it, I instantly fell in love with the music and the escape from life it offered. It was simple making new friends with that musical connection. Meeting people as passionate about it as I was, who also adored the feeling of losing yourself on the dance floor as life seemed to peel away. Some of my friends couldn't get that feeling without the aid of drink or even drugs. Not me. Don't get me wrong, I enjoyed a drink but as long as there was good music playing and a few people on the dance floor to blend in with, I was in my element. Music had always been my drug of choice. While others were dressed up, looking cool, standing around to catch the eye of someone they liked the look of, I was flushed and sweaty on the dance floor. Back then, my idea of dressing up was wearing jeans and a fitted teeshirt. I owned one dress for special occasions, a retro black babydoll dress. I used to love that dress. If I wasn't dancing or harassing the DJ to find out what old song they had just played, I was talking to like-minded people about recent gigs they'd been to or albums they'd bought.

I'd often wondered if that was the career path I should have taken, though not on stage, I never stuck with an instrument long enough to master it. I showed little talent in that area despite trying to learn the cello (everyone else at school dropped out and it wasn't economically viable to employ the teacher just for me), saxophone (my playing was likened to a cat being strangled) and acoustic guitar (I couldn't get beyond the painful calluses it caused). I was content with being the listener, feeling that connection to the musician you experienced when their music became part of your soul too. Once I'd tasted that, food and water were no longer sufficient, I also craved the nourishment music provided. Switching on the imaginary jukebox in my mind to find a song from the extensive catalogue, to suit my mood, its role adapting to my changing life, whether celebrating happiness, relieving boredom or seeking empathy and escapism from anger, confusion or heartache. Music allowed me to understand my innermost feelings when words failed me, kept me company, consoled me, offered me confidence, made me euphoric. Whatever my situation, there was always an artist who had experienced exactly what I was feeling in that moment, expressing it so powerfully through their lyrics and arrangements of music that it counselled me through. Music had always been there for me, it had never let me down.

Michele hadn't shared my passion for clubbing. She had a different passion to focus on, getting pregnant with Adam at seventeen. It was quite the scandal. She had been seeing Ben for about a year when one morning she rang my house in a panic. It was early, I was getting ready for work. She told me that the condom had ripped the night before and she had exams all day so please could I go to the clinic in my lunch hour and get the morning-after pill for her. I did as she'd asked, catching the bus in the pouring rain, pretending I was the one having sex the night before. She took it that evening, followed the instructions to the letter, but it didn't work. She hid the pregnancy from everyone except me, and Ben of course, until she was five months pregnant and elastic bands to extend her waistband and baggy jumpers were no longer able to disguise the truth. I could still remember opening the door to her and Ben when they came round after telling her mum. They both stood, sheepish, like chastised children. I'd never seen Ben look so pale.

Michele had recently started using the tale on Adam, now fifteen and showing an interest in girls, saying condoms were only 98% safe and the morning-after pill only 95% successful. I couldn't help but laugh uncontrollably as Adam's face flushed with embarrassment, turning scarlet, shaking his head, hiding behind his hands as he pleaded with me to make her stop. She'd always finish though by telling him how extraordinary he was. How determined he was to be in this world, beating those odds. That with that determination he could conquer anything. I loved the way she saw the world.

* * *

We walked across to the DJ booth where Max introduced me to his friends Luca and Dante. I could hear Max above the music telling Luca I wanted to dance and naming some of the bands I'd named earlier.

Luca turned and hugged me, placing a kiss on each cheek, his greeting taking me by surprise. 'I love you,' he declared with an Italian accent.

'What did I do?' I asked, confused, looking to Max who was laughing.

Luca put his arm around my shoulders. 'You have amazing taste, just like me. You like The Chameleons. Nobody has ever heard of them.' He gave me a huge grin. 'You want to dance to some fantastic music, you have come to the right place.'

Luca was completely different to Max, polar opposites. I could see why they were friends. Max was quiet, thoughtful and intense. There was a nervousness behind his confidence. Luca seemed carefree, outgoing, the centre of attention, which would allow Max to shelter in the background. The way Michele had allowed me to.

Luca looked over, winking and grinning as the increasing tempo of guitars and drumbeats filled the air, the intro to 'Swamp Thing,' my favourite Chameleons song that I have danced to a thousand times. I closed my eyes and let the warm, soothing caress of the music spread throughout my body, slowly reaching the extremities, beckoning me to let go, to dance. I opened my eyes and saw Max watching me. He nodded his head towards the dance floor.

'Go, lose yourself, I'll be here.' He knew exactly what I was thinking.

I quickly kissed him on the cheek – I was thankful for him coming into my life – before making my way onto the dance floor. As I danced, it felt as though I was hearing the song for the first time. It had always amazed me how a song could do that, take on an entirely new meaning, pertinent to your current situation, making lyrics stand out because of what you were feeling or going though. It was suddenly depicting my inner struggle, trying to carry on with life while battling the grief consuming me.

I danced to song after song after song. It was as if Luca had access to my own private collection. Was Michele really somehow watching over me? I thought back to when Michele and I had created the playlist for our joint thirtieth birthday party, how we'd drunkenly sung and danced around her living room like rock stars as we re-discovered songs we hadn't heard in ages; enjoying the song selection process almost as much as the actual party. I was always more theatrical with Michele, she brought me out of my shell, made me feel like I could accomplish anything.

I kept on dancing, the music taking control of my body. I remembered a man from a local club, years ago. He was a bit of a loner and was always the first one on the dance floor, dancing alone as people stood around, pointing and laughing at him, but I was in awe of him, of his bravery, of how contented he looked, swept away in his own internal joy. I understood that look now, his eyes closed, the outside world a distant place, oblivious to those around him. Escapism. Escape.

Luca played 'Family Tree' by Kings of Leon. Its funky 70s sound always made me dance, even if I was standing in the kitchen in my pyjamas. There was something about Kings of Leon's music, I could never pinpoint exactly what it was, the guitars, Caleb's raspy voice, the combination of everything I guess, but it always made me feel sexy. I found myself glancing over at Max, still in the DJ booth. Our eyes connected but instead of feeling self-conscious, time seemed to slow and my surroundings became a blur as Max momentarily became the only other person in the room, in the world.

The intro to 'Not Nineteen Forever' by The Courteeners started, the pounding beat making the dance floor come to life around me. I saw Max and Luca making their way towards me. They joined me, not really dancing, more singing the lyrics to the first verse and chorus *at* each other. It was fun seeing Max in this environment, he clearly loved it as much as I did.

During the instrumental part, Luca began jumping up and down and over to another group of people dancing. Max was laughing hard then turned his attention to me, putting his arm around my waist, catching me unawares. He had lost all his inhibitions; the magic of the dance floor. He began swaying me in time with the music, our eyes once again connected. I steadied my breathing, my body suddenly fully charged. Max began singing the second verse to me, lessening the intensity, and I joined him in singing along. He looked both shocked and impressed that I too knew the words. I gave him a wink and leant back in his arms, both of us laughing. It was a band I had forgotten to name earlier – well he had stopped me at ten.

Luca reappeared, one arm around me and the other around Max, dancing with us, before disappearing again. As the song slowed, Max pulled me in closer and I rested my head on his chest as he softly sang the end of the song, his mouth next to my ear. All of my senses were heightened.

The next song began, breaking the moment. We released our serene hold and Max took my hand, leading me towards the bar. I was parched after all that dancing and a Heineken was very welcome. As we clinked bottles, he tilted his head and raised an eyebrow.

'So, you like The Courteeners then?' He looked impressed.

'You stopped me at ten bands I've seen live or I would've mentioned them earlier.'

'Of course you've seen them live.' He was grinning and shaking his head.

'Just after they released their first album.' I thought back fondly to the gig. 'It was one of those gigs where the crowd knew every word, sang along to every song.'

'I think you may love music even more than I do,' he said, laughing and ushering us towards two bar stools.

We sat down opposite each other, my knees between his. I was aware we had become closer, our touch more intimate yet comfortable. I was also aware how his touch made me feel inside, awakened yet uncertain.

I noticed Luca watching us. 'So how do you know Luca?'

'Our parents are best friends. My mum met his mum at university. We basically grew up together. We spent every summer I can remember in Italy with Luca's family. His parents have this incredible house surrounded by vineyards. And it's got a pool, so you can imagine as a kid I loved coming here.'

Talking about it made him smile. I imagined a young, carefree Max dive bombing into a swimming pool.

'Is that why you moved here, because of Luca?'

The moment the question left my lips I wanted to take it back, seeing how it shattered the happiness on Max's face, the smile in his eyes replaced by loss. I knew not to delve deeper.

'I guess so, yes.' He looked over to where Luca was standing, his smile returning. 'He's a good friend. Though sometimes he feels more like a brother.'

I nodded, thinking about Michele, as I felt the familiar stab inside. Quickly excusing myself, I retreated to the safety of the toilets. I couldn't fall apart in a nightclub, I needed to be alone until the wave passed. I locked the cubicle door and leant against the wall, wrapping my arms around myself in an attempt to offer comfort. Something I had been receiving from this stranger. I didn't have the energy or want to understand or define the feelings I was having for Max, it was simply enough that he was getting me through today. When I finally left the cubicle I caught my reflection in the mirror and reached inside my bag. Powder, mascara, lipstick, hair brush. Reconstruction. That was better.

I left the toilets and noticed a brunette woman talking to Max at the bar where I'd left him. She was animated, flicking her hair and giggling. I felt a pang of jealousy, surprising myself – how was that even possible, I hardly knew him. I hesitated, unsure what to do. I needed to shake the feeling so headed towards the dance floor, but Luca caught my eye and gestured for me to join him in the DJ booth. Dante was on the equipment so Luca and I sat on a table at the back where it was quieter. As we chatted about music, Luca caught me looking over at Max and offered me a reassuring smile.

'It happens all the time,' he said, throwing a glance in Max's direction.

That didn't actually surprise me, although Max didn't seem aware of his own attractiveness.

Luca continued. 'Women see him alone and think he must be, what's the expression Max uses?' He paused, thinking. 'On the pull, that's it.' Luca giggled, then turned serious. 'He's not like that. The attention annoys him. He's quite the loner is Max. I usually rescue him with a song but sometimes it's fun to watch him squirm a bit.'

Luca laughed and pointed to where Max was standing. When I looked again, looked properly, I saw that Max was noticeably uncomfortable, standing there, silent, picking at the label on his Heineken bottle. I felt an urge to go and rescue him.

'I hear you're quite the loner too,' Luca said, distracting me.

Had Max told him about me? I guess he had. Turning up to his friend's club with a complete stranger would have required an explanation. I wondered if Luca knew about Michele, but before I had a chance to ask, Luca spoke again.

'We're not used to seeing him with anyone. I can tell he likes you.' As he said it, he grinned and playfully elbowed me in the arm, making me blush. I laughed and shook my head, feeling extremely young all of a sudden, but Luca sat up straight and looked at me seriously. 'He's relaxed with you. You're good for him. You make his eyes light up again.'

Before I had a chance to stop myself, the question I had been wanting to ask Max but hadn't for fear of the painful memories it might stir came rushing out of my mouth.

'Why did Max move here?'

What Luca said next finally allowed me to make sense of this day and understand this stranger that seemed to have an insight into my soul.

'Max needed to get away after Kate died. His wife.'

The words struck me inside. Max was married? She died? I turned and faced Luca as he continued.

'They met their first day of college. That was it, he was "smitten," he called it. I remember at his stag party, him drunkenly telling me how he knew from the moment he met her that she was his destiny, she was the woman he was going to marry, have a family with, grow old with.'

Luca's eyes fixed on Max. 'They were so happy, we all aspired to find what they had.' He closed his eyes, shaking his head. 'Then she was gone. It was a terrible time. It was so sudden, you know. They were just beginning their lives together.' Luca looked from Max to me, his face despondent.

I stared at Max as I absorbed what Luca had told me. I felt drawn to him. Our time together replayed in my mind and all the pieces fell into place, the things he'd recognised, things he'd said, he knew because he too had experienced loss. Such horrendous, catastrophic loss.

Luca took a deep breath before continuing. 'So Max moved in with me, left England, rebuilt his life here. He's never been back.'

'When did she die?' I asked, already knowing the answer. My mind racing back to sitting on the bench earlier. I'd sensed his sadness when he'd said it, 'six years ago.' He was searching for somewhere peaceful, somewhere like I had been today. As the next thought hit me I felt overwhelmed. He'd never taken anyone there before, but he shared it with me. His loss hit me, joining mine. I wanted to hold him like he'd held me.

Luca shouted something to Dante, pulling me from my thoughts. I was struggling to digest all he had revealed to me. He stood and shrugged his shoulders. 'Maybe I said a little too much. Max doesn't like to talk about it.'

I nodded to confirm I understood.

'Let's rescue him,' Luca suggested in an upbeat tone, instantly changing the energy between us. 'Go dance with him.'

He gestured to where Max was standing.

'But he's not dancing,' I replied, confused.

Luca smiled. 'Oh, he will be.'

As Luca said it, the sound of drums filled the air, the intro to 'It's the End of the World As We Know It (And I Feel Fine)' by R.E.M. I watched as Max put his drink down on the bar, smiled up at Luca and headed for the dance floor, singing along. He looked carefree. He got the same release from music that I did. Luca gave my back a gentle nudge in the right direction but I didn't need it, my eyes were already locked with Max's. It was as if the people on the dance floor parted for each of us as we met in the middle. Max wrapped his arms around my waist, swaying me, smiling into my eyes as he continued to sing along. Seeing him happy, knowing all he'd been through, it gave me hope. At the chorus, I stepped back and applauded, I was impressed, Max knew every word. I'm a fan of R.E.M. and have heard the song hundreds of times but I didn't know the words to the verses, they're fast and lyric-filled. You've got to *want* to know the verses perfectly – study the album sleeve-notes, or take minutes out of your day to find them online. Max took a dramatic bow and started to laugh before pulling me close again, our bodies moving together, our eyes locked, electricity coursing through me. I felt like I had left my body and was hovering above, looking down at these two carefree lovers, dancing close, mesmerised by each other's eyes, happy. I didn't recognise myself. I returned to my body when Max began spinning me under his arm, throwing me out and pulling me in like a rag doll, both of us singing the chorus to each other. I was dizzy and laughing. If I could hit the pause button it would've been right then in that moment.

We stayed dancing as the song changed to 'Demons' by Imagine Dragons. I stepped back and grinned at Max, clasping my heart for affect.

'They're okay,' he teased, wrapping his arms around me. I rested my head on him and closed my eyes, listening to the desperation and sadness in the lyrics while thinking about all Max must have been through, of the demons he must carry deep inside. I remembered what Luca had said, that I made his eyes light up again. Maybe I was helping Max escape his darkness for a few hours too. I held him a little tighter, like he had held me earlier, and enjoyed one of my favourite songs wrapped in his arms. The song I loved loaning us its lyrics for the night.

As we left the dance floor in search of another drink, Max firmly held onto my hand and put his mouth to my ear. 'This time please don't abandon me,' he whispered. I smiled and gave his hand a squeeze.

Being with Max was stirring feelings I didn't know I missed until that very moment. The way he looked at me and held me, the things he said and knew, he made me feel significant and enough. They were starting to dislodge feelings I had buried deep down inside of me, of being unwanted, rejected, unloved, incomplete. I shook the memory of James away as quickly as it arrived. Max was helping me in more ways than he would ever know, even if it was just for tonight.

'Are you glad you came?' Max asked, as we clinked Heineken bottles.

I was speechless for a moment. How could I express to him how much the time we had spent together meant to me? That he had completely saved me on this day I had been dreading. That this was exactly what I'd needed. That he was exactly what I needed.

'Let's just say,' I began, 'I've had this crazy theory all day, not that I believe in all that, but I think Michele sent you.'

We both smiled and he put his arm around me, placing a kiss on the top of my head. I was happy to stay there, until the next song began: 'Missing' by Everything But The Girl, filling my insides with sadness. Unfortunately, the power of a song worked both ways.

The up-tempo dance music seemed to fade into the background as the lyrics began echoing around my brain like a soaring headache, making me picture Michele's house, now empty without her. Then I saw her, standing in the doorway,

43

waving and laughing, the image so vivid, her voice so clear, making the truth impossible to comprehend. Until Michele in the morgue slammed into my mind. The reality sharpening the pain inside. I closed my eyes tighter, fighting the tears, grabbing onto Max's teeshirt. All I could see were endless images of Michele flashing up in quick succession, then me back at her house, alone, trying to sort through her thirty-two years of possessions and failing, sitting on her kitchen floor and falling to pieces. Then the devastation and fear in Adam's eyes that morning, another image that will never leave me. My pulse was pounding throughout my body, matching the drumbeat, as the taste of bile rose in the back of my throat. I didn't know how but I needed this feeling to stop.

Max held my face in his hands, lifting my head so I opened my eyes, meeting his.

'Let's get out of here.' He took my hand and guided me to the exit.

Once again he knew exactly what I needed; he *got it*.

As we made our way out of the club I focused on my hand firmly in Max's, taking controlled deep breaths, forcing myself to concentrate on each step so my mind remained in the present, not allowing it to stray back into the past, until the wave eventually passed.

Once outside, the cool breeze hit me, bringing with it the sudden realisation that I was exhausted. I let out a huge yawn, which Max caught.

'What do you want to do now?' he asked, concern in his voice.

'To be honest, snuggle up and fall asleep watching some old film, dubbed in Italian but so familiar it doesn't matter.' That's what I'd done last night.

Max smiled. 'Where are you staying?'

When I answered, 'The Palazzo Victoria,' his eyebrows raised and eyes widened.

'Fancy,' he teased. 'So do you want to be alone or–'

'No.' I cut off his question. I didn't mean for it to burst out of me but I really didn't want to be alone. The thing I had recently craved, I now dreaded. I wasn't ready to say goodbye to him yet. 'Unless you need to be somewhere,' I added, looking down.

Max put his forefinger under my chin – it felt like he was electrocuting me with his finger, but in a good way – and lifted my head so I was looking at him. His sparkling eyes drawing me in. 'No, I don't need to be anywhere. Plus, I like hanging out with you. I'm game for a bit of snuggling to a cheesy old film.'

I couldn't hide my smile, my relief. As I began walking, Max called out, 'Where are you going?'

I stopped and turned to him. 'To the hotel.'

He started laughing. 'It's this way.' Pointing in the total opposite direction to where I was heading. I caught up to him and he linked me.

I did a quick hop so our steps were in time, both left, both right, walking in unison. Max tried to copy me to get out of the rhythm but he couldn't do it. I showed him again and he kept on trying and failing, making us both giggle at each failed attempt and his confusion as to why he couldn't master something I made look easy. We were completely at ease with one another.

Suddenly the amphitheatre appeared in front of us. I stopped, staring at it in awe.

'You know,' I began, 'R.E.M. played there. Can you imagine how incredible that must have been, in such an amazing venue.' I was shaking my head imagining it.

'It was,' he said.

'Wait. What? You were there?' I was frozen to the spot as a million questions gathered on my lips. Max started to laugh as I tried and failed to get my words out.

'Yes,' he said, 'and yes it was incredible. Luca got tickets and invited me over.' I noticed his face turn serious as he seemed to drift away in a memory. 'In fact that night is one of the reasons I moved here.' He paused. 'You know that thing you said about going to a gig and getting lost in every song? That feeling you get?'

I nodded, looking at him, but he was looking straight ahead at the amphitheatre.

'It was one of those nights and I really needed one of those nights.'

I wanted to defuse the moment. 'Well I wish I'd known Luca then,' I said.

He smiled but his eyes didn't smile along. I could tell he was stranded in a painful memory. I held his hand, offering him comfort as we walked to the hotel.

As we entered the lift, then my hotel room, I couldn't help but think how it should feel awkward, but it didn't. Nothing about spending time with this stranger had felt anything but natural.

'You don't mind if I take a quick shower do you, after all that dancing?' I checked, putting my bag down.

Max shook his head and picked up the TV remote. 'I'll find us something to watch,' he said, bouncing down on top of the bed and pointing the remote control at the huge wall-mounted television in an antique picture frame.

I had no concerns that Max's intentions would stray beyond cuddling to a cheesy old film. He'd been nothing but a perfect gentleman, somehow managing to make me feel safe and comforted on this day I had been dreading. I couldn't deny my attraction to him but I wasn't ready for some impulsive one night stand.

As I stood under the warm water I looked down and slowly traced the horizontal scar across my bikini line, the permanent reminder forever etched into my skin, shaking away the memories that threatened. Instead, I imagined telling Michele over coffee and cake or during one of our hikes, how I'd met a handsome stranger on her favourite bridge, here in her favourite city, the home of Romeo and Juliet. She would love it. She'd been on at me to get myself out there but I didn't want to meet anyone else, to open myself up to being hurt again. I was safer on my own.

As I imagined my conversation with Michele, the pain re-emerged. It stung, knowing I could never actually tell her. I hugged myself until it lightened, then closed my eyes and thanked Michele for finally bringing me here. She was right, there was something magical about Verona.

I came back into the bedroom wearing a white towelling robe to find Max lying on the bed, grinning, his hands behind his head.

'It's not a film but it's old, it's dubbed in Italian and I bet you know it so well that it doesn't matter.' I moved towards the television as he announced, 'Friends re-runs.' Instantly making me smile.

At home these were always on some channel, offering that comfortable familiarity. He was right, I did know them so well that I could probably interpret the lines. He'd done it again, he was the perfect distraction. The ability he had to effortlessly lighten my mood.

'Do you mind if I take a shower?' he asked.

'Go for it,' I replied.

While he showered, I changed into my pyjama bottoms and vest top and got into bed. It was a huge, comfortable bed with one of those fluffy, airy, hotel duvets in pressed white Egyptian cotton. I snuggled up, listening to Rachel and Ross confide in Italian voices that weren't their own, my eyes getting heavy as I watched their lips move in English, and the sound emerge in Italian. Disconnected, but right now, somehow, perfect.

I opened my eyes as Max switched off the television. The room was dark. I must have fallen asleep while he was in the shower. He carefully climbed into bed next to me, placing a delicate kiss on my forehead and we naturally found our position, like we slept cuddling that way every night. My head fitted perfectly into the nook of his neck. My arm resting across his chest. Both of his arms enveloping me. I closed my eyes, listening to his heartbeat. I felt comforted and safe in his arms, like this was exactly where I was meant to be tonight.

4

MONDAY

Despite being in Max's arms, I woke the same way I had every day since it happened. Resuming consciousness, the initial moment of peace, then the memories began to filter in and SLAM. That sickening, uneasy feeling you get when something bad is about to happen but with the force of a category five hurricane, as I remembered...

I jolted up, sitting, holding myself as the pain consumed me like a lead weight within, escaping through my eyes. I must've woken Max as he was sitting beside me, pulling me to him, his arms wrapped around me, offering comfort as I rested my head on his shoulder and steadied my breathing. Then it was over; well the category five part, anyway. It was a cruel trick to play, to offer those initial moments of peace each morning before you remembered.

I sat back, leaning against the headboard of the bed, composing myself as the waking hurricane passed for another day. Max gave me the space I needed. He didn't stroke my leg, or ask if I was okay. He simply allowed me to have a moment. In fact he'd never asked me if I was okay. He was the only person who hadn't. I found it refreshing as that was all I'd heard these past weeks. I knew people meant well but it caused me to fake a lame smile and say yes, when inside I was really screaming *How the fuck can I possibly be okay, she's gone!* It was something Adam and I had agreed on and even though we knew people didn't know what else to say, it drove us crazy.

Max busied himself looking at something. It was my photographs of Michele. I watched as he looked at each one intently. He flicked to the next one and began to laugh. Even without seeing it, I knew exactly which photograph he was looking at.

'Amsterdam,' I offered.

He looked from the photograph to me with a confused look, then held it up. I nodded. Yes, there it was, Michele and me in hysterics in Amsterdam. It made me laugh, it always did, it held that power. I moved to sit next to him, looking down at the wonderful memory and began to tell him the story behind the photograph.

'We were nineteen, met for lunch one day and were complaining about the mundanity of our lives and this crazy idea popped into our heads. Let's go to Amsterdam. So we did, planned a trip. We caught an overnight coach to London, then a tube...' I shuddered at the memory of a creepy guy in the tube station who'd asked us pervy questions. Nothing had happened, we'd quickly moved away from him but looking back, the situation had made us feel like the kids we really were, in need of parental protection, rather than the worldly, know-it-all adults we thought we were. Even though Michele was already a parent herself, she relied heavily on her mum for guidance in those early years.

'Then another coach, a ferry and a train. We were on a very tight budget, it took forever to get there but it was worth it. We partook of the local delicacies, space-cakes we called them. Now, we know we had an amazing time, there's photographic evidence, but our memories were always very foggy. Those space-cakes were good.'

I looked at Max sitting there, listening to my ramblings, smiling back at me, his head tilted to one side, his swept-back hair now falling onto his forehead, his bare chest. I averted my eyes back to the photograph, looking at Michele and transporting myself back to that moment when we were both happy and carefree.

'We had no idea what had made us laugh so hysterically. Although to be honest, we found everything hilarious. We'd never laughed so much in our lives. Trying to figure out why there were two black balls on the pool table while we were stoned made us laugh. Trying to negotiate a spiral staircase made us laugh. And can I just say, a spiral staircase is the worst barrier to put between two stoned girls and the toilet, but they were everywhere. It was like a constant sobriety test and we failed every time.'

I paused, smiling down at the photograph, looking from Michele's beaming face to mine and back again.

'We both loved this photograph,' I sighed, suddenly feeling serious. 'How hysterically happy we were, captured forever. We could never look at it without laughing. Feeling a little bit of what we were feeling in that moment, whatever we were laughing at. This is how she'd want to be remembered. Happy. Always.'

Even now telling Max, Michele was gone but I could still feel it through the sadness, what we'd felt that day, it was still there.

I picked up the photographs, quickly flicking through them, stopping at the one of Michele on the bridge. The bridge where I scattered her ashes, the bridge where I met Max. I was still struggling to make sense of a world without Michele in it. Maybe that was why I'd found myself drawn back to that bridge yesterday, maybe I'd half expected to find her standing there. If only.

I put the photographs back on the bedside table and saw the time. It was already afternoon.

'We slept,' I declared.

'Yeah but we didn't get in until the early hours.'

He looked just as handsome sitting there with disheveled hair and sleep in his eyes as he had yesterday on the bridge.

'You didn't mind me sleeping here, did you?' he checked, his eyes smiling, both of us already knowing the answer.

I shook my head, smiling back. 'Not at all.' I'd felt completely comfortable in his arms.

'So what do you want to do today? I'm at your service. If you want to hang out, that is.'

His words made my smile widen. Another day with Max was exactly what I wanted.

'Don't you have a job?' It hadn't occurred to me until now.

'I work for myself so I'm giving myself the day off,' he answered, leaving it at that.

My eyes were still hot from crying and I wanted to take a shower and wash my hair, which I told him. The lingering thought that I wanted to look nice for him, I kept to myself.

'Okay, you do that and I'll nip out and get us some coffee and pastries.' He got out of bed and reached for his pile of clothes on the chair.

I followed him with my eyes. He was wearing only boxer shorts. He was tall and slim but not skinny, his body had definition, with dark hair scattered across his chest, but I knew that from my head resting there so comfortably all night. Max caught me watching him as he put on his jeans. He held my eyes, that comfortable intensity between us. I was aware that when I looked at him, it wasn't as a friend.

'Well whatever we do,' he said, sniffing his teeshirt as he went to put it on. 'We need to call at mine for a change of clothes; this stinks.'

I jumped up and retrieved my ten year-old Damien Rice teeshirt from the drawer in the closet, throwing it at Max.

'You can borrow that.' It was the only unisex thing I had.

He held it up. Navy, shabby, a hole in the shoulder, 'cheers darlin'' written in white typewriter font across the chest. The material soft. It was my worn-in-comfortable go-to-piece-of-clothing. I took it everywhere with me.

Max gave me a wink. 'Cheers darlin''

'You're very honoured,' I announced. It was a prized possession. No-one had ever worn it besides me. As he put it on and finished dressing I placed my order, a one-shot latte, then headed to the shower, pointing to the room key on the bedside table next to the pile of photographs.

I stood under the hot water and imagined Michele coaxing me to admit Max stirred feelings inside me. She'd always had a way of getting me to open up. I could trust her with anything and everything. She'd offer advice but still support me even if I chose not to take it. That was the unconditional love we shared. True friendship.

It was Michele I'd sought out immediately after the ultrasound. She had offered to go with me but I didn't think it was going to be a big deal. I certainly didn't expect the woman doing it to reveal so much, I thought I would've had to go back to my doctor for the results, but I knew instantly by the 'oh' that came out of her mouth as she looked at the screen that it wasn't good. I bombarded her with questions. She knew I wasn't going to leave until I got my answers. Afterwards, it was Michele who had helped me absorb and process what I'd been told, along with lots of Googling to fully understand it. She allowed me to cry and allayed my deepest fears, no matter how silly they seemed. It turned out they weren't so irrational after all, although even Michele couldn't have predicted they'd come true at the time. She pieced me back together as I inevitably came to terms with the news – it wasn't like I had a choice – then sent me home to tell James.

I looked down and slowly traced the white horizontal scar with my finger, shaking away the accompanying memories of being altered, abandoned, unwanted.

As I went into the bedroom I was greeted by the extremely welcome waft of coffee and a very pleasing smile as Max looked me up and down. 'You look beautiful.'

Without knowing it, it was exactly what I needed to hear. The way he looked at me made me feel beautiful, something I hadn't felt in a long time. He'd made me feel it yesterday when I couldn't have looked my best. At least today I felt more worthy of the compliment.

'Thank you.' I felt my cheeks blush, I'd never been good at accepting a compliment. I sat down on the edge of the bed and devoured breakfast; I hadn't realised how hungry I was.

Max suggested we jump in a taxi to his as he wanted to change clothes. I thought he looked handsome in my teeshirt but I was excited to see where he lived. He explained that after a year of living in Luca's original cramped apartment they'd found a much bigger place, and that Luca's girlfriend also lived there with them now.

I waited in the lounge while Max changed; no one else was home. It was a mixture of old and new, exposed stone walls, plastered in places. Varnished wooden floors. Heavy wooden furniture and two large, lived-in, leather sofas. I had been expecting a more student-looking place but this was grown-up, sophisticated, stylish and very homely. I tried to imagine which parts belonged to who's taste. There were photographs of what looked like Verona on the walls, quite arty shots. I moved around the large room, studying them. I recognised the amphitheatre, the black and white picture captured its grandeur beautifully. There was another photograph, split into four segments, blobs in various bright colours and graffiti written in Italian. I wondered what it said. I studied each segment but couldn't make out what the photographs were of. I turned my attention to the framed photographs on the bookshelf, several of Luca and his girlfriend, Luca and Max, Luca standing with an older couple who I assumed were his mum and dad, and one of a skinny guy with shoulder length hair sitting next to what looked like his mum. I looked closer, it was a younger Max. He looked completely different, lanky and awkward, before he'd developed muscles and grown into his body. I smiled at the boy with long hair and baggy jeans in the photograph who'd turned into such a compassionate and handsome man.

Just as I turned to see Max re-enter the lounge, the front door burst open. Luca appeared through the doorway first. He shouted my name and, looking pleased to see me, enveloped me in a big bear hug before introducing his girlfriend Aria, Dante again, and Dante's girlfriend, Isabella, as kisses and hugs were exchanged.

'Perfect timing, you guys,' Luca declared, putting one arm around me and the other around Max. 'We're just about to head to the beach. A night under the stars. Max, go grab your stuff,' he ordered.

Max looked to me for confirmation, mouthing, 'You want to go?'

The beach. A night under the stars. With Max. A chance to get to know him better and spend time with the people closest to him. No question. Yes. Was I the same person who'd craved being alone?

As I nodded yes, Luca replied for me, 'Of course she does.'

Luca was such an excitable character. A whirlwind of energy. He filled the room, his mood rubbing off on everyone around him. He was good to be around.

'Don't you all have jobs?' I asked.

'We work at the weekend so Monday and Tuesday is our weekend,' Luca explained. 'Now come on, let's get ready people, let's go.'

As Max disappeared back to his room to grab whatever we needed, I sat down on one of the leather sofas. Dante and Isabella headed off, saying they'd meet us there while Luca and Aria busied themselves filling a cool box. Luca had a friendly face, certainly the biggest smile I'd ever seen. He was shorter than Max with dark brown hair and tanned skin. He wore glasses with thick brown frames that suited him perfectly. Aria was pretty in an effortless way, fair skinned, a round face with soft features and long brown hair casually parted in the centre. She was curvy but slim. You could clearly see from their body language that they adored each other.

Aria turned her attention to me, offering to stop by my hotel on the way so I could grab my swim stuff, telling me how beautiful the lake was. I hadn't packed anything like that, the hotel didn't have a pool or spa. As soon as I told Aria she bustled me off to her and Luca's room on the next level, rifling through her drawer and pulling out a black two piece.

'Perfetto. This will fit you. It's clean. Try it on.' She handed it to me, gesturing towards her en-suite bathroom. She was incredibly sweet and accommodating. It fitted fine and the bottoms came up plenty high enough to cover my scar.

I looked in the mirror, relieved I had chosen a summery, above the knee dress and sandals to wear. I felt more appropriately dressed today.

'Keep it on under your dress,' Aria shouted through the door.

When I re-entered the lounge, Max was carrying a duvet, pillows, blankets and a bag to the car.

'I've got you covered,' he winked, gesturing towards all the items in his hands.

It felt good to be taken care of, not having to think or organise. For once, I could simply relax and go with it.

Max and I travelled the forty-five minute journey with Luca and Aria. I sat in the back with Max, watching the scenery flash by, in my own world, listening to the Italian radio station and the three of them converse in a mixture of English and Italian. It was strange hearing Max speak Italian but I guess it made sense; he had lived in Verona for six years. It was a beautiful language, noticeably different to English as the syllables created a constant rhythm, making it almost song-like. Max would look over to check on me every now and then, giving my hand a gentle squeeze but allowing me to drift away with my thoughts. He knew who I was thinking about.

When we arrived, Max and Luca began building a camp fire for later; Luca pounding his chest like a caveman as everyone laughed. Aria created a seating area around it with logs and scatter cushions while I stood on the sand and took it all in. We were in a secluded cove, sheltered and hidden by rocks and trees all around us, the other side of the lake barely visible in the distance straight ahead. Aria was right, the lake was beautiful. The water clear and turquoise, merging into deep blue. There was no one else around, our own private beach. Peaceful, with gulls overhead and the gentle sound of lapping waves. I had always dreamed of living by the water, falling asleep and waking up to the soothing sound of waves.

My peace was interrupted as Dante and Isabella arrived, bringing with them a football soft enough to kick in sandals. I was happy to sit and watch but Luca insisted I play to even out the teams. Me, Luca and Aria versus Max, Dante and Isabella. Luca kicked the ball to me but Max swung his arm around me, picking me up and moving me out of the way so he could get the ball and score, winking at me and grinning as the three of them ran around, celebrating his goal. Aria then tackled Isabella and passed the ball to me but as I ran to meet it, Max came up behind me and wrapped both of his arms around me so I couldn't move, letting Isabella get the ball instead. Both Max and I were giggling hysterically as Luca protested, shouting 'foul.' I didn't stand a chance against Max but I didn't mind one bit. I much preferred his game, his touch. How he made me feel.

Dante and Isabella stripped down to their swim wear and headed into the water.

'You want to swim?' Max asked, appearing beside me.

'I want to float,' I declared. Max gave me a confused look so I continued. 'You know when you lie on your back, fill your lungs to keep you afloat and relax.'

Max shook his head.

'You've never floated before?' I asked, in disbelief.

'Teach me?' he suggested, as he began to undress, lifting his teeshirt to reveal that tease of flesh above his waistband.

I felt self-conscious as I removed my dress, leaving it and my sandals with Max's heap of clothes on the sand. I'd only worn a one-piece bathing suit since the operation but as I looked down at my toned body, I approved. Mind you, I had worked out a lot this past year, more than ever before, to get back to full fitness. I'd found the recovery incredibly frustrating and hated not being able to do everyday tasks. It took a full eight months before I felt like myself and could do what I used to at the gym. Including the symptoms that made me unwell before the operation, it had actually amounted to a full year. I had been desperate to get back in shape, to feel fit and strong again. I'd never been one of those naturally slim girls who could eat anything. I'd learned to like my curves, to eat properly – well most of the time – and to be active. Michele and I often said if we could talk to our younger selves we would reassure them that we weren't anywhere near as fat as we thought we were. Whenever we looked back at photographs of ourselves, we were always flabbergasted by how much slimmer we actually were than how we'd seen ourselves back then.

I joined Max, chest high in the water.

'Show me this floating then.'

I obliged. Lying on my back and gently paddling with my hands to steady myself as I took a deep breath and filled my lungs, then relaxed and looked up at the clear blue sky above me. I repeated the rhythm, paddling on an out breathe, then re-filling my lungs and completely relaxing.

'Okay, lie on your back and I'll support you until you get the hang of it,' I instructed, standing and holding my arms out.

Max lay back in the water as I placed my hands under him to support him. He was a little clumsy at first, but soon mastered it.

I was deeply aware of how I felt, this close to him, how I felt when his eyes met mine.

'How am I doing?' he gently asked, his eyes sparkling like the water around us.

There was something about him, he was like an addiction, I felt myself wanting more.

'Perfetto,' I told him, resuming my floating position beside him, looking up at the sky, holding hands, or rather fingers. That electrical current being exchanged between our fingertips.

'So where did you discover this floating?' Max asked. His eyes were closed, he looked completely relaxed.

I moved between treading water and swimming as I told him all about the summer I'd spent in America after my first year at university.

'My university friends dropped out and I wasn't going to go but Michele encouraged me to. I remember her asking if I wanted to go and my answer being yes. She said, 'so go then, forget everyone else, do it for yourself, don't have regrets.' It was that simple, and I'm glad I did because it ended up being one of the best summers of my life. All I had was my student work visa, a flight to New York with one night at a youth hostel booked, and a job waiting for me on the Boardwalk in Ocean City, Maryland. When I look back it was quite a brave thing to do considering I'd never flown alone before, never been to America before, had no clue how to get from New York to Ocean City, or anywhere to live once I got there but I figured my new bosses wouldn't see me go homeless.'

'Do you often travel alone then?' Max opened his eyes and looked at me.

'No,' I replied, shaking my head.

I suddenly saw myself through Max's eyes and it made me laugh. I must've looked like this confident woman who travelled the world alone. I remembered I used to be confident and adventurous before James and the surgery. I wanted that girl back.

'Weren't you scared, not knowing anyone?'

'I remember feeling awkward at the airport but then I met another girl doing the same as me on the flight over, except she had a job in Atlantic City. As soon as we arrived in New York we locked our stuff away in the youth hostel and went sightseeing. We were so excited. Neither of us had been to New York before. The Statue of Liberty tour was closed though so we decided to stay an extra day, we phoned our bosses and told them a little white lie that we weren't able to catch a Greyhound bus until the following day. We were desperate for twenty-four more hours in

New York City. We hit the bars that night and did the Statue of Liberty tour the following morning. We had such a great time.'

I smiled, thinking back to that wonderful summer.

'What about you, have you been to New York?' I enquired.

Max nodded but seemed to get distracted by a memory. I wondered if he'd visited with Kate. I desperately wanted to ask if the memories were still painful six years on, I wanted that insight for myself. I hated that thinking about Michele brought pain and sadness, the thought of it still feeling that way in years to come was unbearable, but there was no way I was going to pry. I remembered what he'd told me yesterday, that you somehow learn to live with the pain so it doesn't consume you as much.

'So where else have you been?' Max asked. 'I get the sense you like to travel.'

'I do. When I was younger I had a globe as my bedside lamp. Every night I'd spin it, stopping it with my finger, then fall asleep pretending that was where I was going to wake up in the morning. I dreamed of travelling. Always imagining what my life would have been like if I'd been born in a different country, how where you're born shapes your future.'

Max started naming countries, 'Canada?'

'Yes. Vancouver, loved. Calgary, Banff, Lake Louise, The Rockies. I stood on a glacier in the Rockies, that was cool. Oh, and Mistaya Canyon.' I stopped and took a breath at the memory. 'A short hike from the highway and suddenly it opens out to reveal this breathtaking canyon. It's the most beautiful place I've ever been in my entire life.'

'Even better than my favourite place?' Max teased. 'Anywhere else in Canada?'

'Oh, Toronto. I saw Damien Rice there. He's incredible live.'

'You flew to Canada to see Damien Rice perform?' Max raised his eyebrows, looking at me like I was crazy.

'No,' I giggled, 'he was playing while I was there. It was purely coincidence. I'm not made of money.' I thought, then added, 'Otherwise I'd happily fly around the world to gigs.'

Max was laughing. He knew it was true, I probably would.

We carried on naming countries and sharing stories of places we'd visited, swimming back and forth, floating and treading water. I was enjoying getting to know him better.

Max suddenly stopped. 'Anyway, floating,' he reminded me of the original question.

We both laughed. How easily we'd drifted off onto other topics. I could talk to him for hours. Spending time with him was effortless.

'Yes, Ocean City. I made friends with some people I worked with and moved in with them to a house a few blocks from the ocean. Work didn't start until four in the afternoon so we spent our days at the beach. Nearly three months at the beach. I'd never spent quality time like that in the water before and discovered floating by accident, lying on my back looking up at the sky one day. It's easier in salt water but I still do it at the swimming pool whenever I'm there.' I smiled as I pictured a six year-old Adam. 'I remember teaching Adam, he loved it. He thought he had a super-power.'

Max started treading water, facing me. He looked confused. 'Adam?' he inquired. 'Is he your boyfriend?' I noticed him look at my left hand, my empty ring finger.

'No,' I shook my head. 'I don't have a boyfriend.'

For the first time in years, my relationship status filled me with excitement.

'You?' I casually asked, already knowing the answer but enjoying our flirtation.

'No,' Max smirked, 'I definitely don't have a boyfriend.'

He disappeared under the water, reappearing inches from my face, his eyes meeting mine. I had to catch my breath.

'I don't have a girlfriend either. Just in case you were wondering.'

With that he swam off, leaving me with a hard to breathe, tingling feeling like I'd experienced hiding in the gardens yesterday, and dancing in his arms last night, only this time it was even more powerful. A smile spread across my face, I'd missed feeling like this.

We swam back and forth for a while, exchanging glances and smiles before walking along the beach to dry off.

'So who's Adam?' Max enquired again.

'Michele's son. He's fifteen now.'

'Did he come too?'

'No, he didn't want to. The funeral was enough.' I shook the memory away.

'Do you see him much now he's a teenager?'

'Yes. He plays football twice a week, I take him.'

Max was looking at me intently as we walked, wanting to know more about my life.

'It's our thing. Adam plays at a football club where I use the gym. I've always taken him. I work out while he trains. Or on the weekend, while he plays. One of the guys there is my personal trainer.'

'Oh yes,' Max teased.

I shook my head and smiled. 'No, I'm not into those muscly bodybuilder types.'

Max looked down at himself and laughed. 'I guess I'm all right then.' Referring to his own physique.

I took in his body. Yes, Max was exactly my type.

He stopped and faced me, holding both my arms out to the sides while looking me up and down.

'Tell your trainer when you see him, I like his work.'

I felt my cheeks flush and quickly walked on.

Max caught up, walking beside me.

'Are you close to Adam then?'

His question unexpectedly transported me back to that day, bringing with it the feeling of a lead weight slamming into me. I stopped and wrapped my arms around myself, staring out at the water, taking a moment to catch my breath as I remembered Adam's name flashing up on my phone that morning and everything that had followed.

I nodded. 'I was his "who can we call" when it happened.' Tears surged into my eyes.

'I didn't mean to… ' Max started, regret in his voice.

'You didn't,' I reassured him, swallowing the tears away. I placed my hand on his arm. 'It just hits me sometimes.'

Max gently squeezed my hand. We didn't need to say anything further, he knew exactly how I was feeling. Usually when the pain of a memory struck I would retreat to the nearest place I could find to be alone, but being with Max made me not want to be alone anymore.

5

MONDAY

Luca and Aria appeared, shouting for us to join them as they ran into the water.

'We don't have to.'

I looked at Max, concern on his forehead and in his eyes. Those eyes that gave away his every emotion. I adored his protective nature towards me. I watched Luca and Aria, splashing around, playful. Luca had the power to lift anyone's mood. I welcomed a distraction, a jolt back into the present. Michele had sent me here, to this place, to these people. I could hear her as clearly as if she were standing beside me, *Life's too short, enjoy it while you can*. I momentarily closed my eyes and pictured her, desperately wishing she still could.

'It's exactly what I need,' I reassured Max, taking his hand and leading him back into the water.

We teamed up, boys against girls for a game of water volleyball as Dante and Isabella swam over and joined us. Aria was a natural, which allowed me to stand and watch Max, taking in his body, his captivating smile, the way he laughed and joked with Luca and Dante. I got the impression Max, Luca and Dante spent a lot of time together, they knew each other's ways. I craved that with Michele again, how we could tell what the other was thinking and finish each other's sentences like an old married couple.

I caught Max watching me. The way he looked at me filled my stomach with butterflies. The game came to an abrupt end as Aria accidentally smacked Luca in the face with the ball, hard. She immediately swam over to kiss him better while we all fell about laughing, each of us suffering from that uncontrollable laughter you got when you knew you shouldn't be laughing but couldn't suppress it and the more you tried to, the more it made you laugh.

As I watched Luca take his revenge by dunking Aria, Max startled me by appearing from under the water right in front of me, like he'd done earlier. We were both still giddy from laughing.

'Lie back,' Max suggested.

He put his arms underneath me, supporting me, like I had him. I closed my eyes and completely relaxed, allowing Max's strong arms to support my body and head. It was better than floating.

As I lay there, weightless, I realised I felt happy. Spending time with Max yesterday and today had allowed me to feel happiness for the first time since Michele's death. It brought with it a pang of guilt. Guilt that I could possibly feel joy in a world without her, but if I'd learned anything from Max it was that it was not only possible but also permitted to feel happiness again, despite the fact that those we love were gone forever.

I opened my eyes to find a mischievous look spread across Max's face as he began to twirl me around in the water. When he eventually stopped, I grabbed onto him, laughing and dizzy, wrapping my arms and legs around him. He began spinning me again, holding me tight around the waist. Around and around, faster and faster. I tilted my head back, closing my eyes, letting go, enjoying the freeing feeling it offered. As he slowed down I lifted my head, my arms and legs still tightly wrapped around him, and stared into those sparking, smiling eyes of his. We remained that way, silent, time slowing, holding each other, our bodies pressed tightly together, looking deep into each other's eyes, our smiles turning serious, the intensity building between us, one step further, this time even more heightened. Max moved even closer, resting his forehead on mine. I longed for him to kiss me. Did he want to? Was I reading the situation correctly? I was suddenly filled with self-doubt.

We were interrupted by shouts about food, and both looked over to the camp fire where the others were standing, waving at us. I stood, the moment lost.

Max held my hand and slowly led me back to shore, where two towels were waiting by our clothes. He picked one up and wrapped it around me, pulling me close and whispering in my ear, 'To be continued.' Our eyes met as a smile escaped across both of our faces. We made our way to the others, both wrapped in towels, this secret promise between us as we busied ourselves grabbing a plate, a burger, a beer, sitting across the fire from each other, exchanging looks as we chatted in the group. My stomach was filled with that feeling of butterflies, suppressing my hunger. I gazed across the fire at Max and found myself wanting more.

After we'd finished eating, I went to the cars with Aria and Isabella and carefully changed beneath a towel into my dry underwear and dress, as Isabella teased Aria about hitting Luca in the face with the ball. I brushed my nearly-dry hair and tucked it behind my ears, attempting to tame the natural wave that appeared if I didn't blow-dry it, then applied a little fresh mascara and lip balm; I didn't consider myself one of those girls who could get away with slicked back hair and no make-up. When we returned, Max had changed back into his teeshirt and jeans and was wearing a dark blue hoodie. Luca threw a cushion down in front of the log Max was sitting on, as if encouraging our closeness and offering his approval. I sat down between Max's legs and he wrapped his arms around me from behind to keep me warm. I instinctively eased back, leaning into him, resting against his chest. Being this close to him, wrapped in his arms, somehow felt completely natural. I closed my eyes, momentarily allowing myself to feel it, to feel loved in someone's arms, if only for tonight.

Logs were thrown onto the fire and drinks handed out as Dante re-emerged with a guitar, sitting down next to Isabella and strumming it. Max explained that Dante played in town, which is where they'd met. Dante called Isabella his groupie. They'd been together for almost a year. Our conversation was interrupted as Dante began to sing 'Something' by The Beatles. He looked at Isabella the entire time, dedicating the song to her. You could clearly see they were in love, that he adored her. I missed that feeling of being adored by someone. That beginning of something when the possibilities were endless.

When Dante finished we all clapped as he looked to Luca, who instantly requested 'Wish You Were Here' by Pink Floyd. Dante rolled his eyes and began to play; I guessed that wasn't the first time Luca had requested it. Dante made playing the guitar look effortless and had an incredible voice; I enjoyed hearing these familiar songs sung with an Italian accent, it made them exotic and beautiful in a whole new way. Luca joined in, singing along as I relaxed into Max, focusing on the water to my right, the lapping waves offering accompaniment.

Next, he looked to Max but I didn't hear his request. As soon as Dante started to play though, I instantly recognised it. 'Nightswimming' by R.E.M. I'd only ever heard it played on the piano before but Dante's acoustic guitar suited the ballad, full of vulnerability and sadness. I watched his fingers expertly stroke and pluck the strings, before becoming distracted by the sky, which had turned that stunning deep blue it does at dusk. The sun gone. The air now cool. Max, sensing I was cold, unzipped his hoodie and wrapped me up in it so we were both inside. His arms wrapped around me, my eyes closed, listening to the song. Max's breath tickling my neck as he quietly sang along. It felt as if the crackling fire was dancing all over my body and deep down inside. Another moment where if I could press pause I would.

Dante was looking at me, waiting for my request. I was searching my brain, then I looked at the moon.

'Do you know 'Harvest Moon' by Neil Young?' I asked.

Dante nodded, Max gave me a squeeze and Luca threw me an approving look. As Dante began to play, Luca stood, pulling Aria up and twirling her under his arm. Max followed suit, offering me his hand, which I graciously accepted. He pulled me close, like he had on the dance floor last night and I closed my eyes, enjoying our closeness as Dante serenaded us with the romantic song that sounded like it belonged to an era long ago.

'Do you want to go for a walk?' Max whispered in my ear, as Dante finished playing and turned his attention to Aria.

We walked along the beach to the far end where Max laid his hoodie down for me to sit on. Being thoughtful came naturally to him and those little things he did weren't lost on me. He sat next to me, by the water's edge, and we listened to the soothing sound of the lapping waves and looked out at the water illuminated by the moonlight. I was still captivated by Dante's song, replaying it in my head, when Max spoke.

'I want to know you. What you love. What you do. Why you're not with someone.'

The first part was easy. 'You already know what I love.' I shrugged, smiling.

Max nodded and smiled too. 'Music.'

I gave him a wink to confirm the obvious, then told him about my job as a speech and language therapist. How much I loved working with children and how lucky I was to actually have a job that I loved. How rewarding it was, despite the endless paperwork and long hours. I thought about when we'd met yesterday, how it had made me smile then.

'One of the first things I noticed about you is the way you pronounce your esses,' I told him.

He scrunched his face up. 'Yeah, I've always been aware of that. What would you do to fix it?'

I looked at the amazing man to my left. Fix it?

'Nothing,' I answered him honestly. 'It's part of who you are. You're perfect.'

Max looked pleased with my assessment, his smile widening as he gently nudged his arm against mine, his cheeks flushing.

'What about...' His tone turned serious as he glanced down at my empty ring finger. 'Why aren't you with anyone?'

I looked back out at the water, hugging my knees, taking a moment. I didn't like to go back there but Max didn't have the luxury of finding out about my painful past from one of my friends, like I had his last night from Luca.

'I was with someone for eight years. James. It ended almost two years ago now.'

'Why?' Max was looking at me intently.

I focused on the moonlight, gathering strength from it. This wasn't something I was used to talking about. Did I really want him to know? I was suddenly afraid. Afraid he'd make an excuse to leave, be done with me. I hadn't been in this situation since James and to be honest, until yesterday I was unaware how insecure and damaged I still was from it all. The scar on the outside might now be healed but the mental scars were still very raw. Maybe losing Michele had brought it all back. More loss. Losing the one person who had been there for me through it all. Losing her unconditional love too.

Max took my hand in his, stroking it with his thumb. 'You don't have to tell me,' he reassured.

I knew he meant it, which made me want to be honest with him. Not that it mattered anyway, it wasn't like I was ever going to see him again after Friday.

I took a deep breath and allowed my mind to return to that dark time I'd spent almost two years moving on from.

'Everything was fine between us, James and me. Then I got sick, was sent for tests and had to have...' I stopped, thinking

73

back to what Luca had told me last night about Max and Kate, 'the woman he was going to marry, have a family with.' There it was. I took another deep breath. 'I had to have a hysterectomy. James decided he wanted children more than he wanted me. Funny thing was we were the couple who didn't want children. We were happy, or so I thought. Within a few months he'd moved out, met someone else and got her pregnant. I guess he was checking her body worked before committing. I was heartbroken. My world fell apart. Everything I thought I knew suddenly felt like a lie.' I shook my head, still unable to understand it. 'What made it worse was that I really needed him, to get me through it all, the illness, the operation, my insecurities, but he left. Eight years together and he just walked away, abandoned me when I needed him the most.'

I broke off, staring intently at the moon through my tear-filled eyes, the reality still painful even after all this time, remembering how James had switched off his love for me overnight, that his love for me hadn't been unconditional after all. The fears I'd shared with Michele after the ultrasound, what if James doesn't want me anymore, that she'd reasoned away as nonsense, till they came true. I'd never wanted children before the decision had been taken out of my hands, that wasn't what had devastated me. James suddenly leaving me, being abandoned by the person I loved, the person I planned to grow old with. Knowing that I was incapable of throwing someone I loved aside so easily, especially in their time of need, forcing me to question whether he'd ever really loved me at all. His choice destroying every memory we'd ever created together. That was what had devastated me.

I ran my fingers across my dress where the scar lay hidden. The constant reminder of rejection, of not being wanted, of not being whole anymore, those parts that once made me a woman, made me desirable, gone forever. As the dark insecurities and fears that I was unlovable were unleashed, Max put his hand on my cheek, turning my head so my tear-filled eyes met his, and enveloped me in his arms, holding me, squeezing me tight. Tears fell freely from my eyes. All I could think was how much I'd needed this back then, I would've given anything to be held like this, to be supported, reassured, cared about and comforted in strong arms. To feel beautiful and enough. To feel loved.

I didn't think Max was going to let go. How had I ever been afraid he would run?

He eventually relaxed his hold and searched my face, gently wiping away my tears, shaking his head; he seemed lost for words. I rested my head on his shoulder and he placed his arm around me as we sat looking out at the moonlight dancing on the water.

'Eight years. Were you married?'

'No. It wasn't for us. I'm not religious. We were both children of divorce and understood marriage doesn't necessarily mean forever. I know it's important to some people, a commitment, a way to give your unconditional love to the other person, but we did that in other ways. We'd been together for so long, we were committed to each other. We liked that we woke up every day wanting to be together. We'd talked about it, and children, but we were always happy with our relationship the way it was.'

Although after James had left, I couldn't help but question whether the reason we'd never married was actually because he'd never loved me enough, even though I myself had never wanted to marry. Many irrational insecurities ate away at me,

I was powerless to stop them. It was crushing to suddenly question eight years of your life with someone. To replay your time together and doubt *everything*.

'Do you miss him?' Max turned and asked.

'No, not any more,' I answered honestly. 'For most of the first year I did. Every day. I'd see something I knew he'd like and want to share it with him or go to call him, or turn over in bed to spoon him. I missed him terribly. But then I saw him.'

I thought back to that initial encounter in my local coffee shop. Walking in and seeing them together, James with his new family, holding his baby. The ultimate slap in the face. I remember how my stomach had lurched. How I'd thought I was going to throw up in the shop doorway. My response had been to run. I'd turned and left, thinking he hadn't seen me but he came after me, wanting to check I was okay, wanting to talk.

'Once the shock of seeing him had worn off, I realised it was a stranger standing there, not *my* James. He'd been replaced by this man who looked familiar but I felt nothing for. As I stood there talking to him, I felt nothing. Nothing. No love. Not even anger. I felt empty, numb. That connection we'd shared for all those years, that intimacy, that love, it had all disappeared. The James I fell in love with no longer existed so there was no one to miss.'

I stared out at the water thinking back to watching Dante serenading Isabella.

'I do miss being in love though, being loved,' I admitted.

Max gave me a knowing smile. I guessed he missed that too.

'You never wanted to get married?' His puzzled look made me smile, I'd met that question countless times over the years.

'No, it wasn't my dream as a little girl. I never craved that big day. If anything I'd shy away from it, I'd hate to be the centre of attention. I've been to lots of friends' weddings and they were beautiful. It's just not for me. What's important to me isn't that one big day but every day. Waking up and wanting, *choosing* to be together. Not being able to imagine my world without him in it. Knowing he'll always be there for me and never give up on us, no matter what, even when it gets tough.' I shrugged. 'Marriage doesn't hold you to that. Unconditional love does. That's all I've ever wanted.'

That's what I'd thought I had with James.

I dug my fingers into the sand, thinking. I needed to be honest with Max.

'Luca told me about Kate. Last night,' I explained. 'I didn't mean to pry.'

Max recognised the concern on my face and gently squeezed my hand.

'It's fine, I'm glad you know. I've wanted to tell you, so you know I get it, Michele, what you're going through.' He paused. 'It's just not something I'm very good at talking about.'

'You don't have to,' I reassured him. 'I know you get it. You've already helped me more than you'll ever know.' I gave his hand a gentle squeeze back for emphasis.

We sat, holding hands, enjoying the stillness of the moonlight reflecting on the water.

I don't know why he suddenly began to tell me. Maybe it was because I'd shared so much with him.

'I met Kate on the first day of college and knew straight away she was the girl I wanted to grow old with. Sounds crazy I know, but my life was just *better* with her in it. She lit me up. We were married a few years later. God, we were happy.' Max closed his eyes, momentarily lost in his memories. 'She was late home from work, I hadn't heard from her. I was calling her mobile but it kept going straight to voicemail. Then two police officers came to the door. She was driving home from work and a car moved lanes without looking, clipped hers and that was it. They said she died on impact.' He shook his head. 'For months I kept ringing her mobile just to hear her voice. I tried to reason with it, what if she'd left five minutes earlier or later, or phoned in sick that day. I drove myself crazy. I couldn't believe she was gone. I didn't see the point anymore. I'd lost everything. I guess I hit that *rock bottom* you hear about. Then one day I knew something needed to change, that I couldn't carry on spiralling the way I was. Pushing everyone away. I didn't want to be known as the twenty-something widower for the rest of my life. I needed a fresh start, to get away from the memories but I wasn't sure where to go. Then I remembered the only time I'd felt remotely happy was here, at that R.E.M. concert with Luca. So that was it, decision made. I moved in with Luca.' Max looked at me and smiled, a smile that didn't reach his eyes. 'Pretty insane, I know. But it worked.'

My fantasy of leaving your life behind and starting over, that was what Max had done.

'You don't miss home? England, I mean?'

Max shook his head. 'Far from it. I associate it with the worst time of my life. I don't ever want to go back there. And besides, this is my home now, I've made a good life for myself here.'

'I can see that. You surround yourself with good people.' I glanced over to where the others were gathered by the camp fire. Max followed my gaze and nodded.

'So you haven't met anyone since James?' He seemed surprised.

I shook my head. Meeting someone had been the furthest thing from my mind.

'I've been focused on getting well and getting my fitness

back. It took time. Settling back into work. Starting over. Having fun with friends. Oh, and I bought my own apartment. There's a skylight above my bed so I can lay under the stars.'

We both tilted our heads back and looked up. There were no streetlights, just the moonlight. You could see stars like you rarely ever saw them, thousands of them. It was breathtaking.

'Yeah, it's not quite as spectacular as this,' I laughed, gesturing at the galaxies above our heads.

I thought about Max's question. The times I had been out with friends to bars or clubs, I hadn't been interested in anyone around me. Maybe I was avoiding meeting anyone for fear of further rejection, more hurt. When was the appropriate time to tell someone something so personal about yourself, anyway? A conversation about children during the first date would be upfront, but probably leave a man sprinting for the hills. Yet revealing it after you'd started to fall for one another, when it was actually time for *that* chat about the future, would feel dishonest as the news would change everything. And anyway, James had had eight years of my love, of memories, of intimacy, of knowing everything about me, and he couldn't deal with it. If he couldn't love me, why would anyone else?

I directed the question back at Max. 'What about you, hasn't there been anyone since Kate? All those girls at Luca's club?'

Max shook his head, smiling before turning serious. 'No, it's only really this year I've felt it lift. Contrary to what you see in all the films, it's not something you get over quickly and move on from. Well, not me anyway. Plus, I've never actually met anyone I've wanted to spend time with before. I don't easily connect with people. Their outlook on life tends to be poles apart from mine. I prefer to be alone or with close friends.'

'You don't normally start talking to strangers on bridges then?' I teased.

'I don't normally start talking to strangers at all,' he said, suddenly standing and pulling me to my feet.

Max looked deep into my eyes as he tucked a stray piece of hair behind my ear. I felt a shift between us. A new closeness had emerged.

He slipped his hand into mine and we walked towards the water until our bare feet were paddling in the cold. It felt cleansing somehow, washing away our pasts.

'Aren't you cold?' Max pulled my hands to his mouth, blowing his warm breath and rubbing them.

I was standing there in my cotton summer dress but I hadn't noticed until he mentioned it. 'I'm freezing,' I laughed.

Max wrapped me up inside his hoodie with him, our arms around each other. My head resting on his chest. My eyes closed. We stood that way for some time. Me soaking in his warmth, replaying his words in my mind, 'I've never actually met anyone I've wanted to spend time with before.' Before what, me? Then thinking back to last night, 'I like hanging out with you.' He stayed but didn't have to, I was fast asleep, he could've left. And this morning, 'I'm at your service.' Here he was, spending time with me. As I tried to figure it all out, Max began stroking my back with his fingertips. A trail of electrical current connected deep inside. 'To be continued,' I remembered. Did he still want to? I began to caress his back, then ran my palms up his teeshirt-covered chest, looking up so I could see his eyes.

Max began to trace his thumb down my cheek and across my lips, like I'd imagined doing to him when we were hiding in the gardens yesterday. He continued, down my neck and along my collarbone. I closed my eyes, savouring the moment. His touch awakened every part of my body, stirring feelings inside of me. Feelings I hadn't felt in such a long time. Feelings I feared I would never be able to feel again. As I looked up to meet his eyes I found them focused on my lips. We were in that wonderful limbo moment, the anticipation of a kiss, our bodies filled with longing and excitement. The want, urge, need to consume and be consumed by the person before you. My heart felt like it was going to explode out of my chest. Then his lips were on mine. Those full lips I had stared at as we hid in the gardens yesterday, I had wanted to kiss him then. I had wanted to kiss him earlier in the water. But it felt right now. Now we had laid ourselves bare to one another. Now he knew the truth about me. I was completely immersed in our kiss as we devoured each other, satisfying the lust that had been building since yesterday, and creating more lust deep inside.

When our lips eventually parted we touched foreheads, staring into each other's eyes, panting for breath and grinning, my body weak yet fully charged.

'I've been wanting to do that since we were hiding yesterday,' Max admitted.

I didn't think my uncontrollable grin could get any bigger. Then he kissed me again. A long, deep kiss, changing from soft and delicate to hungry and passionate. My insides were pulsating, the feeling overwhelming, but in a good way for once.

'Come on,' he said, rubbing my cold arms as we made our way back to the camp fire.

The others were setting up ground sheets, duvets, sleeping bags, blankets and pillows. No tents. They really did mean a night under the stars. It was perfect. Max and I took over setting up our bed and got inside, still clothed. Max placed an extra blanket over me to ensure I was warm enough, tucking me in. I was cherishing the way he treated me, his concern for me and the way he made me feel, especially when he looked at me, like I was the only other person in the universe.

We lay snuggled, holding hands in the air as Max pointed out stars and constellations he knew. I pointed to The Plough, or The Big Dipper as he called it, and shared an Arabian myth I knew, about how the stars forming the bowl represented a coffin and the three stars that made the handle were mourners following it. I told him how it had appeared the night of Michele's funeral, framed perfectly in the skylight above my bed. How I lay there staring at it as though Michele herself had placed it there. Michele. With me, Adam and her mum following.

I turned to face Max and smiled as I caressed his cheek. 'Why do I feel like I can tell you anything?' I whispered, our faces almost touching.

'Why does it feel like we've known each other for years?' Max whispered back.

He was right. I'd shared so much of myself with him. I trusted him and felt completely comfortable in his company. There was an undeniable connection between us, it *was* as if we'd known each other for years.

He touched the tip of his nose to mine, wiggling his head, giving me what he called an Eskimo Kiss.

'Inuit,' I corrected, looking deep into his smiling eyes, then his lips were once again on mine. I got lost in our kiss. Had first kisses always felt this powerful? My entire body was alive and tingling. I felt lightheaded, thankful I wasn't relying on my legs to support me. It was incredible.

When our lips finally parted I noticed his expression turn serious.

'What?' I questioned.

'Was tonight really your first kiss since James?'

I nodded as Max shook his head, surprised.

'Why so surprising?' I whispered.

'Because you're you, you're endearing and beautiful.'

I raised an eyebrow and began grinning at his lovely compliment, still not used to receiving them. I almost looked around to see who he was talking about.

Max cupped my cheek in his warm palm, his face still serious. 'You really have no idea how lovely you are, do you?'

He stared into my eyes for a moment as if emphasising it, then leant in and kissed me again.

Max certainly made me feel beautiful; maybe it would do me good to see myself though Max's eyes for a change. I'd seen myself through James' for far too long.

It felt late in such darkness and tiredness set in. We found our position, my head in his nook, my arm across his chest, his arms wrapped around me. The sound of his heartbeat soothing me as we began to fall asleep in each other's arms again. Although I did wonder if I'd actually manage any sleep with the electricity surging through my body.

6

TUESDAY

I am running along the beach. It's Shell Island in Wales. I'm pretending to be a shark, chasing a seven year-old Adam, catching him and pretending to bite him but tickling him instead. He's laughing uncontrollably and shouting, 'Mummy, help.'

I am standing in the doorway of a morgue, my fingers tightly gripping the doorframe, my body refusing to move. My arm is being pulled. I grip tighter, digging my nails in, I don't want to see. I'm led inside. I'm telling myself to breathe, to remain composed. The sheet is pulled back, revealing Michele's face. Her eyes are closed. She looks peaceful, as though asleep. I'm willing her to jump up, to shout boo, that it's all been a sick joke. As tears fill my eyes, I nod to confirm that the dead body before me is my beautiful friend. Her hand is sticking out. I reach out to hold it. It's shockingly cold. My legs collapse from under me and I hit the ground.

I jolted awake, startled from my dream, unable to breathe, pushing my way out from Max and the covers and running down to the water's edge, trying to shake the memory from my mind. How I wished I'd never seen her that way. I desperately wanted to erase it, to stop it haunting my dreams.

I sat down and focused on the sunlight reflecting on the water, matching my breathing to the rhythm of the lapping waves, calming myself, deep breaths. A warm body enveloped me from behind, gently rocking me in time with the waves, kissing my head with such force I knew he wanted to take my pain away.

'It won't hit you hard like this forever. I need you to know that,' Max whispered into my ear.

I turned and hugged him. It was a comfort coming from him, someone with that knowledge, that glimpse into my future. It gave me hope.

As I released him, he wiped my tear-streaked face with his hoodie and looked deep into my eyes, making me feel like the only other person in the universe again.

'Are you aware your eyes go the most beautiful shade of turquoise when you cry.'

He did it again, knew exactly what to say. He couldn't have known but yes I had been told that once before, by Michele; one of the few people to have ever *seen* me cry. She said she wanted to buy contact lenses the exact colour my eyes turned and asked me if she took me to the opticians would I cry so they could see what colour she wanted. The memory made me smile. She could always snap me out of it. It was as if she'd transferred the skill to Max.

He held my hands and pulled me up so we were both standing, his eyes now grinning as he removed his hoodie and dropped it on the ground, slowly lifting his teeshirt – revealing that horizontal line of flesh above his waistband – and removing it, then his jeans until he was standing before me in only his boxer shorts.

'Fancy a morning swim?' He raised his eyebrows, a flirtatious twinkle in his eyes.

I couldn't do anything other than grin back at him. He made me laugh, made me feel young, made me feel sexy. As I took in his body I felt that urge once again stir inside of me. I held his eyes as I removed my dress, standing before him in my underwear. He broke eye contact momentarily as his eyes travelled down my body before taking my hand in his as we walked into the water.

We swam for a while, back and forth, exchanging glances. The water was refreshing, clearing the fog of my dream. Max suddenly appeared beside me, giving me a fright, making us both laugh. I wrapped my arms and legs around him as he pulled me close, embracing in the water, resting our foreheads together, reading the longing in each other's eyes.

'To be continued,' he winked.

It felt different to yesterday though. There was a deeper connection, a new closeness after revealing so much of our pasts. I stroked his cheek with my fingertips and traced my thumb across his lips. Then they were on mine.

As we kissed, I became aware of a new conflict brewing inside of me. My desire to make love to Max, for him to be the first man since James and the surgery. My insides longed for him. But I was also aware that I was developing feelings, real feelings for him and already the thought of Friday gave me a sharp pang in the pit of my stomach. Would taking things further make Friday even harder? Would it be better to say goodbye now? I knew that wasn't an option. As long as I was in Verona I wanted to spend every possible second with him. Time was all we had. I would just have to deal with Friday on Friday.

We embraced in the water, the morning sun warming us. I enjoyed the security being in Max's arms bestowed. When we eventually made our way back to camp, the others were stirring. I headed to the car to change back into my dress, using the now dry bikini for underwear, and overheard Luca ask Max where we had both slept last night. Luca laughed when Max pointed to our makeshift bed; apparently, it only looked like one person had been in there. I smiled. I guess we did sleep closely snuggled.

I sat down next to Max, who instinctively put his arm around me as I rested my head on him; it still surprised me how comfortable we'd become in such a short space of time. I noticed Luca and Aria watching us as they sat opposite, stretching into the new day.

'When do you go back to England?' Aria inquired.

'Friday,' I said, sadly, looking at Max who was staring out at the water, the smile gone from his eyes. Was he feeling that same dread in the pit of his stomach?

As Luca and Aria busied themselves packing up the car, I stood between Max's legs, holding his head in my hands, his sad eyes staring into mine. I hoped he could read the sadness and dread in my eyes too.

'Let's forget there's a Friday,' he said. 'Live in the moment.'

I nodded my agreement and he buried his face in my dress, wrapping his arms around me and holding me tight. I closed my eyes and held him, stroking his hair, not allowing my mind to focus on anything but the moment.

On the drive back, Max sleepily asked what I wanted to do today. He was all mine again. I sat and thought about it as I stared out of the window, my hand in his.

'Will you show me around Verona? I haven't had a chance to see it properly yet.'

'Tourist stuff?' he questioned, his face scrunched up.

'Yes, tourist stuff,' I encouraged.

We quickly stopped off at Max's so he could grab some clothes, then Aria drove us to my hotel. As I thanked Luca and Aria for a wonderful time at the beach, Luca gave me an extra long hug, like he didn't want to let me go. As much as I'd enjoyed being with the others, I was looking forward to some alone time with Max.

We entered my hotel room, tidy and clean, bed made; if only I could get home from work and find my apartment like that. Then we busied ourselves showering and getting ready, me first as I had to wash and blow dry my hair.

As we left the hotel, hand in hand, I found myself imagining we were a regular English couple on holiday. Our first stop was brunch, sitting outside a cafe on Piazza Bra – the main square, dominated by the magnificent amphitheatre to our left and the Palazzo Barbieri, their town hall, to the right, under the shade of the green awnings that ran the entire length of the cafes, and surrounded by grand old multi-coloured buildings with balconies and green shutters. Everywhere was beautifully dressed with flowers and ornate street lights. I sat back, soaking it in.

Max explained that he normally avoided such touristy places. I understood that. When I lived in America that summer, we used to get hassled by people selling things on the beach every day. It got to the point where we'd scream 'locals' at them as they approached so they'd know to leave us alone.

As we sat in the stunning piazza, a man approached, holding leaflets. Max gave me a knowing, 'See, that's why I avoid touristy places', smile and I gave his hand a reassuring 'Just go with it' tap. The man spoke in English, apologising for disturbing us but wondering if we had plans for today because he still had places on his bicycle tour to a local vineyard that was leaving in an hour.

'There'll be plenty of wines to sample and food to soak it up, you'll learn all about the regional wines, how they're produced, and the bike ride is through some stunning countryside,' he explained.

I turned to Max, who saw my face and realised I was actually interested. He shrugged, giving me the final decision. After we'd signed up and been told where to meet, the man left us to finish our brunch. I turned to Max, laughing. 'He had me at wine tasting,' I admitted.

There were ten of us altogether on the tour. Us, another couple, a group of four friends, the tour guide and an older woman on her own. I wondered if I would have said yes had I been sitting there alone, if I hadn't met Max. How different my week would have been. The next thought surprised me – how lonely I'd feel without him. As we stood around awaiting instructions, it had that uncomfortable 'beginning of a tour' feeling, when everyone kept to themselves and no one really spoke.

We set off riding out of the city, along tree-lined concrete roads, surrounded by wide expanses of countryside, the odd farmhouse in the distance, before beginning a gentle climb as we headed for the hills. I couldn't remember the last time I had ridden a bicycle, besides at the gym, but I soon got the hang of it again. The tour guide was right, the scenery was stunning. Although the views were similar to those I'd seen from the car window on our excursion to the beach, being on a bicycle made them more dramatic, like we were in the painting too.

Max and I stayed at the back, a little behind the others; he felt more comfortable that way. As the hill became steeper, we glanced back through breaks in the trees to enjoy the ever-changing view below, clouds cascading dark patterns on the patchwork of green fields and terracotta rooftops in the distance.

When the road narrowed, the group stopped and decided to walk the rest of the way, pushing their bicycles alongside them. Max turned to me and shouted, 'Race you,' as he took off ahead, laughing. I chased after him, trying to catch him, peddling hard as the incline grew steeper and steeper, my quads burning. It felt wonderful to be able to push myself, for my body to behave the way it used to. Those months and months of recovery after the surgery had been tough, and now I appreciated feeling like myself again every day. Max reached the top first, holding his arms in the air and declaring himself the champion. We got off our bikes, both panting for breath, and collapsed onto the grass, me falling into his arms as we lay cooling down. I looked up and met his eyes, locking into them as he gently brushed his thumb down my cheek. Feelings stirred inside, the electric charge returning. I leant up and kissed him, a continuation of where we'd left off in the water this morning. I could have abandoned the tour right there and then and stayed lying on the grass in Max's arms. That was until our intimacy was interrupted by the others reaching the top of the hill. Max stood, pulling me to my feet, a smile on his face, meeting my eyes. I always loved that about being with someone, that secret you could share with just a look.

We set off again, peddling at a steady pace until we reached the vineyard where we were joined by another group of tourists, who had arrived by minibus. Our peace was interrupted by a very loud man, dressed in a hat, polo shirt, shorts, white socks and Jesus sandals. A camera around his neck. I couldn't help but smirk, he epitomised the word 'tourist'. We all followed the owner, and his dog, as he informed us that we were standing in the Valpolicella territory, he explained his growing methods, type of soil, pesticide alternatives and so on. He spoke affectionately about harvest time, telling us how his family and friends all came together, working solidly before sharing a well deserved meal, and wine of course, around their huge outdoor table. That strangers turned up each year offering to work in exchange for food, wine and a bed. Max and I agreed, that sounded like a wonderful experience. The very loud man was asking lots of questions and trying to be funny, which he wasn't, so Max and I hung back taking it all in, the vast amount of vines and grapes. It was an incredible sight. I felt Max nudge me, directing my gaze to where the owner's dog was taking a poo, right in the middle of the next path. Just then, the group approached, led by the very loud man. Max and I glanced at each other, knowing exactly what was going to happen before it happened, both glued to the spot in disbelief as it played out in what seemed like slow motion. As the very loud man took another step, there was a loud squelch as poo splattered all over his sandal and white sock. He shouted dramatically while doing a crazy dance on one leg, flicking out his dirtied foot, which only made the situation funnier. Max and I tried desperately to suppress our laughter but it was impossible. We both burst out laughing at the

92

same moment, doubling up, trying to pretend we were laughing about something else. Like naughty school children on a field trip. I hid my face in Max's chest until my laughter subsided.

Still giddy, we headed into the winery where the wine tasting began.

'This is more like it,' Max whispered in my ear.

At first we listened intently to how wine was produced and how barrels made from different types of wood were used to create different flavours. It was really quite interesting. But after our third small glass we became giddy again. Max was intent on making me laugh. I held out until he mimicked earlier, flicking out his foot and doing the crazy dance, bursting out laughing. We were in our own little bubble of fun, eventually moving to the back so as not to disturb the others. We sat at one of the picnic tables drinking our fourth glass of wine, the famous Amarone, as Max began making up stories for the other members of our tour group. Apparently, this was what he did when he people-watched. I wondered if he'd done it to me on the bridge.

'What about her, what do you reckon her story is?' I asked, referring to the woman on her own. I found her fascinating. 'That could've been me.'

Max looked at me, confused.

'If I hadn't met you. I would've been wandering around on my own all week.'

Max put his arm around me and kissed my forehead. 'I hadn't thought about that. We'd have met anyway. Bumped into each other somewhere else.'

I liked his fate-filled theory.

He raised his glass. 'Well here's to meeting sooner rather than later.'

We both clinked glasses, smiling.

'So, what will you be doing this time next week?' Max asked.

I looked at my watch but I wasn't wearing one.

'It's nearly five o' clock, so one hour behind, four o' clock on Tuesday?' Max confirmed.

I scrunched up my face at the thought of returning to my real life. 'I'll be back at the office doing paperwork, writing up reports from my day. What about you?'

'I haven't a clue, probably missing you.'

He rested his forehead on mine, making a sad face so I kissed him, making him smile again. We were both quite tipsy.

'Don't you have a job?' I asked.

'Sort of,' he answered.

I raised my eyebrows, indicating I wanted more information.

'You know that club I took you to the other night?'

I nodded.

'It's mine. The bar upstairs too. I own them.'

I was trying to work out if what he was telling me was true, but why wouldn't it be, but how could he have afforded to buy them?

'Kate had life insurance and our mortgage was paid off.' He shrugged.

It was as if he read my mind, again.

'Wow. You've created a place where you can get lost in music you love whenever you want.' I was in awe of the idea.

Max laughed. 'I hadn't thought of it like that, I did it more to save Luca's job and because it was a damn good investment, but yes I guess I have.' He was studying my face. 'You really love your music, don't you?'

I nodded, wide-eyed and smiling.

'Was James the same?'

It was odd how we could now discuss Kate and James so comfortably.

'No.' I shook my head, remembering all those gigs where James had stayed at the bar while I'd pushed my way as close to the stage as I could get. I loved being able to see the musicians play their instruments, see their faces and their expressions close up. 'James tolerated my obsession. He'd come along to gigs with me if I had no one else to go with but he'd want to chat all the way through. He found standing and listening boring. I mean, how is that even possible? I'm talking about seeing incredible bands and artists at huge venues and in tiny rooms, but it didn't move him. How can you watch someone like Damien Rice sing and play guitar close up and not be in complete awe?'

'You can't,' Max simply stated. He got it. He was shaking his head. 'I can't imagine you being with someone like that.'

I had met James through friends at a birthday party. We'd hung out in a group for months, getting to know each other before going on an official one-on-one date. We weren't instantly attracted to one another, we more grew on each other over time. We'd been to several clubs and gigs but I hadn't noticed his indifference because I'd always danced and gone to the front with friends while he'd stayed with the guys. I'd tried to get him excited about music but it wasn't for him. If I was being honest, it had always bothered me deep down that he didn't share my passion but we had other things in common and he was funny, he made me laugh.

Max and I chatted away, getting to know each other until we were interrupted by an American couple from another group sitting down. Everyone was being seated for food. They introduced themselves, Beth, as in Mary-Beth, and Bob. They looked to be in their fifties. Within ten minutes we knew their life story. Where they were from, Pittsburgh, Pennsylvania. How long they'd been in Verona, it was their second day, they were leaving tomorrow for the next part of their European tour, to celebrate their twenty-fifth wedding anniversary. How many children they had, three, plus their names, ages, jobs and relationship statuses. How many grandchildren they had, one, plus name and age. How many dogs they had, two, plus names and breeds. Max was squeezing my hand under the table. I tapped it reassuringly. 'Just go with it,' I was telling him.

'So what about you two love birds?' Beth asked, a big smile spreading across her face. 'How long have you two been together?'

Max jumped in before I could even think of a reply. 'Well we're actually here celebrating our three year anniversary.' He was speaking in a cheesy voice, not that Beth and Bob noticed. He lifted my hand, kissing the back of it. 'Three years with this wonderful woman. I'm the luckiest man in the world.'

I was biting my lips from the inside, trying to stop myself laughing. He had become Max the tourist. I had created a monster. He looked at me and I could tell instantly from his eyes that he too was laughing inside.

Beth continued her line of questioning. 'So where are you from, what do you do?'

I sat back, relishing what was to come out of Max's mouth next.

'Well you could say we live a bit like gypsies. Angelina here is a photographer. She travels all over the world, very glamorous. I'm a sound engineer, on the road a lot too, touring with different bands.'

Angelina? I was dying to ask where he'd plucked that from. I was searching my brain for a name; Brad was too obvious. I had it – Clooney.

'George and I always make time for each other though, don't we darling?' I said, smiling and squeezing his hand as Beth gushed about how exciting our lives must be.

I'd momentarily entered my fantasy of becoming someone else.

We were saved by the arrival of food; baskets of bread, plates of meats and cheeses, and more wine, which Beth quickly turned her attention to.

I leant over to Max and whispered, 'Angelina? Where did that come from?'

'I was trying to think of another name beginning with A,' he explained. Then looked at me mouthing, 'George?' before taking a sip of wine.

I gave him a sexy wink as I mouthed, 'Clooney,' causing Max to burst out laughing and spit his wine everywhere.

It was another one of those moments where we desperately tried to suppress our laughter but to no avail, hiding behind our napkins as Beth and Bob exchanged glances, giggling along like they were in on the joke too.

As I regained my composure I picked up my wine glass and whispered, 'Are we supposed to cycle back?'

Max took the wine glass out of my hand and moved it away from me, laughing. But as Beth went on and on about everything they'd done on their travels so far, he handed it back to me, both of us taking a large gulp.

After we'd finished eating, we excused ourselves and took one last stroll around before leaving, to walk the food and wine off before getting back on our bicycles. When we approached the scene of the earlier incident, Max flicked his foot out, doing the crazy dance again. We burst out laughing, both suffering from that uncontrollable laughter that made you cry. I was doubled up, my jaw aching, grabbing onto him. It had been a day of it.

When I finally stopped, I wrapped my arms around his neck, looking into those beautiful, smiling eyes of his.

'Thank you for playing tourist, I've had a wonderful day,' I told him.

'Me too,' Max agreed, surprised, realising he'd actually enjoyed doing 'tourist stuff.' He pulled me closer and wrapped both of his arms around me, his mouth next to my ear, 'I like who I am with you.' He paused. 'I can't remember the last time I laughed like this.'

I could. It was after my operation. Michele was trying to help me get up off the bed. Such a simple act but every time I tried I screamed out in pain and couldn't get up. It was pathetic but really comical, which made her laugh, which in turn made me laugh, but laughing really hurt after surgery; you don't realise how much you use your stomach muscles. The more we tried not to, the more we both cried with laughter. The pain was worth it though, she filled my days with joy. I closed my eyes, picturing her, desperately wishing I could tell her about my day, about Max. I liked who I was with him too. I held Max a little tighter and he held me right back.

The ride back into Verona was easy. It wasn't late but we decided to go straight to the hotel, both kicking off our shoes and collapsing onto the bed, the exhaustion from drinking in the sun and cycling catching up with us. I couldn't be bothered moving so Max plugged his iPod into the hotel room's dock. I loved that he always carried it with him. The mood of his chosen song, 'Summer' by Courteeners, matched the warm pastel glow coming in through the window. I relaxed into our embrace, glad Max was there, hoping for more adventures with him tomorrow, and sleepily closed my eyes as the dreamy song serenaded us – the singer didn't want to go, he wanted to remain in his lover's arms forever. Had it been written about this very moment?

'Alex, it's just a dream, Alex, you're dreaming…'

Max's voice was pulling me from my nightmare. I'd been screaming with my mouth closed.

I opened my eyes to his concerned face, his hand stroking my hair. My eyes were open but my brain was still lost in the nightmare, taking its time to catch up. Then I was back in the present, in Verona. I was with Max. I was safe. I met his eyes, nodding to let him know I was all right as I slowly sat up, remembering the dream. My body felt drained. I put my hand out to steady myself, hugging my knees into me with the other, desperately trying to suppress the memory and the pain that had struck inside. Max sat next to me, resting against the headboard of the bed, handing me a glass of water. It was dark, the room dimly lit by moonlight coming through a gap in the curtain.

'What can I do?' Max asked.

I looked at the wonderful man next to me who had done so much for me already. 'You're already doing it just being here,' I answered honestly, lying back down, my head in his lap.

Max began stroking my hair, soothing me. 'Where were you, in the dream?' he gently asked.

I found myself starting to tell him. It was something I'd never spoken of before. Still so vivid in my mind, every detail. Every heartbreaking detail.

'I was in school, working with a child, it was my first appointment of the day. My bag kept on vibrating, making me check my phone. I saw Adam's name and instantly knew something was wrong. He should've been in lessons. I gave a story book to the child I was with, a distraction so I could answer my phone. Adam was frantic, hysterical. I kept telling him to calm down, to breathe. I couldn't understand what he was saying. My brain was working overtime on possible scenarios, never for one second imagining it was Michele. I started to pick out pieces from his repeated ramblings. He left for school and saw her car still there, which was odd because she always left before he got up. He went back inside to wake her. He thought her alarm hadn't gone off. He thought she'd overslept. He was shouting at her, screaming 'Mum' but she didn't open her eyes. He was shaking her but she didn't move. He lifted her shoulders but her arms and head fell back, lifeless. He dialled 999. He did everything they told him to, checked for a pulse; they talked him through CPR. The paramedics arrived. They worked on her, they tried, but they said she was already gone. Gone? I couldn't comprehend it. There must've been some mistake. As Adam cried into my ear, I saw someone pass the room I was working in. I grabbed her, calmly apologised and asked her to take the child back to class as there'd been an emergency and I had to go. I closed the door and told Adam to put a paramedic on the phone. The paramedic explained how they'd tried everything, how very sorry he was, that despite all their efforts they weren't able to revive her. Then he said it, made it real. She was dead. That's when I began repeatedly telling myself to hold it together, I was at work, I had to hold it together. I made the paramedic promise to stay with Adam until I got there, I was on my way. I remember sitting down on a tiny blue child's school chair and staring at my phone, willing myself to rewind time, thinking if I hadn't answered it then it wouldn't be real. She wasn't dead. She couldn't possibly be dead. I calmly phoned and cancelled my other three appointments for that day, then my boss. I didn't offer an explanation, just said it was an emergency. When I look back I must've been in shock. I drove to Michele's house, taking controlled breaths, telling myself to hold it together, just a bit longer. I remember feeling helpless that I couldn't get there faster. Willing red lights to change. Considering driving on pavements and the wrong side of the road, anything to quicken the journey. When I pulled up I saw the ambulance parked outside. Seeing it made me panic. Maybe it *was* real. Despite the rain, neighbours were standing around watching. As I got out of my car Adam came racing up and wrapped his arms around me with such force he slammed my back into the car. He was grabbing onto me, sobbing hysterically. I didn't know what to do. I was numb. I just held him, there on the street, everyone staring. The paramedics led us both inside and made us a cup of tea. I remember thinking how no amount of tea could ever make us feel better. I sat holding Adam, stroking his hair. I kept telling myself to hold it together, just a bit longer, that I had to be strong for Adam. He was hugging me with all his might. This teenager who hadn't let us hug or kiss him in years, now too old, was suddenly attached to me... Eventually I went upstairs to use the toilet but found myself going into Michele's bedroom instead. I knew they'd moved her, taken her away. I stood, staring at the unmade bed, the place where my best friend had died, all alone. It was the saddest thing I'd ever seen. I couldn't hold it together any longer, I lost it right there on her bedroom floor. It was the worst day of our lives. I hate that Adam was the one to find her. That he'll carry that around with him for the rest of his life. I'd do anything to take that burden from him.'

I closed my tear-filled eyes and took a breath. I felt numb as I spoke about it. Despite the anguish and the hollowness that her death had caused inside, it still somehow didn't seem real. My brain, my heart, refused to accept it, I wasn't ready to let her go. She was my best friend, my family. The world was a better place with her in it.

Max kept stroking my hair, like my mum used to when I was a child; it was the only thing that used to calm me. Seemed it still did.

'You really love Adam, don't you?'

'I'd do anything for him.' I sat up and faced Max. 'He made me promise that nothing would change between us. That we'd still do our football routine. He desperately craves normality, some stability in his life. Moving in with his dad and step-family has been difficult for him. So much has changed. His world has been turned upside down.'

'Michele wasn't with Adam's dad?'

'No, they split up years ago. They gave it a good go but I guess meeting so young, their interests and dreams changed until all they had in common was Adam and it wasn't enough. They were amicable about it all though, even when Ben remarried and had more children. I always admired them for staying friends, for putting Adam's needs first.'

'Adam's really lucky to have you in his life.'

'I'm lucky to have him,' I corrected, 'he makes me feel close to her.' I shook my head, fighting back the tears that were rushing into my eyes. 'He looks so much like her.'

Max held me as I tried to accept the fact that I was never going to see Michele ever again. Wondering if I'd ever be able to come to terms with it. Devastated that she'd never get to see her son grow into a man. Determined to put Adam's needs first, to ensure he lived as happy and fulfilled a life as possible.

Max lowered me down into bed, pulling the covers over me, back into our position, wrapped up and comforted in his embrace, the sound of his heartbeat soothing me back to sleep.

7

WEDNESDAY

I awoke once again in Max's arms, grabbing onto him as the hurricane passed, then lay cuddling him as I imagined myself back in my own bed, alone. The thought of never seeing Max again pained me. To never hear his voice or feel his touch or his eyes on me, it filled me with a mixture of dread and sadness. The way he looked at me, he made me feel flawless, complete, enough. The very things I had struggled with since James and the surgery. Max made me feel young and carefree. How I craved that life. How I wished I could somehow stay in his world forever, but I knew that was impossible.

I propped myself up on one elbow and watched Max as he slept, listening to the sound of him breathing, memorising every part of his face. I never wanted to forget that face. Tears of trepidation surged into my eyes, threatening to escape. I was going to miss him terribly. I was tired of missing people. How could Max, the person who'd been helping soothe my loss and pain, now become the source of it?

I quietly made my way to the bathroom and let the warm water of the shower merge with my tears, washing them away as I repeated our pact like a mantra. 'Forget there's a Friday, live in the moment.'

I got ready, opting for my striped sleeveless dress. It felt odd dressing to impress, imagining someone else's opinion of an outfit, contemplating which one they'd prefer. Although Max had seen me at my worst, his eyes still lit up when he looked at me, but then he could see straight into my soul.

When I returned to the bedroom Max was still in bed, stretching and yawning. He held out his hand for me to move closer, which I did, sitting on the edge of the bed next to him. He grabbed me and flipped me over him so I was in the middle of the bed, in his arms, giggling. He brushed his thumb down the side of my face. I became serious as I felt that connection between us powering up. The transfer of energy from his eyes, his touch, his mouth on mine. It was hopeless, I was unable to hold back, to restrain my feelings. I was crazy about him, falling hard. Just live in the moment, I told myself as I got lost in his kiss.

As much as I knew I wanted more, we hadn't moved beyond kissing. Keeping our touch to less intimate areas. It was an unspoken agreement to take things slowly. I respected him tremendously for it. No pressure. Plus, I couldn't deny how incredible it felt, the lust inside, charged, overflowing. I wasn't ready to succumb to it yet, I was enjoying it too much.

We both lay, holding, yawning but I didn't want more sleep, to waste those hours. I could feel the clock counting down on our time together. I sat up but Max remained snuggled, his eyes closed, resting back into sleep so I went to where his iPod was docked and pressed play on the perfect song, 'Get Up' by R.E.M., then proceeded to sing along as I jumped up and down on the bed, prompting Max to open one eye. He moved onto his back, his hands behind his head, grinning as he watched me.

'Let's go and do something,' I pleaded.

'What do you fancy?' As he yawned and stretched, the covers fell away to reveal his bare chest.

I stopped jumping and stood, looking down at him, lust in my eyes. What *did* I fancy?

Max grabbed my legs, pulling me on top of him and kissing me passionately, catching me unawares. He flipped me so I was under him again, his body on top of mine holding me in place, his deep brown eyes looking deeply into mine. I adored the way he looked at me, it awakened me.

'Any ideas?' he asked flirtatiously, lust evident in his eyes too.

'Let's go on an adventure,' I suggested as I steadied my breathing, trying desperately to stop my voice divulging what was happening inside of me.

Max smiled and kissed me again, a long, passionate kiss, making me hungry for more.

'Okay, I'll go get ready.' With that, he swiftly jumped up, leaving me lying there listening to R.E.M. alone, breathless and lightheaded, filled with longing and excitement.

Max took me to the cafe around the corner from the hotel, where he'd bought the coffees and pastries from the other day. He ordered, remembering my one-shot latte preference, as I sat down at one of the dark wooden tables. It was cosy and quaint. Exposed wooden beams with a ceiling fan rotating above my head. I noticed an elderly couple on the next table getting ready to leave. As Max sat down, the old man stood and retrieved a wheelchair from the corner. We watched as he carefully helped to transfer his wife from her cafe chair into the wheelchair, his touch gentle and loving. I caught them adoringly gaze into each other's eyes, sharing a moment. Still in love after all those years. I found myself envious of their true, unconditional love. Something I'd discovered almost two years ago I no longer had. Something I could only wish for. I longed to hear their story, wondering what hardships they'd endured and survived. Max reached across the table and held my hand as we both watched them leave the cafe. I wondered if he was thinking about Kate.

I still had half a cup of coffee left when Max declared he had a quick errand to run, a boring bill to pay as he was in town. I didn't mind going with him, but he insisted I sit and finish my coffee; he'd only be ten minutes. So I did. I sat alone, finishing my coffee, imagining how this would have been my reality if I hadn't met Max. I would be sitting here, probably with a book, half reading and half people-watching. I struggled to remember how I had once found that idea appealing. Even with the growing dread inside of me, if I were to time-travel back to that moment on the bridge I would still say yes and go off with that handsome stranger. There was something about Max, I'd felt it when we met, a familiarity, a comfort and definitely an attraction. Although I could never have predicted we'd become this close or that I'd develop real feelings for him.

Max reappeared, making me appreciate him even more. 'Ready?' There was evidence of a grin on his face, like he was up to something.

I stood and enquired, 'Where are we going?'

He held my hand, lifting it to his mouth and softly kissing it. His eyes were smiling. 'I have no idea, you wanted an adventure.'

Max led me into a taxi and back to his place. I stood in the doorway as he grabbed the keys to Luca's car, which he explained he also used sometimes. Luca was still asleep, so Max left him a note. As we drove out of town, Max placed my hand on the gear stick so he could hold it while driving; I enjoyed the little things he did. He stopped at a junction and pointed to the signpost, reading the options out loud, foreign place names I'd never heard before, asking which I liked the sound of. That was how we continued, reading the names and choosing the one I liked. The way you might choose a horse to bet on in The Grand National. Or we'd each pick a direction, left or right, and play 'rock, paper, scissors' to decide. It was fun, impulsive, fitting. An adventure left to fate.

After a while, we stumbled upon a small village. It was market day, the centre a hive of activity. We decided to stop and look around, but got stuck in a traffic jam as Max searched for somewhere to park. I was focused on a tree up ahead to our right, the leaves in one small section at the top had started to change colour. The dramatic orange contrasting against the blue sky was stunning. I noticed Max becoming restless so pointed it out, explaining that when I was stuck in a traffic jam or queueing in a shop, when it was out of my control, I always looked around and found something I would have missed if I hadn't been forced to stop at that exact moment. There was always something to see, maybe a colourful tree or the clouds making a pattern in the sky, or an interaction between two people. When I noticed it, I didn't mind being held up after all. I watched Max focus on the tree, his face relaxing.

'I like the way you see the world,' he said.

I leant across and kissed him, neither of us caring how long we were going to be held up for.

We eventually parked and walked around, hand in hand, surrounded by beautiful old buildings, shutters closed to keep out the sun. Blue and white market awnings stretched out ahead of us lining the street, housing a rainbow of colours from the abundance of food, flowers and spices. A heady blend of exotic fragrances greeted us, along with sweet fresh fruit, earthy vegetables, a hint of the salty sea, and joined by the mouth-watering scent of warm yeast emanating from the freshly baked bread and pastries. We stopped along the way, trying samples and buying what we liked: bread, cheeses, meats, fruit, wine, filling our bag as we moved from stall to stall for a picnic later. Max was speaking Italian and translating for me, teaching me new words and phrases, correcting my pronunciation. We were in our fun bubble, living in the moment. As we passed the flower stall, I stopped and ran my fingers across the soft petals of the red Gerbera Daisies, my favourite flower. I'd never seen them in such a rich, dark shade before. I walked on, perusing the pottery on the next stall when I felt Max embrace me from behind, whispering, 'Your favourite, I believe,' as a single red Gerbera Daisy appeared in front of my face. I turned around, unable to hide my grin. Max looked so pleased with himself. His thoughtfulness was boundless. As I took the flower I began to kiss him, but we were interrupted as the old man behind the stall got animated, gesturing towards us as he repeated something in Italian, 'giovani amanti, giovani amanti.'

'What's he saying?'

'Young lovers,' Max translated, smiling and wrapping his arm around me as we moved on.

I suppose to anyone watching, we looked like any other couple on holiday. No one could see the clock counting down on our time together or the sickening feeling it brought with it. I imagined what it would be like if that were the case for all relationships, if you could see the timer counting down, dictating when you were going to split up or when one of you would die. I wondered if I'd have done anything differently with James or Michele had there been a big ticking clock constantly reminding me that our time together was about to end.

As we reached the end of the stalls, I noticed a church. It looked centuries old. You could tell it was central to village life by the collection of people gathered around the cramped noticeboard.

'I'll be back in a minute,' I told Max.

The coolness hit me first, along with the familiar smell of incense. Straight ahead were two sections of wooden benches separated by a central aisle that led to the altar lit by candles. I knew what I wanted to do as soon as I saw it. I slowly walked towards the altar. I had a tradition: whenever I came across a church or cathedral abroad, I would go inside and light a candle. I wasn't religious, but I found these places, filled with history, evoked thought and peace, an opportunity to take a moment and remember those no longer with me. In the past it had been grandparents, Michele's father, my aunt. Now though, the only person in my thoughts was Michele. I dropped a few coins into the slot and placed a candle on the very top row, lighting it, the blurred flame illuminating the tears in my eyes. The pew creaked under my weight as I sat down. There I stayed, staring at the flame, hypnotised. It was how I'd spent the entire funeral, staring straight ahead at the flame on the altar. Holding Adam's hand as we moved with the congregation from seated, to standing, to kneeling but never once looking away from the flame. I couldn't. I didn't want to see the coffin. I couldn't bear to think of Michele locked inside, all alone. I was afraid I would've gone insane and prised open the lid to let her out. No, I dared not look at it. I needed to be strong for Adam.

I sat, enjoying the silence, contemplating how our lives had begun on the same path but veered off in completely different directions, and yet we'd remained perpetual friends. Michele was always dating different boys at school, whereas my only interest in boys at that age was as friends. Michele had become a mother at an age when I had just discovered going out, socialising, travelling, and had started university. She'd found love early, only for it to end. I'd found love later on, or so I'd thought, only for it to end. Despite everything we'd never grown apart. In fact, we complimented each other, allowing the other a glimpse into a different world. We'd remained constants in each other's lives throughout, shared everything. Michele had been the significant relationship of my life. There would never be another like it. She was my best friend. She was my family. Through all the joy and tears, we'd been there for one another. I couldn't imagine my life without her in it. I wasn't sure I would ever be capable of accepting that she was really gone. Every time I tried, sadness and loneliness consumed me. I'd never felt hollow like this before, I didn't know how to think about her without being stricken with it. I remember as teenagers, the profound years, she had a saying: 'my life is on a cloud but then the sky stretches forever.' Typical teenagers, assuming we were invincible, that we'd live forever, never once contemplating any other alternative. Why would we?

I returned to the present, taking a breath, dabbing my eyes and putting on my sunglasses as I emerged into the warmth and brightness outside. Max was sitting on a low wall to the right, eating an apple. As I approached, he rested the core on the wall and patted his knee for me to sit down, placing his arm around my waist as I rested mine around his shoulders. He pushed my shades up onto my head to reveal my eyes.

'Turquoise,' I admitted, shrugging. 'When will I be able to think about her without feeling like this?' I was desperate to be able to. Would I *ever* be able to?

Max looked bewildered by my question.

'I don't recall exactly when it was. I just caught myself in the moment, thinking about Kate but I didn't feel that deep anguish. Obviously there was still sadness, but it was bearable. But then just as you think you've turned a corner, it unexpectedly hits you again, something in a film you're watching or a song you hear. Even now.' He looked at me. 'Kate will always be a part of my life, will always be in here.' He placed his hand over his heart. 'Just like Michele will always be in there.' He placed his hand over my heart.

I placed my hand over his, holding them both close, drawing comfort from it. I felt gratified that Max could talk openly to me about Kate. That we could be honest with each another. I gazed into his eyes, those eyes that sucked me in, drawing me closer, and thought about two days from now, but immediately replaced it with the here and now, resting my head on his as we sat, contented, the warmth of the sun on us, soaking in the bustle of the market in this magnificent historic village we'd stumbled upon.

On our way back to the car, Max led me through a restaurant's outdoor seating area. At first I thought we were going to sit down and order a drink but Max stopped and hugged me, very

111

unnaturally. I wasn't sure what was going on until I heard the bag rustle and looked down to see him place one of the cutlery sets from the table into it, before moving on.

'We need to cut the bread with something,' he grinned.

'Trespassing and now theft,' I teased, shaking my head, feigning disapproval.

We drove on, surrounded by greenery and vineyards, hills in the distance, blue skies above. Max and I holding hands on the gear stick. Sometimes talking, Max telling me how he'd never driven this far out before. Me telling him how I'd been to Rome and Florence but never this far north. Sometimes sitting in comfortable silence, appreciating the beauty around us while listening to the Kodaline album he was playing for me.

Max slowed the car to a stop as an incredible sight stretched out to our right. We both got out, staring in awe. All we could see for miles were sunflowers. A sea of yellow. Thousands of them. It was hypnotic. We walked into the field a little, the car door open, Kodaline's sunny melody following us.

'I'm going to take a photograph,' I said, holding my hands up to create a frame around a portion of the sunflowers, like Max had shown me the other night. After a few seconds, Max turned me around and stepped back, holding his fingers up, framing me surrounded by sunflowers and pressing 'click.' As his eyes held mine, his smile disappeared, our excitement extinguished by sadness. I wondered if he was thinking it too: *I never want to forget you.*

Max grabbed me, wrapping his arms around my waist and spinning us both around as the harmony of a mandolin, whistling and a harmonica danced over to us from the car speakers, the intro to 'Love Like This' by Kodaline.

'This could be our song,' I announced as we sang along to the up-beat chorus that was telling us to live in the moment, to enjoy our romance, even though we knew it couldn't last forever: this song I loved now the soundtrack to my life. Max started spinning me under his arm, both of us laughing uncontrollably. I was trying to be carefree and forget there was a Friday but as I stopped dancing to catch my breath and looked across at Max, I knew that actually I did mind that this wouldn't last, he really did light up my heart, I couldn't remember ever feeling this way. As much as I was trying to push it from my mind, the reality was that I was dreading saying goodbye to Max on Friday… but I needed to keep my emotions hidden so I didn't spoil the time we had left together.

We went back to the car and continued our adventure, eventually parking in a field by a river, where Max placed a blanket under a tree and laid out our food, wine and stolen cutlery.

'You couldn't have stolen a couple of wine glasses?' I teased, unscrewing the wine bottle and taking a swig.

After devouring most of the spread and a few gulps of wine each, Max sat back, leaning against the tree trunk as I lay on my back, resting my head in his lap. I paid attention to how I felt in that moment. Relaxed. Contented. Happy. The stillness of the tree above, flecks of sun peeping through gaps between leaves and branches. The sound of the river. Max stroking my hair.

'You know when you had the operation,' Max started. I wasn't sure what he was going to say. 'You weren't alone, were you?'

I was overwhelmed by his question, that he was even thinking about me back then, that he genuinely cared. I shook my head and smiled.

Max instantly understood and smiled too. 'Michele?'

'Yes.' I nodded. 'She was incredible. I had to be there for four, my operation was that evening. I'd never been in hospital before so I didn't know what to expect. She drove me there and waited with me. We thought the time would drag but as soon as they showed us to my room, it was full on. Nurses doing checks, the surgeon came to see me, then the anaesthesiologist. Each asking the same questions and getting me to repeat the procedure I was having, I don't know if that's some sort of acceptance technique they use. When it was finally time, I'd started to cry. I'd been holding it in all day, keeping myself busy to distract my thoughts, but I was petrified, certain I wasn't going to wake up. I was convinced I was going to die on the operating table.'

The realisation suddenly hit me, making me sit up. I'd never thought about it before. I carried on talking, but my mind raced back to the hospital with Michele.

'I remember looking at Michele and hugging her, not wanting to let her go, certain it was the last time I would ever see her. Trying not to cry but unable to stop myself.'

My body was overcome, that fearful feeling from back then briefly returning as a single tear escaped, the reality hitting home again.

'But I didn't die. Michele did.'

I was caught in the memory of my final farewell. How terrified I'd been. How I hadn't been ready to die. How Michele hadn't been ready to die. How she had no one to hug goodbye. How she had died all alone. I hugged my knees into my chest, the searing pain taking hold.

'Hey,' Max soothed, wrapping his arms around me.

'She was all alone, she died all alone. She had no one with her in her final moments.'

Max held me tighter as I struggled to breathe, stifling the threatening tears.

'She wasn't alone. She was loved by you and Adam and her mum and her friends, all the people who came here to Verona. She knew she was loved. It's not those final moments that are important, it's all the moments that led up to them that count. Trust me, she wasn't alone,' Max reassured me.

I thought about Kate alone in her car. He was right, they knew they were loved.

I nodded as I met his caring eyes, in awe of his wisdom.

My entire being was drawn to him. I was helpless to stop it.

I lay back down, my head on Max's lap, looking up at the tree and the tessellating blue sky. I began to smile as the memory of Michele reprimanding the nurse popped into my mind. As if Michele herself had placed it there to cheer me up. She'd always known how.

'What's making you smile?' Max asked as he stroked my hair.

'The nurse walking me to theatre saw I was crying and asked if I already had children, assuming that was the reason, not my fear of imminent death. Michele was livid, she told the nurse that she should think before engaging her mouth and sign up for some sensitivity training. Then she instructed the nurse to telephone her the second I was out of surgery with an update, gave me a hug and got in the lift. The nurse turned so pale I felt like I needed to hold her hand the rest of the way to theatre.' I couldn't help but laugh at the memory. 'Michele always had my back. She knew how much I needed to get out of my old rented apartment, the one I'd shared with James. My new apartment completed a few weeks after the surgery, but I wasn't going to move in. As much as I needed a fresh start, to move on, I could barely lift a kettle, never mind pack. Michele became my project manager. I chose and she organised, the cleaning, decorating, carpeting, new furniture, removal men, everything. She made those next few months so exciting, took my mind off the surgery and James, gave me something fun to focus on. She and Adam packed up all my worldly possessions, then unpacked them at the other end, shouting at me every time I tried to do or lift anything. I remember walking into my new apartment and everywhere being homely. She'd even paid Adam and his friend to build my new bed. I lay there that first night, looking up at the stars and thinking how there was nothing I could ever do or say that would let her know how truly grateful I was for everything she'd done for me.' I held Max's hand to my heart. 'I hope she knew.'

I thought about how I was now faced with packing up all of *her* worldly belongings, how I had failed at the task so far, the pain too great. I resolved to do it when I got home. It was the least I could do.

Max kept stroking my hair, holding my hand, reassuring me that Michele definitely knew. I could reveal my darkest thoughts to him. I didn't have to pretend to be light and easy or be the strong one, Max offered me strength. No matter what I told him, he accepted me. He understood me. It was effortless being with him. He made me feel important, wanted, happy and beautiful. I could feel a confidence growing inside of me, dislodging those insecurities left by James. I wished for every second between now and Friday to feel like an hour.

As Max cleared away the rubbish to the car, I shook out the blanket and lay back down under the tree, the sound of the river keeping me company until Max returned and lay down next to me. I reached across to hold his hand but instead he placed something into mine. I brought it up to my face to look. It was a box, the kind a necklace or bracelet would come in. We both sat up, Max facing me, watching me intently as I carefully opened the box to reveal a heart-shaped silver locket with a single diamond in the centre, made to look like a star. I picked it up between my fingers. It was elegant and delicate. Beautiful. Definitely something I would wear. I turned it over and saw the inscription 'Always' etched on the back.

'Open it,' Max prompted.

I was confused. Were there pictures inside? Of him, of us, how? When I opened it, I froze. It took my breath away. There before me was Michele how I always wanted to remember her, laughing hysterically, me by her side. That moment in Amsterdam captured forever. I was overwhelmed.

'I had the idea when you were telling me about the photograph,' Max explained. 'How you always want to remember her that way. The power it holds. You can wear it and whenever you need her, open it up, she'll always make you smile.'

'But how did you…?' I couldn't finish, I was truly overcome, tears swimming in my eyes.

'I took it while you were in the shower. When I went to get us coffee on Monday. It was ready today. Remember I had to run that errand earlier?'

Even on Monday he'd cared enough to do something that monumental. I thought back to earlier in the cafe, his excuse that he didn't want me to go with him to pay a boring bill. He'd returned with a huge grin on his face, like he was up to something. It all made sense now. I was speechless. I had a million thoughts swirling around my head but I was unable to voice any of them. I couldn't stop staring at it.

'You do like it, don't you?' A worried expression was spreading across Max's face. 'I know the engraving's a bit off-centre, he did it by hand and he's getting on a bit n–'

'I love it,' I interrupted, throwing my arms around his neck.

'Wait, whoa, no.' He pushed me back so he could see my face, concern on his. 'I didn't mean to make you cry.'

'But this is good turquoise,' I told him, laughing through my tears and wrapping my arms around his neck again, hugging him tight. I put my mouth to his ear and told him, 'And this,' I said, dangling the locket, 'is the most wonderful, beautiful, thoughtful, meaningful gift anyone has ever given me. Thank you. I will treasure it, always.' Tears filled my eyes again as I held this wonderful man, never wanting to let him go. Never wanting Friday to come.

Max secured the locket around my neck and we lay cuddling, him on his back, me on my side, in his nook, exactly how we slept.

'Besides Michele, I think you've seen me cry more than anyone else in the whole world.'

Max squeezed me tighter as we lay in our comfortable embrace, being serenaded by birdsong around us.

'What about your other friends?'

'God no, I'm not usually this emotional, you seem to draw it out of me.'

Max laughed. 'Right, yeah, cheers, so what you're saying is I make you cry.'

I started to laugh too.

'So if you'd, say, had a row with James, you wouldn't tell your friends?'

'Well, in a matter of fact, James is doing my head in type of way but I wouldn't go into detail, I'd just leave it at that. If I needed to vent, I'd talk to Michele.'

'So Michele knew all your secrets.'

'Everything,' I paused, 'except for thinking I was going to die in surgery, I hadn't told her that.' I gazed up at Max. 'I hadn't shared that with anyone before today, you're the only person in the world who knows about my irrational fear.'

I rested back into Max as he placed a kiss on the top of my head, his arms wrapped around me.

'So tell me something about you, something nobody else in the world knows,' I prompted.

He didn't respond for a few moments.

'When Kate died, she was pregnant.' Max exhaled loudly. 'I've never said that out loud before, not in six years.'

As his words hit me, he secured his arms tightly around me. I was unable to move my head to look at him, so I looked straight ahead at his chest rising and falling, holding him as he spoke.

'She was five weeks pregnant, we'd just found out two days before… It was only the size of a sesame seed but the moment she told me, our child's future played out in my mind, like a video on fast forward, I saw it all. I was going to be a dad.' He paused. 'I didn't just lose Kate that day, I lost our child too, my family, that future I'd seen.'

We lay in silence as the enormity of his loss struck me.

'Why didn't you tell anyone?'

'I didn't think it was fair. Losing Kate was already enough, they didn't need any more pain.'

I had no words, all I could do was lay there and hold this selfless man as I tried to somehow comprehend the senseless cruelty.

After a few minutes, Max relaxed his hold. I leant up on one elbow, caressing his cheek with my hand.

He looked at me. 'Sorry, I didn't mean to get all deep and morbid. I'm guessing you would've settled for "I stole chocolate bars as a kid." No one else knows that either.' He smiled, attempting to lighten the mood, but his eyes were filled with loss.

I moved so my face was next to his. 'I'm glad you told me, you've already carried that around for far too long.'

We searched each other's eyes, before finding each other's lips. A kiss filled with grief, loss, passion and longing. I desperately wanted to take his pain away.

We walked down to the river where Max began collecting pebbles and throwing them. I watched his body twist, the concentration on his face as the pebbles bounced and skimmed across the surface of the water as he tried to get them all the way across to the other side, then his triumphant smile when he succeeded. He was gorgeous. Max tried to teach me but I was hopeless, although I did enjoy him holding me close as he modelled the correct stance. I sat down on the river bank watching him as he told me how his dad had taught him as a young boy in the river near where he grew up. He was an only child. That he used to practice when his dad took him fishing and get into trouble because he would scare all the fish away. How it used to drive his dad crazy.

'Do your parents still live in England?'

Max nodded. 'In Bedford, the house I grew up in, not far from where I lived with Kate.'

'Bedford?'

Max laughed at my lacking geographical knowledge. 'North of London, in between Oxford and Cambridge, near Milton Keynes.'

I nodded. I'd never been to that part of the country, just bypassed it on the way to London.

'What about yours, do they live in Manchester?' Max asked.

'My dad and his wife live just outside Manchester but I rarely see him now he's retired, they're always with her family or off on holiday somewhere.'

Max turned and grinned. 'That's who you get it off.' Then carried on throwing pebbles. 'What about your mum?'

'She lives in a remote village in the north of Scotland. She moved there years ago, it's where her husband's originally from, his family live there.'

'Do you see her much?' He turned again to look at me.

I shook my head. 'No. It's bloody miles away. And it's always freezing.' I shivered at the memory of my last visit, being greeted by thrashing cold rain after a ten-hour drive. 'We call each other. Only on the landline though. She's a bit like you,' I giggled, 'none of that mobile phone nonsense. She's all about the good old reliable landline.' Max giggled too, pretending to throw a pebble at me for teasing him. 'What about you. Do you see your parents much?'

'Yes, they come over a few times a year, otherwise they'd never see me. Oh, and to visit Luca's parents too.'

'You've never been back to visit them?' My voice was a mixture of surprise and confusion.

Max stopped mid-throw, his face turning serious. He dropped the rest of the pebbles and wiped his hands on his jeans as he walked over and sat down next to me.

'I tried once. It was their thirtieth wedding anniversary, I was going to surprise them. I knew it'd mean the world to them to have me at the party. Turned out I gave them quite a different surprise.'

'Why, what happened?'

Max exhaled and ran his hands over his face. 'I was sat on the plane, people were still boarding. I started to feel hot and clammy, I thought it was because the engine wasn't on yet, you know when the air con's not running? Anyway, then I felt this tightening in my back and neck, which I put down to all the sitting around. Then my mouth went dry, so I called the stewardess to ask for some water but as I tried to speak my words came out slurred. She was looking at me like I was hammered but I'd not had a drink. So I tried again but they were still slurred. That's when I started to panic, I thought I was having a stroke or something. Within minutes, I was burning up, sweat started pouring off me, I was struggling to breathe, my heart was pounding, I was completely freaking out. I couldn't get my breath, I thought I was going to die. All I remember after that is people staring at me as I was carried off the plane by paramedics.'

'What was it, were you okay?'

'An anxiety attack. I had quite a few mild ones for a year or so after Kate died but nothing like that, it scared the hell out of me. And of course the hospital rang my mum and dad, as they're my next of kin. At that point they didn't know what was wrong so Mum and Dad cancelled their party and jumped on the next flight.' He shook his head, rubbing his face again, as though hiding behind his hands. 'It was a nightmare.'

'Do you still get them?'

Max shook his head. 'I learned to know my *triggers.*' He air-quoted the word. 'That's what the doctor called them. Going back to England, where I'd lived with Kate, trigger. I haven't flown since, not anywhere. Fortunately, living in Italy I have incredible cities, architecture, lakes, countryside, mountains, all on my doorstep so there's no need.'

'You certainly picked a beautiful place to live a stress-free life.' As we focussed on the rolling hills in the distance, the reality that this knowledge brought with it sank in the pit of my stomach, quashing any hope I might have been secretly clinging to of seeing Max again.

We continued our walk beside the river, hand in hand. Max put his arm around me and pulled me close.

'Who'd have ever thought, meeting you on that bridge on Sunday, that we'd be here now.'

'I know,' I agreed. 'It feels like I've known you a lot longer.'

'That's because we've crammed in two months' worth of dates.' He held up his free hand while speaking and began counting on his fingers to emphasise his point. 'My view, one. The club, two. Hanging out at your hotel, three. Daytime at the beach, four. Night time at the beach, five. That would have been two dates,' he explained, justifying his thought process that he could see me about to question. 'Piazza Bra, six. The vineyard, seven. Brunch today, eight. The markets, nine. And our picnic here is ten.' He stopped walking and faced me. 'See, it's the equivalent of a lot of dates.'

I started to laugh. I could see he'd put some thought into it. Maybe to make sense of it himself. To somehow justify how we were feeling what we were, the connection between us growing deeper and stronger. We had shared so much with each other in this short time.

I wrapped my arms around his neck, taking in the moment, the way he felt, his smell, the way he held me, the river, the hills, the vineyards, the blue sky, the birds flying overhead. Today was turning out to be even more fabulous than I could ever have imagined when I was jumping up and down on the bed this morning. Our adventure was already incredible. Another day I would remember, always.

As the sun faded, we went back to the car, music playing, both of us singing along. I could tell Max was still amazed I knew the words to many of his favourite songs, but they were my favourites too. His taste, like mine, was a mix of old and new. He was playful and silly when he sang along to a song he loved, just like I was, comfortable enough to be ourselves in front of each other. 'Please, Please, Please, Let Me Get What I Want' by The Smiths followed. I started to tell Max how I'd studied Art A-level, not because I'd intended on doing anything with it, but simply because I'd enjoyed it. We'd looked at the use of art in film and one clip, set to that song, was from a 1980s film called 'Ferris Bueller's Day Off', which had since become one of my all-time favourite films. The character was staring at a child in the painting 'A Sunday Afternoon on the Island of La Grande Jatte' by Seurat. The closer he looked, the less he could see, depicting how the character felt like he was disappearing. It was because the painting was composed of tiny dots that you couldn't see until you looked closely. It stayed with me for years, I was fascinated by it, finally visiting The Art Institute in Chicago to see it for myself first hand.

'And, did it live up to your expectations?' Max asked.

'Surpassed them,' I answered. 'I remember sitting on a bench in front of that huge painting for well over an hour and feeling like I had accomplished a life dream. Is it really pathetic that I listened to this song on repeat while looking at it?' I cringed.

Max shook his head, smiling. 'No, I probably would've done the same.'

He got it.

We drove on, fingers entwined, Max stroking the back of my hand with his thumb. With every moment, our touch became more intense, more insatiable, like being electrocuted but in a good way. Max caught me looking at him, caught *how* I was looking at him. I reached across and placed my hand on the side of his face, stroking his cheek with my thumb. He indicated and pulled over, switching off the engine. There wasn't another vehicle in sight. It was almost pitch black, no streetlights, just thousands of stars and the moon gently lighting his face, allowing me to make out his glistening eyes burning into mine, reading each other's wants and needs.

'Thank you. It's been a great adventure.' I touched the locket with my free hand. 'And thank you for this. I really will treasure it, always.'

Sadness hit me, but not about Michele, I felt like I was saying goodbye to Max, well getting ready to, anyway. I knew I would treasure the locket and these memories I had created with him for the rest of my life. There were certain people you knew would always own a piece of your heart, however fleeting their time with you, the connection so strong it would be simply impossible to forget them. Max was one of those people.

He leant over, putting his hand on the side of my face. I moved into it, closing my eyes, pushing back the tears threatening, memorising his touch. Then he kissed me, hard and passionate. I undid my seatbelt and moved onto his side, sitting on his lap, straddling him. I held his face in my hands, tracing his lips with my thumbs before slowly running my hands down his chest and under his teeshirt. My body was alive, electricity surging throughout me. We found each other's lips, kissing, holding, caressing, consuming and being consumed. He was allowing me to take the lead. Waiting for signals that I was ready. I enjoyed the feeling of being able to dictate my own future for once.

We finally parted lips, resting our foreheads together, panting, both feeling exactly the same. Craving to take things further.

'Take me to your place,' I breathlessly commanded, kissing him once more before returning to my seat and buckling in.

We drove the rest of the way in our comfortable silence, his hand on mine, relishing in the anticipation, lust overflowing. My body was aching for him.

8

THURSDAY

It was after midnight when we arrived at Max's, no one else was home. He held my hand and led me through the lounge, straight to his bedroom. His gentle thumb strokes seemed to resonate throughout my entire body; my senses heightened in the darkness. As he switched on the lamp and walked over to his iPod dock, I closed the bedroom door, trapping the anticipation inside with us.

He turned to face me, reaching for my hand and pulling me to him, slowly moving us in time to the music. I closed my eyes, enjoying being in his arms, his body against mine.

'This is our song,' he whispered, his breath tickling my ear.

I looked at him, smiling as I recognised the familiar song. 'Lovesong' by The Cure.

Max smiled. 'They say it better than I can.'

I snuggled back into Max's embrace as Robert Smith sang to us about being with someone who made him feel whole again, who made him feel young, fun and free, who he'd always love no matter how far away they were or how much time passed. I looked into Max's wanting eyes and nodded my approval at his song choice. It was perfect. We stood for a moment, the warm glow of the lamp making his eyes appear an even deeper shade of brown, the air between us charged. The moments we'd shared – from hiding in the gardens to kissing in the car earlier – that had ignited this lust and finally led us here to Max's bedroom. I'd known at the beach I wanted to make love to him and now here we were. My excitement was suddenly joined by nervousness, it had been two years since I'd been with a man, and I didn't know if my altered body would respond in the same way as before.

As if sensing my nerves, Max smiled reassuringly and tucked a piece of hair behind my ear. He put his hand on the small of my back and pulled me closer so our bodies were tightly pressed together. A heat seemed to radiate from the epicentre where we connected, making the rest of me yearn for his touch. I ran my palms down his torso to the edge of his teeshirt, my fingertips lightly brushing against his warm skin as I lifted the teeshirt above his head, removing it and dropping it on the floor. Max watched me as I caressed his naked chest, taking it in. I wanted to touch, kiss, taste every part of him. I trailed my palms across his smooth skin, moving down his toned stomach. He was beautiful. I traced my fingertip around his navel and down even farther to the V where his abs met his hips – he was so sexy – then horizontally across where his hair began, just above the waistband of his jeans sitting low on his hips. My favourite part of his body, besides his eyes. My breathing grew shallow, knowing what was inches below my touch, I was losing all restraint. Max closed his eyes and inhaled sharply, I enjoyed seeing his pleasure from my touch, his craving matching my own. I began placing kisses across his chest, up his neck, onto his cheek, finally finding his mouth. Max returned my kiss hungrily, his tongue meeting mine. He took my lead, running his fingers down my arms, my sides, my thighs, his gentle touch making my pulse quicken as he found the hem of my dress and lifted it, our mouths momentarily parting to allow him to remove it. I pressed myself into him, surprised by how responsive both of our bodies were to each other's touch. Max embraced me in his strong arms as his lips found my cheek, my neck, my collar bone. I gasped with pleasure as his kisses left a cool trail, which connected deep inside. Every pore reacting to his delicate touch. I tilted my head to one side, offering him easier access as he slid my bra strap down my arm and kissed my shoulder, up my neck, I could feel his breath on my ear, the sensation overwhelming. The entire left side of my body was frozen, yet alive. My breathing grew louder. I wanted to feel him against my naked chest.

I stepped back, standing before Max in my underwear, enjoying his eyes on my body, how powerful and sexy he made me feel, patiently waiting until they met mine again, before slowly removing my bra and letting it fall to the ground. Max's eyes remained on mine as he sat down on the edge of the bed and held out his hand for me to move closer. It was only when I stepped towards him that his eyes travelled down, then I felt his hands and mouth on me. I entwined my fingers in his hair, pressing myself against him. I felt alive. I wanted more. My hands on his shoulders, I pushed him so he was lying down. As I stood looking at him laid out before me, I couldn't remember ever wanting someone so much. I swallowed hard and moistened my lips, moving on top of him, straddling him, leaning down and kissing him on the mouth, our kiss growing more passionate as we pushed ourselves together, separated by underwear and jeans, our hands exploring each other. Without taking his lips off mine, Max flipped me so I was underneath him, and then he was between my legs. He trailed kisses down my neck, my breasts, my stomach. My back arched at the touch of his tongue, my body completely aroused, my skin so sensitive it was as if an ice cube were touching me. But as Max began to remove my knickers, my hand instinctively rushed down to stop him, afraid of him seeing the thin, pale line etched across my body. He took my hand in his and gently kissed it as he looked into my eyes to offer reassurance. I hid behind my arm as he began to trace my scar with his kisses. A single tear escaped, running down the side of my face, disappearing into my ear. Max removed the arm I was hiding behind so his eyes were once again on mine. 'You're perfect,' he whispered, erasing the path of my tear with his thumb. I grabbed him and kissed him like he was my oxygen.

As our kiss grew more urgent, I reached down and unbuttoned his jeans, my fingers eager and clumsy like a teenager. Max helped until we were skin to skin, our fully naked bodies finally pressed together, our hands searching each other. My entire body was tingling. Max held himself above me, his strong arms on either side of my head, his eyes level with mine. He brushed my hair off my face, checking I was ready. I'd never been more sure about anything in my life. I impatiently raised my hips to meet him, lightly digging my fingers into his backside, pulling him towards me. I needed to feel him. Max slowly lowered himself, prolonging the moment, and I wrapped my arms and legs around him, enjoying his weight on top of me. A breath caught in my throat as we became one, as he finally completed me, our bodies moving in rhythm, our breathing mapping our satisfaction, our hands exploring and caressing, intent on pleasing each other. Max's eyes searched mine, reading my desires and wants, as he made my body experience feelings I wasn't sure I'd ever feel again, as two years fell away, dissolving into passion, giving ourselves completely and crossing the line where passionate sex became making love, all-consuming passionate love.

We eventually collapsed into our embrace, sated, exhausted and relaxed, the desire that had been building between us now released, the need deep within now nourished, a deeper connection shared. I was aware as I lay in Max's arms that I had a constant smile on my face. I wasn't sure if it was because I hadn't had sex for two years, or because that was the best sex of my life, or because I'd just discovered that post-surgery orgasms were still wonderful, if not more so. Although maybe that was down to the man in my arms. Everything was heightened with Max.

We shared that sleepy, intimate pillow talk. Both confiding our innermost thoughts and fears since James, the surgery and Kate; it felt as if we'd taken each other's virginity. As I drifted off to sleep in his arms, I remembered what Luca had said at the beach, how it looked like there was only one person in the bed because we slept so close, waking up exactly how we'd fallen asleep. I'd never been able to fall asleep like that with anyone before, preferring to spoon or stretch out, but somehow with Max it was comfortable, we just fit.

* * *

I woke a few hours later, wrapped in Max's arms, immediately thinking about Michele and gaining strength from his hold as the wave passed. Then I imagined waking up without his comfort and strength wrapped around me. My stomach clenched as it filled with dread. I tried to push it to the back of my mind. I needed to accept it for what it was and be thankful, not get carried away with unrealistic dreams I knew could never come true, it's not like I could stay in Verona forever. My home, my job, my friends, my life was in England. Most importantly, Adam was in England. I had responsibilities, I couldn't just pick up and go. I had to be practical, not let myself get carried away with romantic fantasies. I'd declared I would spend as much time with this wonderful man as possible then return to my life tomorrow. That was just the way it had to be. But as I lay there in Max's arms, staring at the clock, imagining myself on a plane home this time tomorrow, I couldn't escape the sadness as it crept to the backs of my eyes, constricting my throat. As if reading my thoughts, Max began stroking my hair, soothing me. I swallowed hard, blinking away the gathering tears as I looked up to kiss him good morning, the memory of hours ago putting huge grins on both of our faces.

'Good morning, beautiful.'

I kissed him again, then settled back into our position and we lay cuddling in silence. I enjoyed the stillness, the sound of his heartbeat, his chest hairs ticking my cheek. His scent. I buried my nose into his neck and inhaled, memorising his smell – caramel and coconut. Wrapped in Max's arms was exactly where I wanted to spend my final day in Verona, there was nowhere else I'd rather be.

Max's movement pulled me from my sleepy embrace.

'Back in a minute,' he whispered, kissing me.

When he came back from the *en suite* bathroom, I watched with disappointment as he put on his black jeans and a black teeshirt, running his fingers through his hair. I'd never known a man look so good in jeans and a teeshirt, I couldn't take my eyes off him. Although I would have preferred it if he were taking them off.

He tilted his head to one side, studying my expression, then bent down and placed a long kiss on my lips. 'I'm just going to make us coffee, I will be right back, don't move.' He winked before turning and heading to the kitchen.

I lay back down, smiling, flashbacks from last night replaying in my mind, my entire body awakened.

I eventually sat up and looked around his room. It could have passed for a New York loft apartment, it certainly had that feel. The bed I was sitting on had an industrial feel, made from metal and wood with two matching single-drawer cubes for bedside tables. Charcoal bedding. A dark wooden floor with a huge, cosy grey rug. His walls were mostly exposed brick. I noticed two large frames leaning up against an empty wall, looking like they were waiting to be hung. There was a dark wooden dresser that housed his music, iPod dock, CD player – and he had a turntable like me. There was something about playing vinyl; I even loved the crackling. Although not so much when the needle stuck, repeating the same line over and over, especially when I was in a bubble bath and had to jump out to fix it. Next to his dresser, in the corner, was a retro leather swivel chair and footstool. It looked well used. I imagined Max sitting there, listening to music.

I headed to his *en suite* bathroom and opened the cabinet – a man of few products – picking up the Uppercut hair wax and twisting the lid off the large metal tin. I held it under my nose. That was Max's smell – coconut and caramel. I closed my eyes and breathed it in.

There was an unused electric toothbrush head, which I attached and used. When I'd finished, I automatically placed it in the holder next to Max's, such a little thing but it stopped me dead in my tracks. I couldn't help but wish it was my reality, our toothbrushes together, our lives together. I shook the thought from my mind, splashing cold water on my face and combing my hair with my fingers.

When I opened the door, Max was sitting in bed, shaking his head disapprovingly.

'It's supposed to be breakfast in bed,' he teased. 'Get back in.'

I smiled and darted back into his bed, pulling the covers over me as he placed the tray down between us. Two coffees, mine very milky how I liked it, two fluffy croissants and a tall glass, acting as a vase, containing my Gerbera Daisy, the one he'd bought me at the market yesterday. I touched the soft petals before planting a long kiss on the lips of the man opposite me.

After we'd finished eating, I moved the tray onto the floor and knelt up before Max, my eyes level with his, letting the covers fall away. I ran my fingers through his hair then traced his face, his shoulders, his biceps. He began to slowly trace his fingertip down my cheek, across my lips, my chin, my neck, along my clavicle and down my side, just brushing my breast. The craving deep within returned in full force. I was sure I could exist on the energy surging through my body from his touch alone and never need food again. We stayed for a few moments in that blissful anticipation before letting go, our mouths consuming each other, our bodies coming together, that connection again, looking into each other's eyes as we made love.

We lay in our embrace, satisfied and relaxed, my body felt completely weightless. My head resting comfortably in his nook as he stroked my hair.

'My mum used to stroke my hair,' I told him. 'When I was nine I went through a phase where I dreaded school. Every

Sunday night I would get this horrid panicked feeling. She'd lie on my bed, stroking my hair until I fell asleep. It was the only thing that used to soothe me. She did it every week for months and months.'

'My mum used to tickle my back and write words on it. I'd have to guess what she'd written,' Max shared.

I looked up at him, confused. I didn't know that game. 'Do it to me?'

We adjusted our positions so my back was facing Max and he began to write a word, one letter at a time. I said each letter out loud as he etched them into my back.

'M – a – x. That's easy, Max.'

He rubbed my back, which he called rubbing it out, and began again.

'A – l – e – x,' I spelled out. 'Alex.'

He rubbed my back for the next word.

'S – t – a – y.' Did he mean what I thought he meant? I shot around and met his sad eyes.

'Stay,' he gently said, feigning a smile. 'I can't imagine waking up and you not being here.'

It was like a punch to the stomach. Hearing him say the thing I had been secretly wishing for, knowing that he felt the same way. But also knowing it was impossible.

'I can't.' I was shaking my head, looking into his eyes, already missing the smile that was gone.

'Just a few more days.'

'I can't. I have plans with Adam. I can't let him down and I'm back at work on Monday and I *have* to be there.'

'But you can come back for long weekends. Just think, you can jump on a plane after work on a Friday and a few hours later we'll be in my club, dancing.' He said it with such conviction he made it sound possible. 'We could book it now, take the edge off tomorrow.'

Our energy couldn't have been more different, he was filled with making plans and excitement while I was filled with hopelessness and sadness.

'Max, I can't. I spend my Saturdays with Adam, he needs me. Plus, I have to clear Michele's house and… there's just so much to do and I can't take any more time off work. I've used all my holidays. You only get half a day bereavement leave when a friend dies, a sister gets you five days but Michele wasn't officially my family. I was a mess. It was all such a mess, Adam was–' I shook my head at the memory. 'He regressed into a little boy those weeks that followed, I was the only person he'd talk to, he needed me. My boss was amazing but I also had an 18-week absence on my record from the surgery. As lovely as she is, there was only so much she could do for me. She's allowed me to take this week as unpaid leave but that's it now until we finish for Christmas. No leave, no sick days. Plus, I can't afford to take any more time off, I've got my mortgage to pay.' As the practical side of my brain took over, I placed my hand on his. 'Max, this week, meeting you.' I struggled to put into words how much it had meant to me as I swallowed back the threatening tears at the thought of goodbye. 'I wish I could come back. I'm going to miss you so much.' I looked deep into his eyes, willing us both to be strong. 'Forget there's a Friday and live in the moment, remember.'

'But when I said that I didn't know I… that was before.'

I took a deep breath as I looked at his puzzled face, unsure how to make him understand.

'If I lived in Verona, or you lived in Manchester it'd be different, but we live a thousand miles apart and as much as I want to come back, I can't.' I paused, squeezing his hand, wishing he'd say he would visit me instead, though I knew that wasn't a possibility for him.

'So we'll keep in touch.' He shrugged.

I didn't say it out loud but I didn't want to become his friend and hear about him meeting someone else after me, I didn't want to see him look at her the way he did me. I selfishly wanted to hold onto our memories and how he made me feel. I needed to. I couldn't face ever being hurt by Max or regretting this week. A clean break would be easier, then nothing could ruin what we had.

'Let's just have our wonderful week together. You will forever remain the handsome stranger I met on a bridge in Verona.'

Max was shaking his head. 'No, tomorrow can't be it.'

'But it is,' I said sadly. I didn't want to talk about it or think about it any more, I just wanted to enjoy the little time we had left together.

'But we can email.'

'I don't see–' I took a breath. I'd already worked through every possible scenario in my head, I couldn't come back, he couldn't come to me, I didn't want to hear about him falling in love with somebody else. I guess I'd had time to prepare myself for goodbye, Max just needed to catch up. 'Let's just enjoy our last day together,' I pleaded.

He stared at me, as if waiting for me to change my mind. I watched as his eyes became pools of tears, as the realisation finally sank in. 'You don't want to keep in touch, do you?' His voice was barely a whisper.

It was painful to see the hurt on his face, the sadness in his eyes, knowing it was because of me. I shook my head. 'I just think it'll be easier this way, for both of us.' I really did, I just needed to hold onto that.

Seeing he couldn't change my mind, he pulled his hand away from mine, his sudden movement surprising me. His words cut through the silence. 'Maybe it'll be easier for both of us if you just leave now.' With that, he stood and walked into the *en suite* bathroom, locking the door behind him.

I followed, stopping and leaning my forehead against the closed door. I wanted to charge in and throw my arms around him, but I knew we'd just end up going round in circles again. I didn't want it to turn into a fight, to ruin our incredible week. I wanted to remember *us*, not this. Wasn't that the whole point?

I took a breath to steady myself and got dressed. Trying to convince myself that it was better to say goodbye now, why string it out? I needed to focus on Adam, on myself, I couldn't face being hurt again, especially not by Max.

As I went to walk towards the bedroom door, I found myself rooted to the spot, staring at the unmade bed, my head filled with memories from hours before. How had we possibly gone from that to this? I looked at the closed bathroom door, willing him to come out. I didn't want to leave, not like this, but I knew there was nothing I could do or say. With tears escaping down my face, I turned and left.

I half walked, half ran. Half wanted Max to come chasing after me, half wanted to be alone. I saw a taxi and flagged it down, getting in and saying the name of my hotel. The constant motion and ever-changing scenery helped me to order the thoughts and questions swirling around my mind as I replayed every possible scenario.

I thought back to a previous relationship, before James. We'd been dating for just over a year when he finished university and moved back home to Cornwall. We were in love, swore we'd travel back and forth, we were so important to each other and couldn't imagine not being a significant part of each other's lives every day. But it eventually fizzled. We didn't mean for it to happen, we simply got on with living our lives, found our weekends filled with other things that left no time for a ten-hour round trip. I remember in hindsight wishing we'd left it at goodbye instead of watching our new romances play out on the internet. That way we could have avoided the dwindling that ended up overshadowing our wonderful memories. I couldn't face that happening with Max, maybe I was being selfish but I needed to hold on to how incredible he'd made me feel, to the happiness I'd felt this week.

As I stared out of the window of the taxi, I recognised Michele's bridge and shouted for the driver to stop. He turned, gesturing and speaking in Italian, throwing some English words in, 'No. Hotel. No yet.'

'Here is fine,' I reassured him, giving him a kind smile and a generous tip before getting out.

I rushed to the spot where Michele still stood in the photograph, where I'd scattered her ashes, peering down at the river below, half expecting to see remnants. I remembered what Max had told me and opened the locket. It worked. Seeing her beaming up at me instantly made me smile. I thought about Max, his face full of confusion and sadness. I never wanted to hurt him. Neither of us could have predicted we'd develop these feelings, not in such a short space of time. I had tried to suppress them, rationalise them, make excuses that my emotions were heightened because of Michele, but the way Max could read me, sometimes knowing what I was thinking or what I needed even before I did. His love for music. His kindness and thoughtfulness. It was easy with him, natural, the way it was supposed to be. We could be ourselves around each other, no pretence, no games. I adored him. He made my heart flutter, gave me butterflies. There was an undeniable connection between us, far beyond anything I'd ever felt before, not even with James. If he lived in Manchester there would be no question, but I was simply being realistic, it was easier this way, well it would be in the long run anyway. Was I an idiot for letting it happen, for allowing myself to feel that way? No. I wouldn't go back in time and change anything about our time together. We don't get to choose when we feel it or who with. Max came into my life when I needed him most. He'd also allowed me to lay to rest two years' worth of demons. I would always be thankful for that. I was leaving with memories I would cherish forever. Maybe knowing we could never go beyond the very beginning was what made it so powerful and beautiful. It was safe to let myself get swept away, knowing it had an expiration date and could never cross over into my real life. No future meant no risk. I could remember the chemistry and passion, the attraction and lust. We'd never get to that stage when we'd argue, when those things we once found endearing about each other would start to annoy us. Max could never hurt me or let me down. I'd never have to face the disappointment and heartbreak if it didn't become that true unconditional love that stood the test of time.

No amount of rationalising could alter the fact that my insides felt like they were being ripped apart every time I imagined never seeing him again, but I knew once I got home that would fade. I turned and looked to my right, picturing Max, remembering our beginning. My smile was joined by tears. I didn't want that to be our end. I wanted to go back to him but I had no idea how to find his house. I looked across to where the taxi had dropped me; he could take me back to where he'd picked me up and maybe from there I could retrace my steps. But the taxi had gone.

I rested my arms on the ledge of the bridge, looking down at the water below as I continued to regret, question and rationalise. I pictured my iPod in the hotel room safe, wishing I had it with me, I needed a song. I closed my eyes and flicked through the jukebox in my mind as I searched for the perfect song to console me and counsel me through.

'You're not going to jump are you?'

The voice startled me. I looked to my right, expecting to find myself alone, my brain playing tricks on me. But there he was. Max. My heart leapt at the sight of him but I couldn't make out his expression, the bright sunshine behind him was casting his face into shadow. Until he moved closer. Sadness and regret.

'I'm sorry. I don't want that to be our last memory of each other,' he said, grabbing me and pulling me into his embrace. I held him tight. It felt incredible to hold him again, to be held by him. We stood that way for several minutes, before letting go. He looked at me, stroking my cheeks, wiping away the remnants of my tears, his face serious and apologetic. He shook his head. 'I never want to be the cause of your turquoise eyes. I just don't want tomorrow to be it.'

'But—'

He lifted his finger to my lips. 'I know I can't change your mind. Just listen to what I have to say because I really need to say it.'

I nodded.

'I know you think a clean break will make it easier but I think you're wrong, I think we should stay in touch. I understand the timing's off, that you have commitments and of course Adam's your priority, but I don't think us emailing would make it harder, surely it'd make it easier. Not ever talking to you again won't help me forget you.' He sighed. 'Alex, I don't *want* to forget you.' He caressed my cheek with his fingertips and studied my face as though he was reading my thoughts. 'I'm really going to miss you.'

'I'm going to miss you too.' I threw my arms around him and held him, our arms wrapped tightly around each other, fighting the tears away.

'What do you say to spending the rest of your last day with me?'

I squeezed him tighter. 'I think that's a wonderful idea.'

Max smiled at me, the sparkle finally returning to his eyes.

'I'm sorry, I shouldn't have left like that, I wanted to come back but I didn't know how to find... Wait, how did you know I'd be here, am I that predictable?'

Max grinned. 'Well it was either here, your hotel or the view but I knew there was no way you'd be able to find that on your own, not with your sense of direction.'

We laughed as we leant against the bridge, thinking back to the moment when we first met.

'Sunday seems like a lifetime ago,' Max said, shaking his head.

'What made you start talking to me?'

'You fascinated me,' Max admitted. 'I noticed you in that sexy black dress in the middle of the day and tried to make up your story, but nothing fit. Then I saw your face and there it was. Loss. I recognised it instantly. I had this urge to know you, the beautiful woman standing all alone, filled with sadness and loss.'

Beautiful. Sexy black dress. I began to laugh. It was my funeral dress. I loved the way he saw me.

'When we started talking, I knew exactly how you were feeling,' he explained, 'I saw myself in you. I just wanted to hold you, comfort you somehow. Take the pain away. When you mentioned escaping to somewhere peaceful, I knew I had to take you, share my favourite place with you.'

'Have you really never taken anyone else there? Not even Luca?'

Max shook his head. 'Not even Luca.'

I wrapped my arms around his neck. 'I'm honoured you shared it with me.' I met his eyes so I could emphasise it to him. 'You know that, don't you? Everything you've done for me, every moment we've spent together, I'll never forget any of it, it's meant more to me than I can ever express with words. I'll never forget you.' I was hanging on with all the strength I had, desperately trying not to let my emotions come pouring out of my eyes as I told him, but it was important he knew what he'd done for me. He had helped me through such a terrible time, had made me feel beautiful and enough. I needed him to know what a truly incredible man he was. I pulled him close and held him tight, suppressing the sadness and dread building inside.

'I wish you could stay,' he whispered, squeezing me tight.

So did I. I already missed him.

I needed to lighten the mood before I fell apart.

'Just so you know, I wanted to kiss you too when we were hiding in the gardens,' I admitted.

In one swift move he turned me around so my back was pressed up against the bridge, his body against mine, mimicking how we'd hidden in the gap between the houses.

'What made you come with me? I could've been an axe murderer.'

'That did actually cross my mind but I figured my day couldn't get any worse,' I teased, laughing, before turning serious and continuing. 'I thought I wanted to be alone but you made me not want to be alone anymore. Does that even make sense?'

Max nodded, his eyes serious. 'More than you know.'

As I wondered what he meant, he placed his finger on my lips, just as he'd done in the gardens. I was rooted to the spot again, that current surging inside. I managed to move my arm and this time I did trace the creases that appeared when he smiled, I did touch his full lips. Then they were on mine. We had come full circle.

It was another beautiful day so we strode hand in hand around Verona; I hadn't really seen it properly yet. As we walked, Max pointed out buildings and bridges, naming them and telling me stories behind them. He was incredibly knowledgeable.

He took me to the amphitheatre where we walked under arches supported by columns created from huge slabs of pink and grey stone; I felt tiny. Inside, it opened out into a perfect round, taking my breath away. We climbed to the top step and sat so I could take it all in. Not only was the actual amphitheatre beautiful but also the original wall that jutted up into the sky in one section, the views beyond of ancient buildings and rooftops, and the sky. It was as if the sky were part of the design. I could imagine how it added to the drama of an event, dictating the mood, especially when Max told me they staged operas there.

'I wish I'd seen R.E.M. play here,' I sighed.

Max stood, offering me his hand and pulling me up. He put one earphone in my ear and the other in his, hitting play on his iPod as he turned me so my back was to him, pointing out where the stage had been and wrapping his arms around me from behind.

'Close your eyes and pretend,' he said, as we joined the middle of the R.E.M. song 'You Are the Everything' he must've had paused.

I closed my eyes and imagined stars above my head, a stage below to the right, and the whole amphitheatre filled with people singing along to this beautiful love song as Max gently rocked me from side to side, singing in my ear, squeezing me tight as he emphasised certain lyrics, using the music as poetry between us. It made me think back to the old couple in the cafe, of being in love and growing old together. If there weren't so many barriers, I would happily grow old with Max. I could gladly stay here with him and be his everything.

'Do you think R.E.M. will ever play here again?'

'If that's what I've got to do to get you to come back.' Max winked at me. We both smiled but we felt it, our hearts heavy. It was impossible to ignore.

I rested my head back on him and closed my eyes, desperately trying to forget there was a tomorrow.

'Will you take me back to your favourite place?' I turned and asked. 'I want to see it one more time.'

Max nodded. 'Of course, but I've got somewhere else to take you first.'

As we left the amphitheatre, I noticed the shops were touristy, filled with pointless memorabilia and tacky gifts. Then I saw a sign for disposable cameras developed in thirty minutes. I ran in and bought one. I had to. I reappeared to find Max leaning against a wall, his arms folded, his knee bent, wearing his 1950s sunglasses. He could have been a model posing. I quickly wound the film to ready and took a photograph of him, moving closer to take another one. He finally saw me and chased me, grabbing the camera, laughing.

'When you've got no phone you've got to go old school,' I declared, laughing too.

He started to take some of me, then grabbed me and held the camera at arm's length to take a selfie of us both, then another with him kissing my cheek, then my lips, then me kissing his cheek, then giggling hysterically as we found the fact that we had no idea what he was taking and that he had to keep winding the film on so funny. A couple offered to take one for us. We posed, our arms around each other. Max turned me to face him. I placed my hand on his cheek, captivated by those eyes, before finding each other's lips. As we pulled apart, he rested his forehead on mine and I noticed the couple were watching, giggling, still taking pictures with our camera. I turned away embarrassed as Max retrieved the camera and thanked them.

I took the camera from him and looked at the dial: five left. Taking his hand and leading him to a quiet corner of the street. I desperately wanted to capture his eyes. Those beautiful eyes that sparkled when he smiled. Then I remembered my other favourite part of him.

'Reach up to the sky,' I instructed.

Max looked confused, so I modelled what I wanted him to do.

'Go on,' I encouraged.

He did as I'd asked, his teeshirt lifting. I grinned as I took a photograph.

'Pervert,' he laughed, walking over to me and taking the camera. 'Okay, just take off your dress,' he instructed, teasing me about my previous request.

I blew him a kiss as he finished the film. 'I will be right back.' I took the camera and ran back to the shop, handing it to the old man behind the counter and gesturing at the 'developed in thirty minutes' sign.

He gave me a pen and envelope to fill in.

'Hotel?' I asked, pointing to the address box.

'Indririzzo, casa.' He was shaking his head.

Address, house, I translated. I looked out of the window to ask Max his address but I couldn't see him.

'Casa, casa,' the old man repeated, tapping the box with his finger.

I took the pen and wrote my home address in England. It was my casa. He rolled his eyes but accepted it.

'Mezz'ora.' He pointed to the thirty minutes sign.

'Grazie,' I replied. Happy to leave the confusion of not speaking Italian and excited to return in half an hour to see our pictures.

I found Max and we decided to get an ice cream while we waited. Me, coconut and mint chocolate. Max, pistachio and salted caramel. We sat on a bench in the sun, tasting each other's while soaking up the bustle around us. Verona was such a beautiful city. Even the modern shops felt ancient, set among colourful buildings that were decorated with shutters and ornate balconies. I sat and watched the passers-by, my head resting on Max's shoulder, the sun warming my skin, happy to stay there. That was until I noticed thirty minutes were up and eagerly raced back to the shop while Max stayed seated, exchanging Euros for my treasure. I was excited to see them, making me appreciate how much we took digital cameras and mobile phones for granted. An instant photograph to check, delete and take again if needed. It was strange not knowing the outcome, it offered more excitement. Although I could imagine being hugely disappointed if they didn't turn out.

I opened the envelope and took out the wallet containing the photographs. We looked through them together one by one. Max looking sexy leaning up against the wall. Me smiling, looking really happy; I hardly recognised myself. A selfie of Max with a bit of me, then our lips kissing taken far too close, then a gorgeous one of Max looking at the camera with a smug grin on his face as I kissed his cheek. The ones the couple had taken were incredible, I couldn't help but feel thankful, even though I had been embarrassed at the time. I melted when I saw the next one. A close up of Max, his eyes sparkling, capturing the way he looked at me; I wanted to remember that forever and how it made me feel. I held it to my chest. Max tutted and shook his head, teasing me as he looked at the one of him reaching up, his teeshirt lifted. I began to laugh and gave him a sexy wink. As we looked at the final one of me blowing him a kiss, he put his arm around me, pulling me close, placing a long kiss on my head. More memories to treasure, always.

Max stood and held out his hand to help me up, like an actor in an old film; he was the perfect gentleman. We walked through narrow cobbled streets to Casa di Giulietta, the famous balcony from 'Romeo and Juliet'. I would've walked past it if I'd been on my own, the entrance wasn't obvious, one simple sign outside that could easily be missed. We walked through a crowded dark tunnel that opened out into a courtyard. Chatter and laughter echoed around the enclosure. The famous balcony was to my right on a beautiful, medieval looking building. To my left was an abundance of overhanging greenery, adding some dramatic colour to the courtyard. A bronze statue of Juliet stood straight ahead. People were having their photograph taken grasping the right breast of the statue. I nudged Max, who informed me that apparently it brought good luck to give her right breast a rub. I asked how that had started but he didn't know, doubting if anyone did. There was a long queue of people waiting to go up to the balcony to have their photograph taken by their Romeo. Max explained how he found the place fascinating. Romeo and Juliet were fictional characters. Their love impetuous. The play was set in the 1300s yet the balcony was only added in the 1930s. Despite all that, people flocked there, seduced by the hope of finding true love. Films had been made about the love letters people left stuck to the walls of the tunnel we had walked through as we entered. It had been so crowded I hadn't noticed. I led Max back towards the tunnel, my hand in his. I enjoyed listening to him tell me the history of the place. How people had previously stuck notes to the walls using chewing gum but it had become such a mess the council had imposed new laws and fines, trying to tidy it up. They'd created a designated area for leaving letters, which he added, volunteers replied to, offering advice. I thought back to the photograph frame hanging in Max's lounge, the four sections containing colourful blobs and graffiti.

'Those four photographs in your lounge. Were they taken here?' I asked.

Max nodded, explaining how he'd taken up photography when he'd moved here, how he'd taken all of the photographs on his walls at home, making me wish I'd studied them more closely when I'd had the chance. 'I took the set of four before they cleaned all the chewing gum away. I loved the message, a lyric, written in different places across the walls but I got it, that they were linked.'

'What does it say?' I remembered the Italian writing but obviously hadn't been able to read it.

'Rescue me, from the darkness, take my hand-' Max began.

'Set me free,' I interrupted, instantly recognising it.

Max squeezed my hand, smiling, shaking his head in astonishment. It was another song we both knew and loved. I played the song in my head, it was exactly what we both needed – rescuing from the darkness.

We searched the graffiti-filled walls together. They were covered in sticky notes and plasters; I assumed a Band-Aid was easier to remove than gum. Most contained two names written together.

'A bond made between lovers to last for eternity,' Max translated.

He started speaking to the couple next to him in Italian. They handed him a sticky note and a pen. Max wrote my name then handed it to me, smiling but serious. I wrote his name then drew a love heart around them. We stuck it to the wall together as we both said 'for eternity,' such a teenage act but a fitting tribute. Max looked at me, the sadness returning to his eyes. I felt the heat build at the backs of my eyes and quickly looked away.

'Take me to your favourite place,' I asked, squeezing his hand.

We both took one final look at our names on the wall of love before heading off. How I wished I could return next week to see if they were still there. I wondered if Max would.

9

THURSDAY

We decided to buy sandwiches and drinks to take with us. Dinner with a view. My last supper. The walk wasn't familiar at all. I thought it was because my mind had been in a manic state the first time Max had taken me but we were in fact coming from a completely different direction. I had a terrible sense of direction. Max knew that and kept his arm tightly wrapped around me as we cut through a cemetery. It wasn't like any cemetery I'd seen before, there were rows of ancient crypts, all individually designed, like miniature detached houses lining wide gravel streets. And areas where giant trees stood spreading their shade upon statues and sculptures, angels and busts. Each grave a work of art, chiseled out of marble or stone and adorned with metal ornaments. Some barren and forgotten, others decorated with recently laid brightly coloured flowers. Most of the etchings were written in Italian but the dates, like the surrounding trees, confirmed the place was centuries old. Michele hated the idea of being buried, but I found the thought of having somewhere to visit a person, well their memory anyway, quite consoling. Somewhere to take them flowers, to sit and talk.

As we walked in silence, accompanied by the rustling of trees and birdsong, I found myself captivated by one of the graves and stopped. It was poignant and beautiful. A life-size metal sculpture of a couple laying together, like they were in bed, on their backs, holding hands on top of the metal sheet that covered their bodies, their heads turned in towards each other, their foreheads touching. They looked like they were sleeping, peaceful and in love, inseparable. A truly touching tribute to whoever these people were. I searched for a date, an age, wondering if they had grown old together, dying within a few days or weeks of each other, like you hear about. Immortalised as these young lovers for eternity. I could only hope for such love. Max's fingers entwined with mine as he stood beside me, captivated by it too.

As soon as we reached the outer wall of the gardens I recognised it, remembering how aware I had been of Max's touch as we'd peeked inside and the feelings he'd sparked in me. I looked across at that stranger who had somehow become so much more as he took my hand in his and led me into the gardens, but this time there were no interruptions as we darted through to the far wall. I was thankful for the interruption last time that made us hide in that narrow gap, our bodies pressed together. It was a moment I would never forget. We climbed over the wall, me once again struggling in a dress.

'You really need to start dressing for scaling walls,' Max teased as he helped me. I stopped as the view appeared before me. It was just as fabulous as I'd remembered. I wanted to check, because that whole day had been an emotional fog but I was in no doubt now, my mind hadn't exaggerated anything.

We sat on the bench, enjoying our sandwiches with a view, the best view in Verona, discussing how people would pay good money to sit and eat there.

'It needs a name,' I said, 'your favourite place doesn't do it justice.'

'*Our* favourite place,' Max corrected.

I knew it wasn't his intention, but hearing him say 'our' reminded us both of the inevitable again. Max reached inside his pocket for his iPod and plugged me in as I sat, looking out at the view, anticipating what song he was going to play to lift our mood, smiling at how similar we were, how we shared that musical connection, how lyrics spoke to us. To us, songwriters were modern-day poets.

Max placed his arm around me and I rested my head on his shoulder as the familiar piano filled my ear, 'Come Home' by One Republic. He'd amazed me when he'd quoted the exact lyric I'd been playing in my mind, making me certain even then that he could somehow read my thoughts. I closed my eyes and listened, but the song that had previously put my problems into perspective was now breaking my heart. The someone I'd been missing was Michele, but the song was suddenly speaking to me about Max, filling me with dread and sadness as my entire being willed me to stay. Max began squeezing me tighter, emphasising lyrics that sang that he needed me here... but Adam needed me more. I tried to focus on the beauty straight ahead, instead of in the heart of the man sitting next to me. I couldn't look at him.

It was dusk, lights were switching on in the distance. I looked around, we were completely secluded. I picked up the iPod and changed the song to 'Beautiful War' by Kings of Leon before standing and pulling Max to his feet, wrapping my arms around his neck, my body pressed up against his. He had that look on his face, the same look I had, he knew exactly what I was thinking, as he always did. He moved his hands down my back, resting them on my behind, moving us in time to the song that ached with passion, matching our own. He studied my face as if memorising it before kissing me, trailing his kisses down my neck, his lips making my skin tingle. Clothes were hastily removed as we lay down with an urgency to satisfy the insatiable appetites we'd awoken last night. I'd never experienced pleasure like this before, the passion, the connection, the intensity as our bodies became one.

As I lay, holding him, I could feel the growing dread building in the pit of my stomach, each second making the thought of goodbye even harder. I wanted to be the person I was with Max every day. I hadn't felt happiness like that in so long. With Max I was content, confident, a better version of me.

I held him tighter as I pushed the thought of tomorrow away and instead enjoyed the moment, lying under the stars in Max's arms, Kings of Leon still singing to us. I smirked, I had always thought 'Mechanical Bull' would be a good album to make love to; seemed I was right. Max began tickling me until I gave in and shared my theory with him.

'So, Kings of Leon gets you in the mood. I'm making a mental note of that,' he teased.

I hid my head in his chest, embarrassed.

'I could fall asleep here,' I said, yawning, 'but it's our last night, no sleeping yet.'

Max helped me to my feet as we fixed our clothes and hair, hiding any evidence. Our secret.

'Dante's playing at the bar tonight if you fancy it,' Max offered. 'Isabella, Luca and Aria will be there too, if you want to say goodbye?'

My stomach lurched. There it was, the word I had been dreading.

'Okay, let's get this out of the way now.' I took a deep breath and turned to face him. 'I hate goodbyes. We don't need some long drawn-out goodbye tomorrow, it'll just make it harder.' I placed my hand on his cheek, holding his eyes with mine. Eyes I couldn't imagine never seeing again. I swallowed hard. 'You know how I feel about you. You know if there was any way I could stay longer, I would. If I could come back, I would.' A deluge of tears surged to the backs of my eyes. I had to hold on, just a bit longer. I placed his hand on my heart. 'You'll always be in here.'

As Max became a blur, I quickly embraced him, squeezing him, trying to lessen the anguish inside. We stood that way, in silence, for several minutes as I took deep breaths to steady my emotions, composing myself before releasing Max and looking back into his eyes, feigning calm as my insides broke down and sobbed, desperately wanting to remain in his arms forever, for tomorrow not to be goodbye.

'There, done. Like ripping a plaster off. Okay?' I calmly reasoned.

Max stared at me intently, searching my eyes as he cupped my cheek in his palm, gently stroking it with his thumb. He slowly lifted my hand to his mouth, placing a delicate kiss on the back of it, savouring the moment, never once taking his eyes off mine.

'You know how I feel about you?' He spoke softly as he placed my hand over his heart.

I nodded, forcing away the tears, unsure how much longer I could hold on before I fell apart.

'Okay. Like ripping a plaster off,' he agreed, pulling me in and hugging me so tight I knew he didn't want to let go either. 'Please don't forget me,' he whispered.

I couldn't hold it in any longer, tears escaped, rolling down my face. As much as I tried, I was helpless to stop them. I wanted to tell him that I'd remember him, our time, everything, always, that I'd never forget what he'd done for me, that what I felt for him was unlike anything I'd ever felt in my entire life, that all I wanted was to stay in his arms, that he'd brought me real happiness for the first time in months, in years... but I couldn't. I was afraid if I opened my mouth to speak, the sobs forming inside would escape, that I'd never be able to stop crying, so instead I closed my eyes and focused on his heartbeat, allowing the rhythm to calm me.

When we finally let go of each other, I stepped back and breathed a sigh of relief. It was done.

We arrived at Max's bar, above the nightclub he'd taken me to that first night, which felt like months ago rather than days. I looked around at the tables full of people sitting and watching Dante in the far corner, picking at the strings of his guitar and singing. I joined them in watching him from the bar as Max ordered our drinks. He was singing a song I'd never heard before, it had a wonderful melody, carrying emotion as it told a story about letting someone go. I looked across at Max, knowing that was exactly what I had to do in a few hours; let him go. Would I ever be ready to?

Dante caught sight of us at the bar and gave a nod hello in the middle of his song. Luca and Aria appeared, each greeting me with a double sided kiss, Luca adding his lingering bear hug. Max still had Luca tomorrow and Luca could cheer anyone up. I wished even more I still had Michele. I doubt she'd ever contemplated the huge void her death would leave in the world, it was insurmountable. Despite the funeral and ash scattering I still imagined myself calling at her house. Maybe it took time to retrain the brain after all those years. I grabbed my locket, lost in thought, confused that I was now craving support to get over Max, when he was the very person who'd been helping me come to terms with losing Michele. Max placed his hand on my shoulder, bringing me back to the present. I looked up and met his concerned face. Seeing how much he cared for me instantly made me smile, which in turn made Max smile.

'I need to go to the office,' he said, taking my hand in his and leading me too.

Just before his office were the toilets, so I said I'd follow them in. I needed to freshen up after our impromptu moment at our favourite place. The memory gave me butterflies.

I looked at my reflection in the mirror, staring hard at the woman looking back at me, wishing we could somehow split off and live alternate versions of my life. A version where Michele was still alive, where we were holidaying together in Verona, where we'd stumbled upon Max's club and our eyes had met, Michele pushing me to go and talk to him. In that version, I was returning in a few weeks to spend the weekend with Max, Michele was taking Adam to football for me. Adam was still a carefree, happy teenager living at home with his mum, he didn't know grief or pain, nor did he have to carry around the image of finding his mum like that for the rest of his life. His only concerns were school and football, like every other fifteen year-old boy, the way it was supposed to be.

I found myself smearing soap on the mirror to hide my reflection, envious of her version, desperately wanting that to be my reality instead.

I left the toilets and walked through what I thought was the door to the office but it was a small corridor with three doors leading off it. I could hear Max, Luca and Aria's voices coming from the last door that was ajar. As I walked towards it, I heard my name and stopped.

'So what will you do?' I heard Aria say.

Then I heard Max's voice. 'There's nothing I can do. Her life's there, mine's here.' He paused. 'I can't imagine not seeing her every day though.'

'You have spent every moment together since you met. We're used to Loner Max.'

'That's the thing. She makes me not want to be alone anymore.'

'Well I liked her the moment I met her, and I've got excellent taste.' I could tell Luca was trying to make Max laugh. It went quiet for a moment, then Luca asked, 'When does she leave?'

'She flies home in the morning.' Max sounded despondent.

'But you're going to keep in touch?' Luca questioned.

'She doesn't want to, thinks it's easier this way.'

'Maybe she's right,' I heard Aria say. 'You don't expect her to give up her life for some guy she's known for five minutes. Why string it out?'

'I'd never ask her to do that,' Max insisted. 'I guess I'm just not ready to say goodbye yet.'

I had slid down the wall I was leaning against, and now I was sitting, hugging my knees into my chest. It hurt even more, knowing he felt exactly the same way. I already knew, but hearing him say it, realising that was what he'd meant at the bridge earlier – since Kate died, he'd become a loner, but I made him not want to be alone anymore. Me. Why did we live in different worlds? A huge weight was bearing down on my shoulders, like there was a puzzle hanging over me waiting to be solved but no matter how hard I tried, there was no solution. It was impossible.

I stood and took a few deep breaths, shaking the feeling before walking into the office. I could see the sadness on Max's face, he couldn't hide it, not from me. I busied myself looking around: wooden floor, wooden desk, laptop, leather chairs, a leather sofa against one wall. There was a framed poster on the wall above it from when R.E.M. played the amphitheatre. The Accelerate Tour. Arena di Verona. Next to it was the framed set list. I moved closer to read it. They played twenty-seven songs. Wow. I read each title.

'They didn't play 'Nightswimming'.' I blurted out.

Max, Luca and Aria all looked at me, surprised and confused by my outburst.

'Sorry,' I added, realising I had interrupted them.

Max and Luca began to laugh.

'She sounds as outraged as you were on the night,' Luca said to Max, exchanging a look. I knew Max's looks now. It was a 'See, she thinks the same as me' look. I did. We were such similar souls.

'We'll be out in a bit,' Max told Luca and Aria as they headed back to the bar, closing the door behind them.

Max joined me on the leather couch, lying down, his head on my lap, his feet dangling over the arm. I instinctively began to stroke his hair.

'So this is your office.' I looked around. 'I like it. It suits you. Did you do that?' I pointed to the wall opposite, covered in retro album covers.

'Yep.' Max smiled. 'I saw it in a film years ago and always wanted to do it. You like?'

'I love.' I looked from cover to cover, so many of them iconic, recognising some from my own vinyl collection: Nirvana, Pink Floyd, The Killers, The Stone Roses, The Strokes.

'So do you spend much time in here?'

Max nodded. 'There's always stuff to do. Luca takes care of the promotion and front of house and I do all the, 'boring business stuff' as Luca calls it. Yeah, it definitely keeps me busy. And there's a really good sound system in here so I quite often lay down listening to music. Although, there's not usually such a comfortable pillow.' He wiggled his head in my lap, a huge grin on his face. 'I was thinking of having a lyric painted on that wall.' He pointed to the empty wall behind his desk. 'But I can't decide. What's your favourite?'

I didn't need to think, I'd been listening to it a lot since Michele's death in my search for meaning. 'At the moment it's the chorus from 'The Weight of the World' by Editors. The idea that every piece of your life, every interaction goes on being meaningful to someone, even after you're gone. Those brief moments we share go on existing, leaving a part of you behind.'

I looked down at Max. Yes, those fragments of our lives we'd shared this week, they would remain long after I left tomorrow.

'Someone Michele dated at school came to her funeral. He hadn't seen her since we were sixteen, yet he felt compelled to attend, that piece of her life she'd shared with him all those years ago still meant something to him.' I shook my head. 'It was oddly beautiful how complete strangers gathered together with nothing in common except they all shared a piece of Michele's life with her. She was the common denominator.' I stopped. 'Does that sound depressing? It always sounds much more hopeful in my head.'

'No, it's not depressing at all, I like it.'

I carried on stroking Max's hair, his head in my lap, his eyes closed. I began to memorise his face, relieved I had bought a camera so I'd never have to worry about closing my eyes and not being able to picture him.

His eyes suddenly opened. 'I didn't take you to my favourite restaurant.' He looked at his watch, but it was too late and I wasn't hungry.

'Describe it to me. Why's it your favourite?'

Max relaxed back into my lap. Ignoring the pressure of the clock counting down. 'There's a walled garden at the back. They've grown ivy so it makes a ceiling and strewn it with white fairy lights. In the day it's pretty and offers shade but at night when they switch the lights on, it's magical. We always go there for whoever's birthday. It's been run by generations of the same family. The food is incredible. You do like Italian food?' He looked at me, his eyebrow raised.

'Who doesn't? The best meal I ever had was at a restaurant up in the hills in Florence. Away from all the touristy stuff, where the locals go. Popeye Spaghetti it was called.'

'I'll take you for Popeye Spaghetti before the R.E.M. gig I'm going to arrange, after I've convinced them to get back together, that is.'

We both nodded our agreement, smiling. We knew it was just a dream. A wonderful dream though.

'Tell me about your week,' Max asked, 'so I can imagine your world. You know mine.'

'It's not very exciting. I wake around seven. Drive to work with a latte.'

'One-shot.'

I grinned. 'You know me well. Although, a pumpkin spice one-shot latte to be exact. It's nearly that time of year again and I have a friend who works for Starbucks, she sneaks me cartons of the syrup,' I gave him a wink and whispered the last part as though Starbucks might be listening. 'I honestly don't mind rush hour traffic jams if I've got good music and a latte.'

Max was gazing up at me, smiling. I guess putting a positive spin on things was my way of coping and eventually turning things around after James and the operation. I'd bumped into a neighbour one morning. In that brief interaction she'd zapped me of all my energy with her moaning and negativity. It was exhausting. The most frightening thing was that I'd recognised myself in her, or rather who I was becoming. That was the turning point, I started taking time for me, to make myself happy because no one else was going to do it for me, I was in control of that. I began to focus on the positives in life. That was until Michele... Since then, it had been incredibly painful. I resolved right there in Max's office to begin finding the positives in life again when I went home, to focus on living. I was the lucky one after all, I had more time.

'What about next weekend?' Max asked.

'Friday night I'm going to a gig with friends. The Fray. I saw them years ago.'

Max stood and moved to his desk, opening his laptop and putting on their latest album before lying back down, their mix of up-beat and despondent love songs filling his office. It felt like we did this all the time, me visiting Max at work, hanging out in his office, listening to music. I allowed myself to momentarily imagine my life with Max in this wonderful city. I could feel it tugging at me to stay. It was tempting to throw caution to the wind, to stay and see what happened, but then I thought about Adam, and returned from my fleeting fantasy to reality.

'What about the rest of the weekend?'

'I'm going to finish something I've been putting off. Well, trying to do but failing terribly at.' My free hand reached for the locket as I thought about the mammoth task that lay ahead of me. Max was looking at me, confused.

'I need to clear Michele's house, so it can be sold. Adam and her mum have taken everything they want but they couldn't face clearing it, so they asked me.'

It was another request I had been unable to say no to, me, the person who usually had no problem saying no, but I couldn't, not to them.

'I've tried a few times but it keeps overwhelming me. There are too many memories and I can't sort them into piles. I don't want to. They're too sacred for piles. I end up moving things around, constantly changing my mind about the significance of an ornament or a tea towel, trying to remember if it was meaningful to Michele. Then I get sidetracked by a memory and end up sobbing, eventually giving up, going home and drinking red wine.' That was pretty much what had happened every time I'd tried it so far.

'I remember trying to clear Kate's stuff. It was impossible. For months I wouldn't let anyone touch or move anything, but then seeing her things made me furious. Constant reminders of what I'd lost, everywhere. I got drunk one afternoon and set a bonfire in the back garden. I burnt everything, her clothes, make-up, toiletries, books, everything. The neighbours thought I'd gone crazy, finally snapped. I had. I was completely consumed with anger. That was when I knew I needed to get away. I put the house on the market the following day. My mum paid to re-turf the grass in the back garden because apparently a big black hole puts buyers off.' Max closed his eyes momentarily, then looked up at me, a smirk appearing on his face. 'Just to be clear, I'm not recommending you get drunk and have a bonfire.'

'Okay.' I nodded. 'I promise I'll steer clear of alcohol and go with tradition: bin, keep or charity shop. No bonfires.'

What he'd told me gave me a glimpse into his world back then and I understood how bad it must have gotten for him and why he'd never been back.

'Lay down with me,' Max said, moving me into his nook. We lay, silent, in our embrace. I pulled strength from his hold, knowing how much I would need it next weekend. I breathed in his smell, trying to memorise it, as The Fray sang 'Break Your Plans' to us.

If only I could.

As we left his office to go back to the bar, Max pulled me back inside and gently pushed me up against the wall, kissing me passionately. He took me by surprise. I returned his sensual kiss until he eventually stopped and rested his forehead on mine, his eyes still closed. He finally opened them and looked at me intensely as he whispered, 'I never want to forget how this feels.'

Tears flooded my eyes as Max took my hand, walking out into the corridor where I'd eavesdropped earlier. My head was spinning. I didn't want to leave.

We returned to the bar and joined Luca and Aria's table, saying hello to Isabella and Dante, who was taking a break. I noticed Dante and Isabella gazing into each other's eyes. They looked completely in love. I was envious of them: their clock was invisible.

I sat back, watching Max interact with his friends, knowing he'd be fine. He was last week before he'd ever met me, as was I. Well, when Michele was still alive anyway. I touched my locket, replaying this week in my mind. Max had shown me that I could come out the other side, that my grief would lessen and one day I would be able to remember Michele without the deep anguish inside. As well as that, he'd awakened feelings I wasn't sure I would ever feel again. He'd allowed me to rediscover myself, to feel whole and beautiful, to believe it was still possible to meet someone and have a connection. He'd given me hope, even if we were hopeless. Although, sitting there, my hand in his, I honestly couldn't imagine ever feeling that way with anyone else.

I stood. 'Okay, who wants a drink?'

'I'll go,' Max insisted.

'Let me buy a round of drinks.' I grinned.

'But it's my bar, you don't have to buy them.'

I shook my head. 'That's not very business savvy of you. Same again?'

I made my way over to the bar. As I waited, Luca appeared beside me.

'Need a hand?'

'Thank you.' I nodded.

'So, you're really leaving me tomorrow?' There was a seriousness behind his grin.

'Afraid so.' I shrugged, trying to keep it light. My eyes settled on Max across the room, and Luca's followed.

'He's really going to miss you.'

'I'm really going to miss him.'

Luca smiled. 'You two have had quite the week together.'

I nodded my agreement, a smile spreading across my face at our memories.

'Max said you're not going to keep in touch?'

Somehow, Luca could get away with being so direct. I shook my head. 'I just think it'll be easier. I hope, anyway. I need to get my life together when I get home. I won't be able to do that if I'm clinging onto this, knowing it can't go anywhere. Make him understand, Luca, this week, meeting him, it's been the most incredible... If things were different. But my life's in England, and his is here with you.'

Luca nodded. 'I get it. I wish it was different but I get it.'

'You'll look after him for me?' The sadness once again hit me. I picked up my bottle of lager and took a large gulp, swallowing the tears away.

Luca nodded. 'I promise.' He paused. 'But who's going to look after you? Everybody needs someone, you know, it doesn't make you less strong, it just makes you human. Isn't that the aim of life, to share it with someone?'

I felt a pang of loneliness as I pictured my parents, who I rarely see, James with his new family, and Michele gone.

Luca squeezed my shoulder, pulling me from my thoughts and greeting me with his enormous smile. 'You know you've got a friend for life here.' Pointing at himself.

I grinned, clinking my bottle with his as we both said 'salute' before grabbing the drinks and returning to the table. I looked at Max's friends; I was going to miss them, especially Luca and his breezy manner.

I felt Max squeeze my hand; Isabella was asking what time my flight left in the morning.

'Ten-thirty, my taxi's booked for eight,' I told her.

Max looked at his watch.

'Nine hours,' he said sadly, kissing me and resting his forehead on mine. 'What will you be doing this time tomorrow?'

It hurt my head to imagine myself back in my life this time tomorrow. So soon. It was starting to feel like I'd been living someone else's life all week.

'I'll probably be in bed, I have to be up early to drive Adam to football.'

Max kissed my hand. He understood why I couldn't drop everything. Even if I wanted to.

'What about you?' I asked.

'I have no clue,' he replied. 'I'll probably be at home missing you.'

Then there it was again, sadness replacing the smile in his eyes. He kissed me firmly on the forehead as Dante returned to the stage. Everyone re-pointed their chairs towards him, the main attraction. The room hushed and settled as Dante began picking at the strings of his guitar and strumming hard, passionately singing 'The Way it Ends' by Landon Pigg, his Italian inflections altering the pronunciation of the words.

'I swear I didn't request this,' Max whispered, his eyes smiling.

I wanted time to stop, to stay looking into those beautiful, sparkling eyes of his but the clock was ticking louder. The dread inside increasing. As I listened to Dante's song, I replayed my time with Max. I had no regrets, our time together had been anything but meaningless, it had been wonderful. Max had taught me so much about grief, about myself. I hoped I was ready to move on. Not that I had a choice, I simply had to be. I squeezed Max's hand as Dante finished singing his hopeful love song.

'Will you walk me back to my hotel?'

Max nodded then scanned the table. 'You want to avoid goodbyes?'

'Yes.' I nodded. He knew.

'You go first,' he instructed. 'I'll follow you in a minute.'

'But make sure you say it for me another time, I don't want them to think I was being rude. I like your friends.'

I took one final look at Dante, Isabella, Aria and Luca, wonderful Luca, and felt the heat rush to the backs of my eyes. As I stood and left Max's bar, I felt like I was leaving a piece of my heart behind. I leant against the wall outside, taking controlled breaths, telling myself to hold it together.

Max appeared, putting his arm around me as we walked. He started trying to match my stride, like he had that first night, but he still couldn't do it. He knew it would lighten the mood and make me laugh, which it did. We walked that way, skipping, hopping, laughing, until the amphitheatre appeared in front of us. I twirled around, taking in the 360 degree view of the amphitheatre lit up, the ornate street lights on. It was stunning. I was going to miss Verona. I looked at Max. I knew I was going to miss him, that was a certainty. I hesitated before continuing, in two minds, whether to tear the plaster off now or say a proper goodbye in the hotel room. I decided to leave it up to Max.

We walked on in silence through narrow streets until we eventually reached my hotel. I'd never been so sad to see a place. We stood, embraced in the entrance, between the two oversized ornamental ceramic dogs, fighting the sadness.

I placed my hands on Max's chest and looked into his sad eyes. 'Do you want to come up or...'

'Yes.'

He wanted to say a proper goodbye too. I was glad. I still wasn't ready to let him go. Would I ever be? Max placed his hand on my cheek, stroking it with his thumb as if wiping away imaginary tears – the tears I was desperately fighting to hold in.

Once inside my hotel room, Max took hold of me and kissed me, wrapping his arms around me. I did the same, leaning into him, running my hands along his back and shoulders. I wanted to remember how he felt in my arms. How I felt in his.

This time as we undressed, everything was slow, savoured, every movement, every touch delicate, every piece of clothing removed carefully, as though we were made of china and likely to break. I kissed his mouth, memorising how his lips felt on mine, his tongue against mine, his taste, making my way down his body, committing to memory every inch of him.

He wrapped me up in his arms, my body felt slight in his embrace, then lowered me down onto the bed. He brushed the hair from my face so he could see my eyes, looking deeply into them. His were filled with sadness too. He caressed my cheek, his fingertips soft, searching my face as I searched his, remembering every line, every freckle. I was filled with a sense of urgency, afraid of forgetting any detail. I placed my hands on either side of his face and he leant in so our foreheads were touching, his eyes never once leaving mine. This is how it felt to be adored by someone. I would never forget his beautiful eyes, how Max looked at me, how he made me feel.

As we kissed, I tried to push from my mind that this was the last time I would ever feel my skin pressed up against his, the final time I would ever feel his breath on my neck, or his hands and mouth all over my body. I was trying to ignore the gut-wrenching feeling within, like my insides were being twisted and wrung out. I needed to remain in the moment, instead focusing on the touch of his tongue across my breast, his palm moving up my inner thigh, the tingling sensation building throughout my body as he took control of it. The extreme waves of pleasure causing my muscles to tighten; the feeling overwhelming. I pushed my head into the pillow, arching my back, my heart thumping out of my chest. I felt light-headed. My body stilled then began to shake uncontrollably. I held onto him as I melted and exploded at the same time, then collapsed back, my body weightless. Max had given me exactly what I needed, everything disappeared as I lost myself completely in the moment, in his arms.

He moved his weight on top of me and I instinctively wrapped my arms and legs around him, still hungry for his kiss, his taste. I felt alive when his mouth was on mine. He held my gaze with such intensity as we gave ourselves to each other one last time. I tried not to think about anything but the incredible man in my arms, desperate to remember every moment, every feeling, as we attempted to cram a lifetime into this one final night. It was impossible to ignore the sadness between us though, this was a different kind of making love, there was a finality to it. It felt like saying goodbye.

I wrapped myself around him in our embrace, my head resting on his chest, closing my eyes and listening to the soothing rhythm. I imagined myself staying in Verona, sleeping with Max every night, stroking my fingers through his hair as I looked into his beautiful glistening brown eyes whenever I wanted, waking in his arms every morning... but the reality of our situation quickly extinguished my dream; I knew it was hopeless. I held him tighter, nuzzling into his chest, inhaling his smell as the dread consumed me, the thought of leaving tearing at my heart. With every rise and fall of his chest I could feel him slipping away, even though he was still right there in my arms, for a few more hours anyway. I didn't know how I was going to prise myself out of Max's arms in the morning and walk away.

I succumbed to my tears, letting them fall freely onto Max's chest but he didn't say anything, he just held me, still, until I fell asleep in his arms, listening to his heartbeat one last time.

10

FRIDAY

I woke to the startling sound of the alarm, immediately aware I was alone. No Max. No Michele. I sat up, hugging myself, sleepily searching the room before running into the bathroom. He was gone. I felt panicked. I slowly walked back to the bed and sat, willing him to come through the door with coffee and pastries, but there on the table lay the room key next to the wallet of photographs… and a note from Max. I grabbed it, hastily reading it,

'I couldn't face goodbye either
so I'm ripping the plaster off.
I know you said no keeping in touch
but if you EVER need ANYTHING
Maybe just to share a favourite song now and again?
I can't imagine my world without you
I'll never forget you
I already miss you, Love Max'

I already missed him too. Beneath his name was his email address. Tears streamed down my face as I traced my finger across it and held the note to my chest. I had an overwhelming urge to run to him. To stay in Verona. I lay back on the bed, feeling the absence of him above me as my tears turned to sobs. I glanced over at the pillow where hours ago Max's head had lain, reaching out and grabbing it, holding it but desperately wanting to hold him. The pillow smelled of him. I inhaled deeply, imagining he was still in my arms. Why was this so painful? I recognised what I was feeling but how so soon? I wiped my tears and reached for the wallet of photographs, I needed to see his face. I noticed some were missing, the one of me looking really happy, the one of me kissing his cheek, of us gazing into each other's eyes, of us posing together, and the one of me blowing Max a kiss. He must have put them in the envelope and taken them. He wanted to keep some treasure too. I read his note over and over, again and again. Then turned it over to discover more.

'Look up the song 'Always' by The Boxer Rebellion,
there's a beautiful acoustic version I know you'll love,
listen to the chorus, it says it better than I can.
Always, Max'

I smiled through my tears, he was giving me a song to remember him by. I lay back down, grasping the note. I knew he'd done the right thing leaving, it was for the best. I was thankful in a way, I didn't know how I was going to be able to walk away from him, the thought seemed impossible, and I didn't want him to witness this, me falling apart, not again, not because of him.

I turned the note over and stared at his email address. I couldn't think about that right now. My brain wanted to replay our time together but I couldn't do that right now either. It was all too raw. I needed to get it together. I walked into the bathroom and washed my tear-streaked face before busying myself getting ready, packing and triple checking I had everything. The note and photographs safely in my handbag, the locket safely secured around my neck.

I stopped in the doorway, looking back at the room, picturing Max lying there on top of the bed that first night, flicking through TV channels. The bed where we'd slept so close, where he'd held me as I cried, where we'd shared breakfast, and memories of Michele. Where we'd made love only hours before. My heart hurt. I turned and closed the door on our memories, taking a deep breath to steady myself.

I half expected to see Max when I walked into the reception area to check-out, but that would've gone back on our 'ripping the plaster off' pact. As I sat, waiting for my taxi, I reached inside my bag for my iPod, I needed a distraction, a song. As I scanned through my albums I laughed, again a song I loved now becoming the soundtrack to my life, pressing play on 'High Hope' by Kodaline. I sat back and closed my eyes as the uplifting, nostalgia-filled melody filled my ears, the piano and acoustic guitar soothing me, their beautiful poetry counselling me through. Yes our time together had come to an end, and yes the world was still spinning. Life goes on. Hadn't I been told that countless times recently? I came here with much more grief than I was even aware of. I did feel like I was starting again, a new chapter in my life. I was hopeful but, also afraid. Afraid of never feeling the way I felt with

Max with anyone ever again, but we could never translate to the real world and the real world was where I lived.

As the taxi driver lifted my case into the boot, I scanned all around, searching for Max standing there in those 1950s sunglasses, but of course he wasn't there. I didn't expect him to be really, it was just a feeling I had. In fact, I was glad he wasn't; it was already difficult enough. I got into the taxi with a heavy heart. Tears rolled down my cheeks as we drove away, hidden behind my oversized sunglasses.

* * *

I sat at the departure gate in a daze, filled with trepidation and sadness. I imagined Max running up and begging me to stay, like you see in films. But it would be pointless, nothing had changed since last night. When it was time to board I stayed seated, my legs unwilling to move. I had to force them, drag myself onto the plane. As we began to taxi to the runway I imagined myself jumping up and screaming at them to stop, to let me off, getting off the plane and running back to Max. Instead, I sat there, silent, tears slowly escaping down my face. The man next to me noticed and asked if I was all right; I think he thought I was petrified of flying. I didn't answer him, I couldn't. I was far from all right. I closed my eyes and focused on my breathing. All I could see was Max. All I could feel was misery.

PART TWO

11

SEPTEMBER

I felt lost that first night back. I tried to busy myself, unpacking, washing clothes, showering, replying to text messages and emails, messaging Adam, but every distraction failed to stop my mind replaying what I had been doing twenty-four hours earlier, with Max. It was torture. I didn't want to be home, I wanted to be back in Verona. I sat, looking at the photographs and reading Max's note, listening to the song 'Always' by The Boxer Rebellion on repeat, feeling completely miserable and alone. I traced my finger across his email address as my heart and brain battled it out, my brain eventually winning. I knew it was hopeless, nothing had changed. I willed our lives to be at least in the same country but that wasn't our reality, this was. With a heavy heart, I placed the note and photographs in my drawer and vowed not to look at them again until the pain from leaving him had subsided. I hated that thinking about Michele, and now Max, brought misery, our time together meant so much more than that. No, I needed to get on with my life, my real life, focus on the here and now.

Seeing Adam the following day helped. I'd missed him. I could tell he was struggling. He didn't like living at his dad's but I knew in time he would adjust. Ben and his family were lovely, but I understood Adam, it wasn't his home. That was now an empty shell though, it would never be home again, not without Michele. The heart and soul was missing.

I didn't feel like working out, so I sat in the stand and watched Adam play football instead. Watched his troubles disappear for ninety minutes. Football for him was like music for me. After the match, while I was waiting for Adam to change, his coach came and sat with me. I hadn't spoken to him before, we'd nodded hello or goodbye but that was all. He introduced himself as Jake. He looked my age, athletic, light brown hair, blue eyes. He was concerned about how Adam was coping and wanted to let me know he was there if we needed anything. He seemed nice, kind even.

'You hungry?' I asked Adam as we walked to the car.

'You know what I feel like?'

'Erm, let me think. Pizza, by any chance?' Whenever Adam chose the meal it was always pizza.

'Yeah but, pizza with a view?'

I nodded my approval and started the engine. I knew exactly where he wanted to go, it was a favourite of his, well mine and Michele's originally, we'd been countless times before.

Adam busied himself phoning our order through while I drove towards Werneth Low, stopping to quickly grab our takeaway pizza on the way. I navigated the steep roads in second gear, remembering how Michele and I used to hold our breath as we willed her old banger to make it to the top of the hill. Then we'd sit, just as Adam and I were now, enjoying the stillness and looking out at the panoramic views across Manchester as we stuffed our faces.

'Come on.' Adam put the empty pizza box on the dashboard and got out, climbing over the wooden gate into the field.

I joined him, lying on my back next to him, gazing up at the September sky. I looked across at him but his head was turned away from me, facing the empty space beside him. I knew he was picturing Michele there, where she always used to be.

'Tell me again why you started bringin' me up here.'

He knew the story by heart, Michele used to tell it to him all the time, but I knew this was more about him wanting a connection to back then, to her, to relive those times when she was still here telling him herself.

'Well, you were a nightmare baby. I mean, cute as a button, obviously, but you never slept. Your mum tried everything, she had a new fad every month. She saw some daytime TV phone-in that said the motion from driving sent babies to sleep, so she obviously had to try it, but she was too scared to take you out driving at night on her own, so she roped me in. At first we just drove around aimlessly in circles, then one night, I don't remember why, but we decided to drive up here. It became our thing. We'd just sit, engine running, heat on, looking out at the view, enjoying the peace, or listening to music, quiet so it didn't wake you, while you snored away in the back. Your mum triumphant. Occasionally sharing a pizza. Then it became your treat as you got older. Pizza in space.'

We both grinned.

'I used to love it. I really believed I was in space, you know.'

'I know you did.'

He was shaking his head, smiling. 'It's 'cause everything looks so tiny from up here, and I was only a kid.'

'And it was completely believable that we could travel to space, what with the cigarette lighter button turning the car into "spaceship mode."' I couldn't resist teasing him.

We both burst out laughing as Adam covered his face with his hands.

'I was so gullible.'

'Nah, you were a kid with a wonderful imagination. And you believed anything your mum told you.'

We both fell silent, lost in memories.

'Do you feel different?' Adam asked.

I looked across at him; he was focused on the sky.

'Different?'

'Since Mum... Like stuff that used to matter doesn't – don't tell me off for swearing – but like everyone's stuck in 'bullshit mode'? Like the other day, they'd run out of burgers in the school canteen and me mates were bangin' on about it like it was the end of the world. I wanted to scream at them to shut up, it doesn't matter, why are they even wasting time talkin' about it. I don't know, maybe before I'd've cared too, but now...' He paused and shook his head, then looked at me. 'Is it just me?'

'God no,' I reassured him. 'A woman at work surveyed the whole office to see how they pronounced "*scone*." While I was trying to write a report, all I could hear was her, I must've read the same sentence thirty times. I wanted to grab her by the shoulders and shake her and scream at her to shut up, that it doesn't matter.'

Adam looked at me, wide-eyed. 'Did you?'

'Only in my head.'

'Yeah, me too.'

We shared a sombre smile.

'I'm not going crazy, then?'

'No. We've just got a new perspective on life, that's all. We're dealing with this huge thing that's happened, so all the small stuff's become irrelevant. You're not weird or crazy for feeling like that, it's completely normal.'

'Okay.' He took a moment, as if to digest this new information. 'I like it when I'm late and have to rush, then I don't have time to think about–'

I nodded. 'Yeah, I like it when I'm working with a child and I'm completely absorbed, time flies. But it's the moments in between, when I'm driving to the next appointment, that's when my brain has time to think, and miss people.'

'People? Do you still miss James?'

'No. Your mum I mean.'

'Oh.'

I sat up, looking out at the twinkling lights switching on in the distance, my mind travelling back to Verona, to sitting on the bench next to Max.

Adam sat up. 'So, how was it?' He glanced across at me, then back out at the view. We deliberately hadn't talked about it until now, I was waiting until he was ready. I pictured the bridge, all of us gathered, watching her ashes float away. It still didn't seem real.

'It was fine, strange, sad.' I shrugged, unsure how to describe it.

'Like the funeral?'

'Kind of.'

'How was Gran?'

'Sad, but she got through it. Have you seen her?'

Adam nodded. 'She said you were "her rock". He paused. 'You were always Mum's rock too, and mine. It made me think, who's your rock?'

'Your mum was.'

'But what about now? Everyone needs someone, even you.'

The pang of loneliness returned as Adam's words echoed what Luca had said to me that last night at the bar. I stared at the lights in the distance, and felt removed from the world up here, a visitor observing a place I was once a part of. Although recently, that was how I'd been feeling more and more when I was down there too.

'You've got me,' Adam reassured me, as though he could see the loneliness inside of me.

I looked at him and smiled. 'Thank you. And you know you've always got me, I'm not going anywhere.'

'I know.'

We sat for a few more moments, then I checked my watch. 'You ready to make a move?'

Adam nodded. 'Thanks for bringing me here, I just wanted to–'

'I know. Any time.'

We stood and made our way back to the car. It had been a good day, for both of us.

I wasn't prepared for the torture the following days brought with them, as my mind replayed what I was doing this time the week before. I tried to avert my thoughts, staying late at work, binge-watching TV shows to zone out for a few hours, reading until my eyes were so heavy I'd fall asleep, so I wouldn't lie in bed craving Max's touch. I took Adam to football midweek and opted to work out as hard as my body would let me, to stop my mind reliving every moment we'd shared, every feeling, every kiss. Not that I wanted to forget, I cherished the memories, but the heartache from missing Max was overwhelming. I struggled to understand my innate need to be with him, like a magnet drawing me back. How he'd somehow become my world in such a short space of time.

Friday night came. I'd been looking forward to seeing The Fray. I went with the usual group of friends I always went to gigs with. They were an easy bunch to be around because our discussions were light, music-based, it never got personal or about someone's problems. As I stood watching the band, all I could think about was Max. Each song from their new album transported me back to his office, to laying in his arms listening to it. When they played 'Break Your Plans,' the pain inside intensified. I tried to imagine how I would be feeling if I had broken my plans and stayed in Verona. Would I be happy? Why wasn't I happy back in my own life?

After the gig I made my excuses, I didn't feel like going on anywhere. Jumping into a taxi, I found myself saying Michele's address to the driver. It wasn't the first time. The street was silent when I got out of the cab, completely different to that day. That day that was still so vivid in my mind. With each blink I could see it, my brain switching from the quiet night to that devastating day, from an empty street to neighbours hovering, the ambulance parked, Adam throwing his arms around me. I walked towards Michele's front door, putting my hand out to steady myself as the grief crept up on me again, taking a few deep breaths before letting myself inside and slowly walking from room to room – but not her bedroom, I couldn't face it in there. I went back to the lounge and lay down on the sofa, pulling her favourite blanket over me. I wasn't sure why I kept finding myself there. Looking for Michele? Visiting her? There was no grave to visit. Where would I go when it was sold? Was that why I was struggling to clear her house? I couldn't imagine it belonging to someone else. Another family making memories, overriding and deleting Michele's, it didn't feel right.

I lay, holding the locket between my fingers, remembering how Max had surprised me with it. I imagined myself telling Michele all about it, how that had been the point of no return, the moment I'd fallen for him. In my head, I could transport myself back to the riverside, staring into those heavenly brown eyes of his, feeling the happiness I'd felt. I could make Michele appear on the sofa with me, my feet resting on her lap as I shared my tales of Verona. But then I opened my eyes and found myself staring up at Michele's ceiling, all alone. And then the tears came, more tears. I was so sick and tired of my tears, of feeling this way. My entire being was consumed with missing people. If Michele were here, surely I'd be happy. If she were here, would I have stayed in Verona? Adam wouldn't need me. I shook my head at the ridiculous thought. If Michele were here, I would never have been in Verona in the first place. I found it comforting, imagining myself talking to her – untangling my thoughts and setting me straight, she could always do that – until my eyes eventually grew heavy and I fell asleep.

I woke with the resolve to clear as much as I could, thinking that after all Michele had done for me, I owed her. First, I walked down to the local store and bought a latte and a pastry. As I was queueing to pay, I smiled, struck by memories of Max nipping out to get us breakfast, of us sitting in the cafe before he rushed off to pick up the locket to surprise me, of him bringing me breakfast in bed, the Gerbera Daisy in the makeshift vase, how incredible he'd made me feel. But on the walk back to Michele's house, as I looked down at my single latte and pain au chocolate, I felt completely alone. I missed being cared for and thought about. I missed having someone there to simply hold me when I needed to be held. I hated missing people.

I busied myself, starting in the kitchen, working swiftly, boxing or binning items. Moving from room to room. Not allowing myself to think but completely detaching myself from the situation. My new resolve was working. If I felt myself faltering, I reminded myself how swiftly Michele and Adam had packed and unpacked all of my possessions, moving me into my new home. I had also arranged for a charity to carry out a house clearance the following afternoon; I thought if I had a deadline, I'd be forced to get on with it and not allow myself to become distracted.

By the evening I had done the entire downstairs, the bathroom and spare bedroom. Adam's room had already been done when he moved into Ben's. There was just Michele's room left.

Filled with unease, I stood in front of her closed bedroom door, my hand hovering over the handle. I hadn't been inside since that day. I had to do it. It was just a room. My heart was pounding. I took a deep breath and slowly opened the door, stepping inside. Her wardrobe door was open. I held out my hand and carefully ran the tips of my fingers across her clothes. The room had her smell. I looked over at the perfume bottle sitting on her dresser, waiting for Michele to pick it up and wear it again. I instinctively sprayed some on my wrist, closing my eyes and smelling it, picturing Michele. Tears threatened. I opened my eyes and found myself staring at the bed. I couldn't avoid it, the very place where Michele had taken her final breath. Where she'd died all alone. My pulse quickened as sadness and anger surged inside. It still made no sense. Why had her life been cut short? Why did Adam have to grow up without his mother? Why had I lost my best friend? Why her? Why? I frantically threw the perfume bottle against the wall, smashing it into a thousand pieces, to match my heart. Then I dropped to the floor, hugging my knees into my chest and sobbing, imagining throwing everything in the bedroom out of the window and setting it all ablaze. I was enraged. Then I thought of Max, of him making me promise not to get drunk and set a bonfire. It made me smile, allowing me to catch my breath. I closed my eyes and imagined him wrapping his body around me from behind and rocking me, like he'd done at the beach that morning after my nightmare. He had a way of soothing me, of offering comfort and strength. I took deep breaths until the tears finally stopped and I was calm again. I was exhausted and emotionally drained. I looked at my watch, it was nearly eight o' clock. I hadn't eaten anything since breakfast. I climbed to my feet, uncertain whether my legs would support me at first, taking a moment to steady myself before leaving and closing Michele's bedroom door behind me, phoning a taxi to take me home. I would finish it tomorrow.

When I arrived home, I ate, took a hot bubble bath and collapsed into bed, falling straight to sleep. I was woken by my mobile phone ringing. It was dark outside. It took me a few moments to focus on the clock; it was after midnight. I switched on the lamp, momentarily blinding myself, and reached for my phone. It was Ben. Panic hit me. I was instantly awake.

'Ben, what's wrong. Is Adam okay?'

'Sorry to wake you Alex, is he with you, have you heard from him?'

'No, he had an away game today, his friend Tim's mum was bringing him home.'

'Yeah, we spoke to her. He stayed for tea and she dropped him off here just before ten, but he's not here. He never came in.'

'Have you tried his mobile?'

'It's switched off.'

My mind was racing. Where could he be? Then I thought back to last night, to getting in the taxi and saying Michele's address. It was where I'd been going when I needed to feel close to her. Adam knew I was clearing the house, his home, this weekend.

'Ben, let me try a few places. I'll ring you if I find anything.'

'Okay, thanks, I'll let you know if we hear anything.'

'Ben, he's okay you know. We'll find him.'

'I just want him home safe.' His voice was frantic with worry.

I hastily dressed and ran to my car, driving as quickly as I legally could to Michele's. I felt sick. A mixture of worry for Adam and flashbacks from that day, that fucking awful day that started all of this.

As I pulled up, I searched the windows for a light on inside, but there was nothing. I felt afraid as I opened the front door and stepped inside, unsure what I was going to find, turning on the hall and landing lights, first checking the rooms downstairs, but they looked exactly the same as when I'd left them. I ran upstairs, the bathroom and spare bedroom doors were still open, revealing nothing. I opened Adam's bedroom door. Nothing. Where the hell was he? I was really starting to panic. I opened Michele's bedroom door and jumped at the sight of a figure on her bed. I looked closer. It was Adam, curled up, fully clothed, sleeping in the very spot where his mum had died, where he had found her, where he'd tried in vain to resuscitate her. I froze, hugging myself in an attempt to lessen the pain searing inside. It was the saddest thing I had ever seen. He missed her terribly. I wanted to take his pain away, to somehow make it better for him, but I was helpless.

I hesitated, not knowing what to do: leave him or wake him? I carefully closed the bedroom door and crept downstairs, phoning Ben. We decided if that was where Adam needed to be, then we should let him sleep there tonight. He was safe, that was all that mattered. I would sleep on the sofa so he wasn't alone; the very place I came when I didn't want to feel alone. I opened one of the boxes and took out two blankets, throwing one on the sofa for me and heading upstairs with the other. As I placed the blanket over Adam, he grabbed my arm, saying 'Mum' repeatedly. Was he dreaming of her? The bedroom smelled even more of her now I had smashed the perfume bottle. Adam pulled my arm around him, his back to me, asleep but saying 'Mum.' Tears ran down my face. I asked Michele what to do. 'Just hold him for me,' I heard her say in my mind. So I did, I lay down and held him for my beautiful friend who could no longer comfort her son herself. I couldn't sleep, my internal struggle was raging, sadness versus anger. I focused on controlling my breathing, unable to wipe the tears escaping as I stayed completely still so as not to wake Adam.

After a few hours, I made my way downstairs to the sofa. Adam was settled and fast asleep. It took me back to when he was a little boy and I'd babysit, laying on his bed stroking his hair until he fell asleep, being careful to hardly move the bed as I got up to leave so as not to wake him. It was like performing some kind of acrobatic trick getting up sometimes.

I stared at the ceiling lit by streetlights as I contemplated how Michele's death was going to affect Adam's future, trying to work out if him being quiet and withdrawn was a natural phase of grieving. It was for me. Surely it was normal to want to spend some time alone. I'd preferred to be alone, until Max. Max had helped me because he had experienced loss too, he understood. Ben had taken Adam to a support group for bereaved children. Adam knew he could confide in me about anything and everything. I began to question and second guess myself. I was petrified of getting it wrong, of letting Michele down. Should I be doing more or doing something differently? I was clueless. All I had to go on was my own experience of grief, my gut, and my imaginary conversations with Michele.

I was aware I was exhausted but sleep wasn't my friend. I needed someone to stroke my hair, soothe me until I fell asleep. Max. I allowed myself to think of him, to miss him for a few moments, to imagine myself wrapped in his arms.

I must have fallen asleep because I woke to Adam standing above me, saying my name.

'What are you doing here?' He looked surprised to see me.

I sat up, yawning, my head pounding from dehydration and exhaustion.

'Your dad phoned me, he was worried.'

'How did you know I was here?'

I moved to let Adam sit down.

'Because it's where I come when I want to feel close to her too.'

Tears filled his eyes and I wrapped my arms around him, holding him as he sobbed. I imagined Michele standing there watching us, helpless, unable to comfort her son. She'd be wild with anger. I tried to tell her it was okay, I had it, I had him.

After a few minutes, Adam pulled away and wiped his face with the blanket.

'I want to pack her bedroom with you.' His chin was wobbling. He was trying to be brave.

I nodded. 'Okay.'

I held his hand as we climbed the stairs back to the room where she had died. The room where Adam had helplessly tried to wake her. I wanted to rewind time and make it be anyone else but him. No child should have to live with that.

We slowly and silently began putting her clothes and possessions into bags and boxes, both of us handling each item so delicately, as if we were touching a part of her. We showed each other certain items, sharing our memories. Adam held up a dress she'd thought she looked fat in. It made us both smile, momentarily anyway.

When the room was finally bare, Adam sat on her bed, stroking his hand across the spot where she had died, where he had slept last night.

'Where will I go when I need her, where will I go?' he repeatedly asked, tears filling his eyes again.

My heart was breaking as I sat down next to him, trying desperately to be strong.

'I don't know, Ad. I've been coming here too, to feel close to her. So many memories are here but she's not here in this room or in this house.' I was unsure what to tell him. She was gone. That didn't hold much comfort. I thought back to the markets when Max had placed his hand over his heart and told me Kate would always be in there, then he'd placed his hand on my heart, explaining that was where Michele would always be. 'She's in here and here.' I placed my hand on Adam's head and then his heart. 'That's where the memories are, that's where the love is, not in this house.'

Adam nodded, holding his heart.

'No one can ever take that away from you,' I reassured him.

'Will it ever stop hurting?' he asked, as tears escaped down his face.

I grabbed my locket. I was grateful to Max, still helping me even now. 'A very wise man once told me that it will always hurt but we learn to live with the pain so it doesn't consume us as much. He'd lost his wife but he could laugh again, enjoy life. He'll never forget her, he'll always love her and think about her, she'll always be in his heart, but he doesn't feel *this* pain anymore.'

'So I won't always feel like this?' I could tell he was desperate for it to stop too.

'No.' I shook my head, meeting his tear-filled eyes. 'I can't tell you how long it's going to take, but I know it will get easier. And we'll have setbacks, days when it slaps us in the face when we least expect it. And every occasion will be tinged with sadness because your mum won't be there, but she would be livid if she saw us let the sadness take over.'

Adam smiled. He knew his mum's temper. She was incredibly protective over those she loved, like a mother bear in the wild.

He looked down at his hands clasped together in his lap, the sadness returning. 'Like my sixteenth birthday?'

Hearing him say it was a strike to the heart. Adam was turning sixteen in a month. I hadn't forgotten, I'd been avoiding it, not knowing how to handle it, what to do. To be honest, I didn't want to face it. I couldn't. The thought of Michele not being there for it was too painful.

I nodded. 'It's okay, you know, if you want to do something. It's also okay if you don't.'

'I don't.' Adam quickly shook his head.

I squeezed his hand, letting him know that was fine.

'Are you okay at your dad's?'

He continued to stare at his hands in his lap as he spoke. 'Yeah, I just miss her.'

'Me too.'

I opened my locket and looked at Michele, instantly smiling back at her, before showing Adam, who smiled too. He reached into his pocket for his wallet, opening it and pulling out a photograph of him and Michele, their faces covered in birthday cake. I remembered it well, I had taken the photograph. It was Adam's thirteenth birthday, the day he had become a teenager. Michele had decided to bake and ice the cake herself but it was a complete disaster. Adam didn't care, but she was distraught. He'd stuck his fingers in, pulling out a chunk and tasting it, saying 'It still tastes good, that's all that matters, here, try some,' as he shoved it in her face. That was it, they splattered cake in each other's faces, laughing hysterically the entire time. Adam looked from the photograph to me; we were both smiling at the memory. It held the power too.

I sat observing the young man before me, the image of Michele. Almost sixteen, the age when I'd left school, got a job, discovered night clubs and dancing and gigs and drinking and boys. I wondered what his future held.

'You want me to take you home?' I purposely said *home* and not Ben's house.

Adam nodded.

I left him in the doorway being hugged and fussed over by Ben, who was relieved to see he was all right – well, as all right as he could be under such horrific circumstances – before driving back to Michele's to meet the house clearance people. After they'd finished, I walked from empty room to empty room, closing each door and trapping over a decade of memories inside. I stood in the hall, looking up the stairs at the wall covered in rectangular marks where pictures used to hang. Holes we'd drilled in error and hidden behind picture frames now in full view. We'd spent hours perfecting it, lining the frames up, measuring, drilling, screaming with frustration, laughing hysterically at the mess we'd made. It had turned out beautifully though, Michele's 'wall of life' as she'd called it. Now bare.

I sat on the bottom step, hugging the bannister, wishing she would walk through the front door, kick off her shoes and head straight into the kitchen to put the kettle on, something I'd taken for granted for so many years but would give anything to experience one more time, just one more cup of tea and a chat with Michele. I had so much left to ask her.

As I got into my car, I turned and took one final look at Michele's house, memories flashing through my mind as tears filled my eyes. It was difficult letting go but maybe it would somehow offer that closure I kept hearing about. I told myself it was simply bricks and mortar, that the memories were inside of me; the very advice I had just given Adam. I drove away, watching it shrink in the rearview mirror until it disappeared out of view. My heart felt heavy, knowing I'd never return. I dropped the keys through Michele's mum's letter box as she was dealing with the sale of the house. I had pre-arranged this time knowing she wouldn't be home, knowing I wouldn't want to talk to anyone, knowing I'd need to be alone.

I looked down at my key chain. It felt light without Michele's keys, they'd been on there forever. Another concrete reminder that she was really gone. I cried all the way home, tears running uncontrollably down my cheeks as I drove. I didn't eat, just collapsed on my bed and fell asleep. Although the last thought in my mind as I drifted off was Max, imagining him there, holding me and stroking my hair. He was constantly there too, in my mind, in my heart. It was like living with two imaginary friends.

I struggled all week at work, faking the energy and enthusiasm I usually had for my job. I continued to push Max from my thoughts, reasoning that he belonged to 'this time last week' and everything I'd told him I was going to do, like clearing Michele's house, was now done, I could move on. But he was still there. The feelings were still there. The yearning he'd awoken. Along with the pain from missing him. I imagined myself falling asleep with him every night and waking up in his arms every morning. It was so *fucking* exhausting, missing people. I suddenly welcomed amnesia.

I was sitting at the computer, the last one in the office again, staring through the screen in a daze. I found myself Googling The Boxer Rebellion, clicking on their website, then the link for videos. It was the first one, 'Always.' I hadn't listened to it since that first night back. I sat, losing all track of time as I watched some music videos and some live performances. Max was right, I did like them. I clicked the link for tickets and was stunned to see right there at the top, today's date and a small venue in Manchester. I checked the date twice. They were playing in Manchester tonight? I clicked the link for the venue's website and saw 'extra tickets just been released on the door.' It was fate.

An hour and a half later I was standing near the front of the stage, alone but not lonely in the midst of hundreds of others all focused on the four talented musicians before us. About an hour in they played 'Always.' I froze at the chorus as Max's borrowed words tugged at my heart. I grasped my locket as memories of him filled my thoughts.

The next song was introduced, 'New York,' a haunting love song about missing someone, about wanting to return to the place where they'd met. I closed my eyes and pictured Max on the bridge as I got lost in the singer's voice, laden with passion and sadness, his regret and heartache palpable against the rhythmic drums. I stood, mesmerised by the performance, so raw and truthful, these four musicians giving everything of themselves. I wondered what the singer had experienced to compel him to write such songs.

After the encore I leant against the barrier at the front, letting the crowd leave while absorbing the incredible performance. A roadie offered me a set-list, which I gratefully accepted. A keepsake. People began to gather on the far side of the room as the band had come out to sign autographs and greet fans. I hung back until it quietened down, then had them sign the set-list. A woman asked me to take a photograph of her with the lead singer and guitarist. I obliged and she offered to do the same for me. Another keepsake. As I thanked them, I desperately wanted to ask the story behind both songs, who he wanted to remember him when they felt lost or alone, and whether he still missed that person, whether it had gotten easier because he must have experienced it too, what I felt, I could hear it in his voice when he sang.

I drove home feeling lighter; music did still work. I'd been down the night of The Fray and was worried music had lost the ability to counsel me, to distract me from my troubles for a time. It was a relief knowing it was still my release.

When Saturday arrived, I took Adam to football but didn't visit the gym because I'd promised his coach, Jake, that we'd stay for the meal afterwards for the team and family members. Jake really wanted Adam to attend and thought as it had always been mine and Adam's thing it wouldn't feel odd that it was me and not a parent there, which made sense. It was wonderful to watch Adam laugh with his friends, to see the progress he'd made. I felt like I had too, since the gig. Adam still sought alone time, but when he was with people he allowed himself to enjoy the moment. I was relieved I'd been there for him, had been able to offer some advice, some insight, even if I had stolen it from Max rather than coming up with it myself. Max. There he was again, never far from my thoughts.

Jake sat down next to me for the meal. We chatted about random things and he asked about Adam and Ben and how I was coping with it all. As the evening progressed, his questions turned more personal; what I enjoyed doing, if I was seeing anyone. He told me he was single, and all about his last relationship and how it had ended a few months before. At first I thought he was asking my advice, then out of the blue – well to me, anyway – he asked me out on a date, offering to take me to the Josh Record gig on Friday that I'd mentioned, even though he'd never heard of him. I was taken aback, I'd never looked at Jake that way. I took a moment. He was handsome, he had a good body, he was kind and caring, he adored Adam, he lived in the same country. His eyes didn't smile like Max's. I stopped thinking and said yes. Maybe going out with Jake was exactly what I needed to get over Max.

After driving Adam home I flopped into bed, numb.

Wasn't I supposed to feel excited?

12

OCTOBER

As we said goodnight outside the restaurant, Jake leant in and kissed me. I let him for a moment, my eyes closed, but it was Max I was picturing. I was kissing Jake but imagining it was Max. I pulled away, apologising, confused, thoughts rushing through my head.

'I'm sorry, I'm not over my last...' I paused. My last what? Fling? Holiday romance? 'I'm sorry,' I repeated, jumping into the waiting taxi and leaving Jake standing there trying to figure out what had just happened.

I sat, holding my head in my hands. What *had* just happened? I thought going out with Jake would cure me. I'd told myself I should be flattered he was even interested in me but I'd watched him at the Josh Record gig a week ago, indifferent, like James used to be. While I was captivated by the beautiful love songs, Jake was checking his phone. Afterwards, he'd admitted he wasn't really into music. I'd agreed to a further date, let him choose, moved it away from music; not everyone could share my passion. I'd told myself it was good to have different interests.

Every time my brain made a comparison to Max I pushed it from my thoughts, stopped myself imagining sitting with Max instead, in his favourite restaurant with the ceiling of ivy and fairy lights. Jake was handsome, kind, lovely, but it felt like he was playing stand-in for the real thing. I *had* tried, but it wasn't the same with Jake, there was no magnet drawing me to him. I knew when I met Max there was something different, that instant connection we'd shared, things we had in common, an ease like we'd known each other for years. I'd known then it was rare.

I'd often wondered what it was that drew you to certain people. You met hundreds, if not thousands of people throughout your life, most you never gave a second thought to but then there was that minority that drew you in, whether in friendship or romantically, that connected with you, excited you, lingered in your thoughts. The ones you fell in love with, wanted to spend every moment with, made your life brighter, switched you on. Like Max. How had he, above thousands of others, connected with my heart? What was it about him, and why couldn't I feel that way about Jake? Were we susceptible to certain people's pheromones but not others, or was it as simple as looking into someone's eyes and your two souls connecting?

I sank back into the taxi seat, watching raindrops crawl down the window as tears crept down my cheeks. The weather matched my mood, just like in The Great Gatsby. I'd written an essay about F. Scott Fitzgerald's use of weather to depict a character's emotion for an English examination many years ago. Since then I'd often thought he was onto something. It had rained the morning Michele died and the day of her funeral.

Driving in the rain at night had strangely become one of my favourite pastimes since her death. Strange because I had previously hated it, avoided it, found it draining. But I now enjoyed the concentration it required, consuming my brain so there was no room for any other thoughts, and I could just switch off. Other strange things I'd found myself doing were lying on my bed and staring up at the skylight for hours. Knowing I should go and do something, go for a walk, take a bath, watch TV, meet a friend, but I'd simply lie there in an almost hypnotic state, my mind completely blank, as though I were asleep with my eyes open. Or I would sit motionless on the bench in my favourite quadrangle, staring at the wall of ivy with my earphones in, oblivious to the world around me. It was like time had stood still for me while the rest of the world carried on living, bustling by me at a million miles an hour. I could disconnect from reality, from my feelings.

Fortunately, my job and Adam stopped me indulging in this unhealthy escapism all the time.

When I got home, I found myself retrieving Max's note from the bedside drawer. I hadn't looked at it or the photographs since that first night back. I thought by hiding the memories I would be able to get on with my life, that the feelings would lessen. How wrong I'd been. Memories weren't in possessions or places, they lived inside us, Max had taught me that. I'd been home for a whole month. I had managed to clear Michele's house, such a momentous feat, yet I still couldn't get Max out of my head, out of my heart. That was the problem. Why did I have to go and fall in love with him? I didn't want to admit it because it was pointless. I knew there was no future, but that didn't stop it being undeniably true. For weeks it felt as though I'd been merely existing, going to work, being there for Adam, missing Michele, fighting away thoughts of Max.

Yet the entire month it was actually Max who had brought me comfort, especially in the most difficult moments, even helping me to counsel Adam when I didn't know what else to say.

I turned the note over, playing the chorus to 'Always' in my head, telling me if I were ever lost or alone to remember him, to remember *us*. Closing my eyes and picturing him, I could still feel his touch as if he were right there with me. I opened the locket and smiled at my wonderful friend Michele. I'd had countless imaginary conversations with her, sharing my day, talking about Adam. Maybe it was because we'd shared twenty-one years and could read each other's minds, finish each other's sentences, but I always imagined her saying the same thing, 'Just be happy because life's too short not to be.' Then she'd ask, 'What would make you happy right now?'

Max. Max would make me happy right now. I was finally honest with myself. I missed him, I was miserable without him, forgetting him had never been a viable option, I understood that now.

I grabbed my laptop.

To: Max
Subject: Maybe to share a favourite song now and again?
'My Favourite Faded Fantasy' by Damien Rice (click on link)
His words say it better than I can,
I think he's been living in my head.
How are you?
I miss you… still.
Love, Alex
P.S. Damien Rice is the greatest poet ever to walk this earth ;)

I hovered for a few moments, wondering if Max still thought about me, doubting whether I should send it. I thought about deleting the 'I miss you' part but I needed to tell him I still missed him, there was no one else to tell. None of my friends knew about Max, it was part of my compartmentalising plan to get over him. I thought back to our time together, how I had laid myself bare, was able to tell him anything and everything, been completely vulnerable yet he'd never judged me, merely been there for me. I quickly clicked send, turned off the lamp and lay down on my bed, listening to the song I had sent him. Damien's delicate vocals said it all, it really was as if he'd been living in my head, had read my thoughts and written the song for me, my love letter to Max. I closed my eyes, thinking back to Jake's kiss earlier. I'd felt nothing. I thought back to my endless kisses with Max, my stomach filled with butterflies and the feeling deep within still stirred. Jake hadn't stood a chance.

I checked the time. 23:34, so half past midnight in Verona. I tried to imagine what Max would be doing, at the bar, at the club, sleeping? It was pointless, I didn't have a clue. For all I knew, he could be laying on someone else's lap in his office. The thought pained me. I turned the lamp back on and reached for the wallet of photographs, looking at each one intently, remembering exactly how I felt in each moment. How I still felt. My laptop binged, making my heart leap. It was an email from Max. As I grabbed the laptop, I was aware my hands were trembling, my heart was pounding. I was afraid to open it for a second.

To: Alex
Subject: Maybe to share a favourite song EVERY DAY
'Throw Me A Rope' by KT Tunstall (click on link)

She says it better than I can ;)
I think Damien Rice has been living in my head too,
beautiful song.
It's so good to hear from you.
I still miss you too. Nothing's the same without you.
Love Always, Max
P.S. I now understand why people own mobile phones,
much easier to carry around than a laptop for checking
email every second of the day... for a month!

He always knew how to make me smile. Had he really been sitting with his laptop on, waiting for me to email him for a whole month? He'd replied quickly enough, or was it simply coincidence? I wanted to type back and ask but I stopped myself, looking at the subject line he'd changed from 'now and again' to 'EVERY DAY'. Would that make it easier, knowing I had something from Max to look forward to every day? Well, it was certainly working, I was sitting there smiling and excited for the first time in weeks. It offered me comfort, knowing Max missed me too. The same way it had offered me comfort back in Verona, knowing he too had experienced loss. Knowing someone else felt it, understood it. It made me feel less alone. I'd vowed to find the positives in life, to start living again. I'd tried, but it was impossible without Max in my life in some capacity. The way I'd opened myself up to him. He knew more about me than anyone else in this world, well now Michele was gone, anyway.

I switched off the lamp and lay down again, imagining Max there stroking my hair as I listened to the song he had sent me, the soothing melody of the acoustic guitar accompanying Tunstall's tender voice, the lyrics mirroring exactly how I felt – telling me he missed me, that he should be fine but instead he felt alone, asking me to go back and find him… if only I could.

* * *

I woke up lighter, happier, excited to share another song with Max. I had forty minutes before I was due to pick Adam up. I quickly got ready, dreading the thought of seeing Jake and hoping things wouldn't be uncomfortable between us. He'd been nothing but kind to me and Adam, he deserved better, but there was no connection between us, plus I was unsure how to explain I was in love with a man who lived in Verona and who I was never going to see again. I remembered Michele's dating advice: she had a shoe analogy. If she were here, she would say I had tried Jake on and as lovely as he was he didn't fit, and I wouldn't buy a pair of shoes that didn't fit, now would I? I smiled; she was always right, even now. I wondered what kind of shoes Max would be. Those expensive Italian ones with a red sole, that I wanted but couldn't have.

I sat down in front of my laptop. It didn't take long, I'd already written it a hundred times in my head. I pasted the link to the depressing love song I'd been playing on repeat since leaving Verona, reminding me just how long it had been since I'd last slept with Max.

> To: Max
> Subject: I like the idea of a song a day
> 'Black Star' by Radiohead (click on link)
> Most listened to song since I got home. It matches my mood.

I didn't expect it to still hurt a month on.
Love Always, Alex
P.S. I thought you might have forgotten me.

Adam was waiting outside Ben's when I pulled up, and it was clear from his demeanour that something was wrong. He got into the car, headphones on, listening to his music. I decided to let him have some time, get whatever it was out of his system at football and I would talk to him later. As I pulled up at the training ground, Jake was right there. I got out and tried to apologise, explain, but he brushed me off saying it was fine, not to worry about it, that he had to go. He wasn't rude but I could tell I had upset him. I headed to the gym and did an extra long session to work off my guilt. Afterwards, I met up with Adam but football hadn't worked its usual magic, he was the same, sombre and quiet. I offered to take him for something to eat but he asked to be taken to Ben's house, still refusing to call it home, even though everybody else did. He'd been doing better since we'd packed up Michele's room together. I wondered if it was his impending birthday. The first of all the milestones in his life he would now have to face without her.

When I dropped him off, I made sure to tell him he could talk to me about anything, to text or call whenever, the time didn't matter, that I was always there for him, unconditionally. He got out of the car muttering he was fine and slammed the door behind him. I wasn't used to being shut out, Adam and I had always been able to talk about everything, even during his difficult teenage years.

There was an email waiting for me when I arrived home. It was exactly what I needed.

To: Alex
Subject: I like the idea of a song a day too
'Leaving New York' by R.E.M. (click on link)
Most listened to song since you left.
I know, I didn't expect it to still hurt either.
Love Always, Max
P.S. How could you ever think that? Although, I thought
you hated me.

The song was familiar but now it was Max's borrowed words to me, a song filled with loneliness. I thought back to the airport, to crying on the plane. It definitely wasn't easier to be the one leaving than to be the one left behind. I read 'I thought you hated me' over and over. How could he have ever thought that? Why? Because he left the hotel that morning before I woke up? But he did the right thing. Because I didn't email for a month? I should've emailed sooner, but I was trying to get over him. I wanted it to be tomorrow so I could tell him, reassure him. I thought about instantly replying but we'd agreed on once a day. I knew it still couldn't go anywhere between us, nothing had changed, I was living in the real world after all. I needed Max in my life, needed some contact and now I had it.

I busied myself, making something to eat, opening a bottle of red wine and creating a Spotify playlist of the songs we'd shared, our playlist, finally ready to revisit all of the music I'd been avoiding. I sat in a bubble bath with another glass of wine and enjoyed my work, getting lost in our memories, knowing exactly what to send Max tomorrow.

* * *

I woke up and immediately reached for my laptop to compose the email I'd written a hundred times in my head, but was interrupted by thoughts of Michele. I grasped my locket and took a few deep breaths until the feeling of emptiness subsided, then continued with the email to divert my thoughts, attaching the photograph the woman had taken of me after The Boxer Rebellion gig.

To: Max
Subject: A song a day
Attachment: Photograph.jpeg
'New York' by The Boxer Rebellion (click on link)
I looked The Boxer Rebellion up. You were right, I do like, in fact no, I love them!
This is my favourite song of theirs, it reminds me of you ;)
What is it with us and songs about New York?
You may recognise the lead singer and guitarist in the attached photograph.
They played here a few weeks ago and were incredible live.
Thanks for the tip!
I just saw Josh Record, look him up. I think you'll like him.
Love Always, Alex
P.S. I hate that you ever thought that, I could never hate you. You know how I feel. Never doubt it. X

I didn't have to wait very long before my laptop binged with his reply.

To: Alex
Subject: A song a day
Attachment: Photograph.jpeg
'The Weight of the World' by Editors (click on link)

Let's stop with the New York songs, I nearly sent you Jay Z LOL

I knew you'd love The Boxer Rebellion. Nice choice ;)

I went back to where we last met... Remember my office wall?

You like? You inspired me.

Love Always, Max

P.S. I'm glad you don't hate me. I know, me too. Don't ever forget it. X

P.P.S. Groupie! Should I be jealous? ;) I wish I'd been there with you... Always X

I will look Josh Record up.

I looked at the title of the song he'd sent, 'The Weight of the World,' remembering telling him my favourite lyric was from that song and wondering if he'd put it on his office wall. I clicked to open the attached photograph but wasn't prepared for what appeared before me. It took my breath away. It was incredible. I touched the laptop screen with my fingertips as I tried to take it in. A large square frame split into six segments, each containing lyrics from the chorus and photographs of places I instantly recognised.

The bridge where we met, the blue sky and vibrant buildings.

Our favourite place where he'd taken me, where we made love on our last night, that beautiful view taken at sunset, pink and peach streaks in the sky.

The beach with the moonlight dancing on the water, where we revealed our pasts and shared our first kiss.

The sunflower field where we stopped and danced to Kodaline, that glorious sea of yellow as bright and wonderful as I remember it.

The tree by the river, where he gave me the locket. Where I fell in love with him.

Our names written on the sticky note, encased in a love heart, that we stuck on the wall of love together for eternity. He had gone back and it was still there.

It was truly magnificent. Overwhelming. My favourite lyric brought to life. Max had revisited and taken photographs of the places where we'd shared so much, that were meaningful to only us, that continued to mean something to Max even though I was gone, each memory preserved for eternity. It made me fall in love with him all over again. I couldn't wait for tomorrow.

* * *

I opened my eyes and focused on the clock. 8:41, when it suddenly hit me, it wasn't the weekend, it was Monday morning. I had been hitting snooze as part of a dream. I leapt out of bed and was ready in ten minutes, running out the door. I was going to be late for my first appointment. As I drove to work, latte-less in my rush, it hit me that I hadn't woken haunted by the memory of Michele and the searing pain that went with it, remembering what Adam had said, how he liked it when he was running late as it didn't give him time to think.

It ended up being one of those days where I was chasing my tail from beginning to end, all the while feeling grotty and desperate for a bath or shower. My plan had been to send my email before work, knowing I had twilight training after. To wake, shower and email Max leisurely, over a latte, telling him how wonderful his photographs were, how much I loved his creation, that it was a work of art. Instead, it was half past seven in the evening when

I finally got home. I opened my laptop and immediately wrote to him.

To: Max
Subject: A song a day
'I Don't Want To Change You' by Damien Rice (click on link)
My favourite poet has just released another beautiful song about us ;)
Crazy day. Woke up very late, was late for work, had twilight training, only just got home!
Re: Photograph Art... I love. It's the most beautiful, incredible thing I've ever seen. I couldn't stop staring at it. You amaze me. I wish I could go back to all those places with you. I do in my head... a lot.
Love Always, Alex
P.S. No jealousy required, no one comes close to you X

I listened to the beautiful love song I had sent Max while taking the bath I had desperately craved all day. The gentle violins and guitar slowly building, the raw emotion, as Damien sang about adoring someone no matter how far away they were, about looking into a stranger's eyes and it feeling like home. I smiled as I remembered the moment I'd met Max on the bridge, how I'd glanced across at him as he'd removed his retro sunglasses to reveal those beautiful, intense brown eyes of his, holding out his hand for me to shake. He'd been merely a stranger that day, yet he'd somehow become so much more.

When I eventually got out of the bath I saw his reply.

To: Alex

Subject: A song a day

'For A Nightingale' by Fionn Regan (click on link)

Damien's new song is beautiful but 'The Animals Were Gone' is still my favourite.

I think he should be paying us royalties for the material he's getting from our heads :)

I heard this song (attached) and it made me smile, made me think of you. X

No worries, I know you're busy and have a life.

I have to admit though, your emails have become the highlight of my day.

I knew you'd love it, it takes pride of place in my office... though nowhere's the same without you.

Love Always, Max

P.S. You either X

I read his words over and over. As pathetic as it sounded, his emails had become the highlight of my days too. I snuggled up under the duvet and listened to the sweet song he'd sent me. The melody and lyrics encompassed our time together perfectly, it was like listening to our soundtrack. Once again, Max managed to put a smile on my face and fill my insides with warmth, replacing the hollowness for a while.

* * *

The following morning I quickly sent my next email before leaving for work. It was a night I'd replayed countless times in my mind since getting home.

To: Max
Subject: A song a day
'Lovesong' by The Cure (click on link)
Favourite memory ;)
Your song made me smile too :)
NEVER too busy for you X
Re emails: I know, yours are the highlight of my days too.
We need to get a life!
Love Always, Alex X

Then spent the entire day waiting for his response, constantly checking my email between appointments.

To: Alex
Subject: A song a day
'Beautiful War' by Kings of Leon (click on link)
Yes, that is a favourite but there was something about the outdoors… and I remember what Kings of Leon does to you! ;)
I went back there today. Sat on the bench missing you.
Love Always, Max X

I'd replayed that night countless times too. I imagined Max back there, sitting on the bench alone, placing myself next to him, my hand in his, my head resting on his shoulder. I could feel the happiness I'd felt, allowing myself to remain there for a few moments before returning to reality.

* * *

The following morning I was rushing to make an early

appointment so decided to email later, after I'd dropped Adam home from football; I didn't want to rush it. Plus it meant I wouldn't spend the entire day continuously checking for Max's reply like an addiction.

I picked Adam up straight from work and drove him to training. I was eager to see him as all my text messages since Saturday had gone unanswered, only receiving the single word 'yes' that morning to confirm he still wanted a lift. He sat with his headphones on, which I knew meant he didn't want to talk. Jake and I nodded hello to each other, like we used to months ago, before any of this happened. I visited the gym and worked out but I couldn't clear the fog in my head from worrying about Adam. It was unfamiliar territory to me, I'd always been able to get through to him, but this time felt different. I was desperate for Michele's guidance.

Football once again failed to work its magic. Adam stayed silent on the way home, forcing me to pull the car over and switch off the engine to elicit a reaction from him. He finally took off his headphones, wondering why I'd stopped the car.

'Adam, I feel helpless. I need you to let me in. What's going on?'

'Can I stay at yours tonight?'

I was taken aback. 'Of course you can.' I knew Michele wouldn't mind, but then it wasn't Michele's permission I needed, it was Ben's. 'As long as your dad doesn't mind,' I added, before driving to Ben's house to ask and so Adam could pack an overnight bag and collect his school uniform. Ben wasn't keen on the idea at first but I convinced him. Apparently, Adam had become increasingly distant with Ben, Melanie and their two younger children, so maybe a night away would help.

Adam didn't speak all the way home. Once inside, he walked around my lounge, picking up the framed photographs of Michele and me, of the three of us. The photographs he and his mum had unpacked and placed on my side tables. I wondered if he was remembering that.

'They don't talk about her. They change the subject. It's like they're pretending she never existed but I want to talk about her.' He picked up a framed photograph of me and Michele when we were teenagers.

'Who, your dad and Mel?' I enquired.

Adam nodded and sat down next to me, staring at the picture he was holding.

I understood why they were avoiding talking about Michele; it was common. They feared upsetting him, but as painful and unbearable as it was, avoiding it was like trying to erase her memory. I knew from my own grief that I needed to talk about her and remember her, despite the pain.

'Well if you want to talk about her you've come to the right place.'

Adam looked at me and returned my smile, but the sadness was clearly visible in his eyes. It was painful seeing him that way.

'What was she like when she was at school? When she was my age? After her dad died?'

I looked down at the photograph in Adam's hands. Tears gathered in my eyes as countless memories filled my head, painful from missing her but they contained happiness too. I sat cross-legged, facing Adam as I began to tell him all about his mum as a schoolgirl, about her life during her dad's illness and after he'd died. How painful it had been, and the happiness she'd felt again even though he was gone; offering us both some fragments of hope for the future. We sat talking about her, sharing stories, laughing and crying into the early hours of the morning. I knew he had school and I had work but this was more important than anything else. Adam was more important.

* * *

I probably wouldn't have made a very good parent because I phoned Adam's school and my boss, saying we were sick the next morning. I knew I'd be in trouble but I couldn't leave Adam. I'd managed to get out of bed when my alarm went off at seven and had tried to wake Adam, who had taken over my spare bedroom, but he wasn't in any fit state. Neither was I if I was being honest. I told Adam to go back to sleep and went back to bed myself for a few more hours.

I woke to Adam sitting on my bed, holding out a latte for me. I sat up, taking a large gulp. It was nice having someone bring me coffee in bed. Instantly, I thought of Max and felt a pang inside as I remembered I hadn't sent him an email.

'I want to ask you something.' Adam looked serious as he pulled an A4 sheet of paper from his pocket, unfolding it and passing it to me.

It was a print-out of two pre-paid fast-track tickets for a theme park, dated today. I looked at Adam, confused.

'Mum bought them before she... we were going to go for my birthday. You know, our annual mum and son fun day. We didn't want to go at the weekend 'cause it's too busy, so she picked today. She was going to phone in sick for us both.' The corners of Adam's mouth turned upwards as he began to grin, indicating what I'd already done. I was stunned I had somehow managed to carry out Michele's plan of phoning in sick today, she hadn't had chance to tell me, it was pure coincidence. I laughed, relieved I wasn't so bad after all. Adam was looking at me, anticipating my response. 'Well, will you come with me?'

I placed my latte on the bedside table and hugged him, trying not to cry as I imagined Michele and all she was missing out on. 'Of course I will.'

We quickly got ready, ate breakfast and drove the hour and a bit there. Adam spent the journey flicking through my music, asking questions about bands and songs. I liked that he was showing an interest in music and decided I would definitely take him to a gig soon.

When we entered the theme park, Adam led me straight to a roller-coaster with fourteen loops. I looked up at it and suddenly felt extremely woozy. Michele had always been much better on rides than me. I knew exactly what she would have been thinking when she'd planned today, to have fun with her son before it was too late and he was all grown up and too old to hang out with his mum. She could never have anticipated it would already be too late. I took a deep breath. I could do it for her. I had her back on this one.

'Come on,' Adam encouraged, ushering me forward.

We spent the day moving from ride to ride, covering the main thrill rides, Adam's favourites, plunging into vertical drops, reaching G-force speeds, spinning upside down, being catapulted around, dropping face forward into oblivion, all the while laughing and screaming hysterically.

Mid-way through we took a break for food, although I wasn't sure how Adam could possibly be hungry. I was a mixture of exhilarated and seasick. I must be getting old, because it felt good to sit still and put my feet on solid ground for a few minutes. While Adam was getting our food, I took the opportunity to call Ben and explain. I was apprehensive, afraid he would be angry with me but he understood and was actually relieved Adam was having fun. I think it helped that it had been Michele's plan and not mine. Ben mentioned they were planning a casual family meal to mark Adam's actual birthday on Sunday as Adam didn't want a fuss. He also discussed putting some photographs of Michele and Adam around the house instead of just in Adam's room, which I agreed was a good idea. Ben and Mel had been avoiding talking about Michele to spare his feelings, they didn't know it was actually having the opposite effect. I reassured Ben I'd have Adam home early, finishing the call just as Adam returned with two huge slices of pizza and drinks.

Adam directed us to the final ride he wanted to go on before we headed home, 'The Ripsaw.' I looked up at people being swung around, dangling upside down, all the while being squirted with water. Adam saw my face and started to laugh. I think I'd turned green just looking at it.

'It's okay, I'll do this one on my own. You take photos.'

I let out a huge sigh of relief and grabbed Adam, taking a photograph of us both giggling. It felt good to smile and laugh again.

On the journey home he appeared lighter, less burdened after spending the entire day remembering Michele and enjoying her birthday present to him. When we pulled up outside Ben's house, Adam looked across at me. 'Thank you, I've had a great day.'

I almost fell apart, seeing that smile on his face. 'You look just like your mum.'

For a split second it was as if she were sitting there in my car next to me. I grabbed my locket, desperately pulling strength from it as I pushed the tears away and hugged Adam.

As Adam waved goodbye and went inside, Ben jumped into the car, saying he wanted a quick word. He'd been thinking and had decided that now Adam lived with him he wanted to start taking Adam to football training and matches, to help develop their bond. I knew his intentions were good and he probably thought he was doing me a favour but I couldn't deny it hurt; football had always been mine and Adam's thing, for years. Not that I vocalised any of that to Ben, I simply smiled and agreed. What else could I do? Reasoning that the most important thing was that Adam could carry on doing what he loved, I told myself I simply needed to adapt, things were different now Michele was gone. Plus I knew Adam would love having his dad there watching and supporting him like the other boys. His happiness was all that mattered. Although I couldn't ignore the lingering fear that without it, we would drift apart.

As Ben got out of the car I asked what time for the meal on Sunday. He looked awkward, informing me it was 'just family,' meaning Adam, Ben, Mel and their two young children. I apologised and brushed it off, waving goodbye as I hastily drove away. Though I only made it around the corner, safely out of sight, before I was forced to pull over, gripping the steering wheel as I broke down, sobbing uncontrollably. It felt like Ben had driven a knife through my heart, twice. Sunday would be the first birthday meal I had ever been excluded from since Adam was born. Michele and I were closer to each other than any blood relative. She and Adam *were* my family. I had spent the most wonderful day with Adam, but was driving home petrified I was going to lose him too.

Once home, I sat staring into space, I felt numb. I looked across at my laptop – I still hadn't replied to Max – opening it to find a new email from him, sent that afternoon.

> *To: Alex*
> *Subject: A song a day?*
> *'Find Her Way to Me' by Josh Record (click on link)*
> *I think Josh is living in my head now. X*
> *I know it's your turn but I couldn't wait.*
> *I bet he was incredible live. Wishing again I could've been there with you.*
> *Love Always, Max*
> *P.S. I hope nothing's wrong. X*

Tears began streaming down my face as I clicked on the song link. Tears about missing Michele. Tears about Adam. Tears because I still missed Max. And tears because I felt more miserable than I'd ever felt in my entire life. As I listened to the lyrics, my tears turned to sobs. What was Max trying to say with this song... I'm all he wants... should he wait for me... will I find my way to him. Was he asking me? I tried typing several replies...

> *I knew you'd like Josh Record. He was incredible live. I wish you could've been there with me too... but then I wish you were here with me every day.* **DELETE**

If I'm all you want then jump on a fucking plane. **DELETE**

You're all I want... I love you. **DELETE**

...eventually giving up. I knew Max would be waiting but I couldn't gather my thoughts enough to send anything. I needed to wait until I was thinking straight, not take it out on Max. The internal struggle of anger and sadness was raging inside of me. The hollowness more extreme than ever. Everything I loved was either gone or slipping away. I lay down, hugging myself, sobbing. Feeling completely lost and alone.

13

FRIDAY, 24ᵀᴴ OCTOBER

I had been counting on the sayings being true, that all I needed was a good night's sleep, that I'd feel better in the morning, but I woke feeling exactly the same. It was tempting to lie staring up at the square window above my bed all day, but instead I dragged myself up and busied myself getting ready for work, letting the mundane routine occupy my mind so I could avoid thinking about anyone. It was another day spent on auto-pilot, channelling colleagues I admired to ensure I acted like them, professional and enthused about my job, keeping my true feelings hidden from the world. Early afternoon, after an uncomfortable meeting with my boss who thankfully believed I had been too ill to come to work *from the look of me*, I received a text from my friend, Claire, inviting me out tonight. A distraction was exactly what I needed, to have fun and live in the moment. To close my eyes and dance, let all those feelings fall away for a few hours.

We met after work in our local pub before heading into town to a noisy bar, the kind where conversation was impossible so instead we drank tequila and danced, meeting more friends and moving onto a club we often went to as it guaranteed music we loved. I was aware I'd drunk more than usual but I still couldn't escape the weight bearing down on me, not even on the dancefloor, the very place where I usually went to forget my problems for a time. I sat down at our table and laughed along, though I wasn't sure what I was laughing at, eventually sitting back and watching my friends, chatting and animated. I felt completely detached. I didn't understand why I felt that way, my friends were wonderful yet I had an overwhelming urge to leave. I scanned the room for an attractive man, briefly considering a one-night stand as a way of losing myself for a few hours, but I didn't want *any* man. I knocked back another shot of tequila and immediately regretted it as I held onto the table with both hands, willing the room to stop spinning, looking over at my friends, each one of them blurry, like their identical ghostly spirit was trying to escape. I excused myself and headed to the toilets, where I locked myself inside a cubicle and began heaving into the toilet bowl. As I sat there – on the dirty toilet floor, wiping my mouth and clammy forehead, feeling utterly pathetic – I tried to work out why even though I had great friends in my life, I felt more alone than I'd ever felt. I knew we didn't share that deep connection I'd shared with Michele, no other friendship came close to that, but I'd always enjoyed their company. I rested my head against the cubicle wall and closed my eyes, imagining what Michele would say if she could see the state I was in. Tears flooded my eyes, the feeling of missing her magnified by the tequila. Even when James left, although devastated, I never felt completely alone because I still had Michele. But losing her had thrown me off course, my axis had shifted, I no longer recognised my world, it felt empty without her.

I eventually scraped myself up off the toilet floor, made my excuses and jumped into a waiting taxi, returning home a little after one. I showered and brushed my teeth before drinking a pint of water and collapsing into bed. I lay there in the dark, listening to Damien Rice while analysing and questioning why things that previously came naturally to me now seemed completely out of my reach, why things that used to bring me joy no longer did, why no matter what I did, my life was lacking. The song 'The Box' captured my attention, making me sit up as Damien's voice and acoustic guitar were joined by violins and cellos, the passion and pain of the music uniting with the pain in my heart. A clarity washed over me as the lyrics epitomised my struggle and I recognised… I no longer fitted into my own life. I felt like an imposter, play acting through my days, putting on an act at work or when spending time with friends, relieved when the final curtain fell so I could come home to be alone. Which in turn was loading me with guilt. How dare I feel dissatisfied with my life when I was the lucky one, I was alive, I had the gift of more time. Yet no matter how much I tried to reason with the logic, I couldn't claw my way back to contentment with my life.

I touched my locket, desperately wishing I could talk to Michele so she could unpick my thoughts and set me straight. I pictured her there, sitting at the foot of my bed, smiling at me. Tears surged into my eyes, the alcohol intensifying my misery.

'When was the last time you were happy?' I imagined her asking.

'I don't know.'

'Think.'

At the theme park with Adam, but even then I was trying to be a more parental version of myself, judging my decisions and second guessing if what I was doing or saying was correct.

'When were you last *you*, the Alex I love?'

I kept replaying the time since her death in my mind, searching for when I last fit, when life last felt natural, when I'd last allowed myself to be the real me with no pretence. I grabbed my laptop.

To: Max
Subject: Are you there?

It was 2:40 in Verona, the middle of the night. What was I doing? I hadn't emailed him since Tuesday, I couldn't have him wake to that. I needed to send a further email to explain, it wasn't fair to make him worry, to keep him waiting. It had been selfish of me to send it. I'd heard of drunk dialing but drunk emailing... I jumped as my laptop binged. It was Max, he was awake.

To: Alex
Subject: Yes. Is everything all right?

To: Max
Subject: Just thinking about you, missing you. I'm sorry I haven't emailed.

To: Alex
Subject: I miss you too. Busy couple of days?

To: Max
Subject: Tough couple of days. I didn't mean to wake you. I'll email tomorrow, I promise.

To: Alex
Subject: No, I'm awake. Why tough?

To: Max
Subject: Adam's birthday. Missing Michele. Missing you.
It's hard to explain. Damien does a better job (he's been
living in my head again).

To: Alex
Subject: Which song?

To: Max
Subject: 'The Box'

To: Alex
Subject: Are your eyes turquoise? Tell me the truth!

To: Max
Subject: Yes

To: Alex
Subject: We can't talk properly like this, give me your
telephone number RIGHT NOW... please

It made me smile, his assertive command immediately followed
by politeness. I didn't think or debate it, just sent it, before
slowly walking downstairs to retrieve the phone that no one
but my mother ever called me on. It startled me as it began to
ring in my hand. I sat down on the stairs, automatically saying
hello.

'Alex?'

'Max.' I closed my eyes, grasping the telephone like I was holding a part of him. I knew I missed him but hearing his voice, like he was right there next to me, it emphasised the hollowness inside, the pain from missing him constricting my throat. It was as if all my emotions reached a crescendo, heightening my tears.

'Hey,' he soothed, 'talk to me.' His voice was soft and caring. I could hear 'The Box' quietly playing in the background. 'What's going on?'

I wasn't sure where to start. 'That's the thing, I don't know what's wrong with me. I just can't seem to settle back into my life since Michele, since I got back, and I feel guilty because I'm the lucky one, I'm still alive, I'm still here but I don't know how to, I just feel so, I'm just not. I can't even explain it. I'm sorry.' I finally gave up rambling, shaking my head, more confused than ever.

'What did I tell you that first day we met, when we were walking to *our* favourite place?' Max questioned.

I thought back to breaking down in front of him, to him wrapping his arms around me. I remembered it well.

'To punch anyone who tells me a cliche about death in the face?' I answered. We both started to laugh.

'That's what you remember. All my wise words and that's what you took away with you,' Max teased.

'Why, was there something else?' I teased back.

His voice turned serious. 'I told you to never apologise for feeling.'

'I remember,' I reassured him, 'I remember everything you told me.' I'd certainly used his wise words enough times since coming home, they were constantly offering me help and comfort.

'Tell me what's been going on the last few days?' His voice was gentle and soothing.

I filled Max in on my time with Adam on Wednesday and Thursday. Why Adam had been upset, how we'd stayed up late talking about Michele and phoned in sick the following day, which unbeknown to me had been Michele's plan all along. How we'd gone to the theme park for his birthday… without her, the first of many painful milestones. Followed by my fears of growing apart from Adam now he was living with Ben, now everything had changed, how I feared losing everyone I loved and was helpless to stop it. Max listened and helped me unpick my thoughts, reassuring me that sixteen years wouldn't disappear, that what Adam and I shared was much too strong for that. I could only hope he was right.

'That's why you didn't email. I thought maybe I'd scared you off, all those songs trying to convince you to come back. I know you can't,' he sighed softly.

I thought back to last night, to listening to the Josh Record song he'd sent as I tried to respond but had ended up falling apart instead.

'I did try to email you back but luckily for you I deleted them,' I admitted.

'Them? Why, what did you write and delete?'

'You really don't want to know.' I wasn't sure I wanted to be that honest.

'Tell me. You know you can tell me anything.'

I hesitated, considering it for a moment. 'Okay, but you have to keep in mind I was already an emotional mess when I read your email and listened to the song you sent.'

'Okay, I'm prepared. Go on, tell me, what did you nearly send?' I could tell he was intrigued.

'Well my first attempt was overly sloppy and emotional, something about wishing you were here with me too.'

'Sounds fine to me,' – a smile audible in his voice. 'And the second?'

'Ah, well at that point my sadness had kind of turned to anger. It was something along the lines of… If I'm all you want then why don't you jump on a plane. Although I may have typed "fucking plane." But of course I know why. It was stupid, which is why I deleted it. I told you, I was having a meltdown, I was alone and missing you. Pathetic, I know.'

'Wow.' He went silent, I guess he was taking it all in. 'Although I think I win on the pathetic front. I was the one carrying my laptop everywhere waiting for you to email. How ridiculous is that?'

We both laughed. I thought back to his first email. He hadn't been joking.

'So let me ask,' he paused, 'why a month? What made you finally email me? I loved the song, by the way.'

'I knew you would, it was written for us.' I was unsure I wanted to share what had prompted me to finally email him but he deserved an honest explanation. 'It wasn't as though I purposely waited a month. It was pure coincidence. That night when I emailed you, I'd erm, been on a date. He'd kissed me goodnight but when I closed my eyes all I could see was you.'

The line went quiet.

'Are you still seeing him?'

'No. I managed one gig and a meal. He even had living in the same country as me going for him but it wasn't the same.' I closed my eyes and thought back to our first kiss, under the stars, the waves lapping at our feet. 'He wasn't you,' I sighed. 'All I could think about the entire date was you.' I took a deep breath, squeezing my eyes closed as my feelings made their way to the surface.

'You don't know how much I wish I could hold you right now.' I could hear despair in his voice.

'I do,' I managed through my tears. 'It's so good to hear your voice again, I never thought I would.'

'I know, and yours.' He went quiet. 'I still feel it you know, nothing's changed.'

Hearing his words, the pain from missing him overflowed like waterfalls down my cheeks. 'I still feel it too,' I admitted, my heart aching for him.

We stayed on the line, both silent, as I caught my breath and steadied my breathing.

'Tell me everything you've done since I left.' I slowly made my way upstairs and lay down on my bed, his voice calming me.

'Well, I spent a month afraid I'd never hear from you again. I was convinced you hated me for leaving a note and disappearing.'

'No, you did the right thing, ripping the plaster off, remember?'

'Yeah? I was afraid I'd really hurt you when you didn't email.'

'No. I was just trying to get over you.'

'So, your clean break, it didn't work then?'

'No,' I admitted.

'See, I already knew you wouldn't be able to live without me.'

I giggled as I pictured Max's jubilant face. In Verona, I really had believed it would be easier to leave it at goodbye. It seemed it was in fact Max who knew better and me who needed time to catch up.

We both stayed silent for a few moments before Max spoke. 'I thought about driving to the airport and begging you stay, like in the films, but I knew I couldn't change your mind.'

I smiled as I thought back to sitting in the airport imagining the exact same thing. 'I thought about making some dramatic scene and running off the plane, but instead I sat and cried, in public. The guy next to me thought I was a lunatic.'

Max was laughing, then he went quiet. 'I watched you get into the taxi outside the hotel.'

I thought I'd felt his presence. He was there. The knowledge struck me inside. 'I looked around for you.'

'I know, I saw you. I wanted to stop you so much but–'

'I know,' I cut in.

'Even though you said 'no' to keeping in touch, I was convinced you'd email that first week. Then definitely the second. When you didn't, I wasn't sure what to think.' He paused. 'There's no way I could forget you that fast.'

'Oh, no, no, no. I could never forget you. No. It was the complete opposite.' I was desperate to make him understand. 'Every moment we'd shared kept on replaying over and over, it was torture. I couldn't slip back into my life. It didn't make any sense why after such a short space of time I had all these feelings, why I missed you so much, why I thought about you constantly.' I hesitated. 'Why I still do.'

It felt good to be honest. Honest not only with Max but also with myself.

'I know, me too,' Max sighed. 'I stupidly took you everywhere. I can't escape the memories. Not that I want to and I know it sounds crazy, but you've left quite a void in my life.'

'If it's any consolation, you've never even been to my world but I constantly imagine you here, holding my hand when I'm driving, lying in bed with me at night.'

Max laughed. 'Oh yes, tell me more. Any Kings of Leon?'

He still knew how to make me smile.

'You sound calmer,' he said.

'I am, thank you. How's everything there? How are you?'

'Besides missing you, fine.'

'Is Luca looking after you? How is he?'

Max laughed. 'He's fine.'

'Where are you?'

'At home.'

'Where?'

'Guess.'

'I'm picturing you on the swivel chair in your bedroom, feet up.'

'Very good, have you been secretly spying on me?' He was laughing. 'So let me guess, you are lying on your bed looking up at the stars?'

He remembered everything. 'Correct but no stars, too cloudy here in England.'

There was another comfortable pause. I focused on the black square above my bed while listening to Max breathing. It still soothed me.

'Did you manage to clear Michele's house? I was thinking about you that weekend, and watching BBC World News for stories of fires.'

I had missed his effortless ability to make me laugh. 'I did. No fires. Just a smashed perfume bottle. There's already been an offer accepted. It's strange not going there anymore.'

'How's Adam coping with it?'

'Better. You helped me with him.'

'I did? How?'

'We were both struggling to let go of the house, to let go of all the memories we'd created there. I didn't know how to reassure him, then I remembered what you told me at the markets that day, how Michele will always be in my heart. It really helped. Thank you.'

'Glad I could help.' He went quiet again. 'I've missed you so much.'

I could hear it in his voice, exactly how I was feeling, reflecting back at me.

'I'm sorry I didn't email sooner. I didn't mean to hurt you, that's the last thing I'd ever want to do. I thought it was the only way to,' I paused, 'break the chains and walk without you.'

'Are you stealing lyrics from Josh Record?' he laughed.

'Ad-libbing,' I corrected, laughing too. I knew he'd get it.

'Hang on,' he said. I could hear movement and rustling, then the song 'Wide Awake' began to play. 'Listen with me. Close your eyes. I'm laying down, my head's on your lap, you're stroking my hair,' Max set the imaginary scene for us.

I closed my eyes, smiling, picturing us together while listening to Josh Record's beautiful love song.

'I didn't mean to make it harder for you,' Max said, 'that day on the bridge, I just wanted to help you somehow. I never expected we'd spend every second together or that saying goodbye would be so painful.' He paused, hesitating. 'I didn't know I was going to fall in love with you.'

His words struck my heart as tears began to fall uncontrollably. Hearing him say it. I'd barely admitted it to myself.

'I know,' I sighed, 'I went and fell in love with you too. That's why it hurts so much.'

We both stayed silent for a few moments, sharing the pain. I could hear Max was crying too. I wiped my tears away, trying to be strong.

'Your office wall, the photographs, they're incredible.' I stopped myself saying, 'It made me fall in love with you even more,' though I wanted to.

'I didn't want to forget us, the way you made me feel.' His voice was tender and loving.

'Do you remember how you kissed me that last night, before

we left your office?' I thought back to that moment five weeks ago when Max said, 'I never want to forget how this feels.'

'Like it was yesterday,' he answered.

'See, just remember that.' We both fell silent, lost in memories. 'We're not doing very well, are we?' I said, half smiling, half crying.

'Pretty hopeless,' he agreed.

I let out a yawn, which Max caught.

'You're tired,' he said, concern in his voice.

'Yes,' I admitted, 'but I don't want you to go.' Panic struck me at the thought of saying goodbye.

'Hey, I'm not going anywhere,' he reassured. I heard him get up off his chair and move. 'Are you in bed, under the covers?' he asked.

'Yes,' I replied, pulling the duvet over me and closing my eyes.

'Okay, I'm in bed too.'

I wasn't sure where he was going with this. 'Are you going to ask me what I'm wearing next?' I laughed. I heard Max laughing too.

'Bet you can guess what I'm wearing, have been every night since you left.'

I didn't know what he meant. 'No, what?'

'Your Damien Rice teeshirt you gave me.'

'Lent,' I swiftly corrected. I hadn't even noticed it was missing. I had forgotten to get it back off him. I'd had that teeshirt forever, although it was nice knowing it had offered him comfort, the way his locket had offered me.

'Put the phone next to your ear and close your eyes,' he gently commanded, 'I'll stay until you fall asleep. I've got my arms wrapped around you. I'm stroking your hair.'

I smiled as I imagined myself back in Max's arms, comforted and happy. It was wonderful hearing his voice again, I had missed him so very much. My eyes were heavy as I focused on his breathing, the familiar sound soothing me to sleep.

* * *

I woke the following afternoon – the telephone on the floor where I'd placed it after briefly waking to hang up hours after falling asleep with Max. I stroked my locket as I thought about Michele. Then grabbed my laptop to email Max, to say thank you for being there for me. I hated that he'd ever doubted how I felt. I'd never make him wait again.

He'd already beaten me to it.

To: Alex
Subject: Close your eyes and listen
'Be Still' by The Fray (click on link)
You're never alone.
I'm here, Always.
Love Max X

I lay down, closing my eyes as instructed, listening to the gentle piano. It was beautiful, Max's borrowed lullaby to me, telling me to simply think of him and I'd never be alone, that he'd always be with me, even in my darkest times. Tears escaped as I lay, I was helpless to stop them. My heart grew heavier. Sadness consumed me. I didn't know it was possible to fall in love with him any deeper or to miss him any more than I already did. In that moment, even though I knew it was impossible, I wanted to leave the life I no longer fit, quit my job, sell my apartment and return to him as I knew that was where my happiness lay, with Max. He was what was missing, he filled the void inside, he made me happy. But I also knew I could never leave Adam.

I composed myself as I reached for the laptop, certain of one thing: forgetting Max had never been a plausible option, he held too big a place in my heart.

To: Max
Subject: Thank you
There's no song I can send to match that!
It's beautiful.
Thank you for always being there for me.
Thank you for last night. I truly mean that.
I only just woke up! I sleep better with you, but then I always did.
Love Always, Alex X

I eventually got out of bed, unsure how to spend the rest of my day. Normally I'd be working out or watching the second half of Adam's football match. It felt odd not being there. I showered, dressed and sent Adam a text message asking the final score. My laptop binged with an email from Max.

To: Alex
Subject: Let's do it again tonight then
I see you're on Skype. I've added you.
It'll save me going bankrupt from my phone bill ;)
Are you in later?
Can't wait to 'see' you.
Love Always, Max X

I opened Skype and accepted his request so we could video chat later. The thought of seeing him again, his beautiful eyes, gave me butterflies. I actually had no plans until my phone beeped with a text message from Adam.

'We won 2-1. Me and Dad going to TC for food, you coming? Meet us there in 30???'

Did Adam know I was feeling lost? It was a wonderful gesture on his part, which I gratefully accepted. Then quickly emailed Max before setting off.

To: Max
Subject: Definitely
I've accepted you.
Am just going to meet Adam and Ben for food.
Will turn Skype on when I get back so you know I'm home.
Can't wait to 'see' you too.
Love Always, Alex X

I arrived home just after nine, checking myself in the mirror before opening Skype. Even though Max had seen me in all states, this was the first time in over a month, I wanted to look good – the pressure of Skype. I tried not to sit waiting for his call but I couldn't help it, although I didn't have to wait very long. My hand was trembling as I answered. Then there he was. I thought I'd be nervous but seeing him instantly filled me with calm, he felt like home, even though that made no sense. Although they did say *home is where the heart is*.

'Hey beautiful. How's your evening been?'

He looked directly into the camera as he said it. Those eyes. How I'd missed the way he looked at me.

'It was good. Yours?'

'Fantastic.'

'Yeah, why?'

'I had this Skype date to look forward to. I've not seen her for awhile.'

'Oh, how does she look?'

'Just as I remember her, beautiful but slightly puffy eyes still. I think I need to work on that.'

'Really, what do you recommend?'

'I think a daily Skype session may be required.' He gave me a wink and my smile widened. 'See, it's already working.' We stared at each other, both grinning from ear to ear. 'So how was it with Adam and Ben?'

'It was great. Things seem good between them. Adam's so sweet, he wanted to check I didn't mind his dad taking over football because it's always been our thing. He was so excited to have his dad there watching him. I felt guilty, all Ben's done is make Adam happy.'

'How can you possibly feel guilty for wanting to spend time with Adam? He's a lucky guy.'

'Thank you. So tell me what have you done today?'

'Not much, drinking coffee mostly, someone kept me up late.'

'Yeah, sorry about waking you.'

'You didn't. I was already awake listening to music and looking at photographs of us.'

'Really?' I wasn't sure if he was teasing me.

'Really.' I noticed him blush, embarrassed by his honesty.

'Hating me because I didn't email you back? I'm sorry.'

'No, I could never hate you. I just couldn't sleep. I thought you were psychic when I got your email.'

'Maybe I am. I noticed you took some photographs.'

'You didn't mind?'

'Of course not, they were ours. I liked that you wanted to keep some.'

'You seem a lot happier today,' he observed.

'I am.' I smiled, captivated by his beautiful eyes that I never thought I'd see again, his face, his smile. 'I've missed that face,' I admitted.

Max sighed. 'I've missed yours too.'

We both paused, taking in the moment.

'Let's do this every night,' Max announced, 'before we go to sleep, it doesn't matter what time or if it's only to say goodnight, let's check in, share our day. What do you think?' His voice was hopeful, like in his bedroom when we'd discussed keeping in touch.

'I think it's a wonderful idea,' I agreed. Back then, I was afraid of ruining our memories. I didn't know how empty my life would be without him in it.

Max asked for a tour of my apartment, a piece of my world, so I walked him from room to room. He especially liked my gig ticket art, a frame I'd filled with tickets from concerts I'd been to over the years, and the fact that I too owned a turntable and vinyl records. We talked into the early hours. When we finally succumbed to tiredness and it was time to go, we ended the call smiling, saying 'see you later,' happy because this time it wasn't goodbye.

14

FRIDAY, 19TH DECEMBER

I sat on my bed drinking a large glass of water to sober up, still wearing the party dress I'd bought especially for Friday Christmas cocktails to celebrate finishing work for two whole weeks. We'd all left work early so we could race home, leave our cars, change and hit the town. It had been a great night, an opportunity to leave the stresses of work behind and laugh. My friend, Jenny, had encouraged me to join her in trying a cocktail from every page of the menu – and it was quite an extensive cocktail menu. I'd opened Skype so Max would know I was home. This is what we did, had done every night since that first phone call two months ago. No matter what plans we had, we spoke every night before bed, me at home, Max either at home or his office. We never lacked conversation, always sharing how we'd spent our day, plans we had coming up. We knew each other's schedules inside out. Discussing bands or songs we'd discovered and the occasional gig either of us had been to. We'd watched each other's all-time favourite films, mine being 'The Thing Called Love,' 'Reality Bites,' 'About Last Night,' 'Before Sunrise' and of course 'Ferris Bueller's Day Off,' and Max's being 'The Shawshank Redemption,' 'Pulp Fiction,' and 'High Fidelity,' then chatted about them like we'd watched them together. Luca sometimes popped in to say hello; he was still a whirlwind of energy. I'd see something I knew Max would like and want to tell him about and I could, that night. I no longer missed him because I saw him every day. We often fell asleep together, lying down next to our laptop or iPad; I always slept much better when I could hear Max breathing next to me. The nights when he was at his office and we were forced to say goodnight, I'd lie in bed afterwards, imagining myself there with him. On the one night my broadband was down we'd chatted on the telephone instead. We never missed a night. I still experienced days when missing Michele overwhelmed me but every night I could talk it through with Max. I hadn't looked at another man; Max sometimes teased me by asking but still no one came close. To be honest, I couldn't imagine ever meeting anyone who could make me feel the way Max did. As depressing as that sounded I was okay with it. Max had enabled me to find elements of joy in my life again. I was no longer consumed by the hollowness inside. Did I let myself day dream about what could never be between us? Yes, all the time. I loved him even more now than I did in Verona but nothing had changed, his life was there and mine was here. Did I still have doubts that I was prolonging the painful inevitable if Max met someone else? Yes, all the time, but then we'd Skype and my doubts would fall away. Or I'd replay Michele's question in my mind, asking myself when I was last happy and the answer was always the same. Max was the one person in the world I could rely on, tell anything. My world was simply a better place with him in it and if life had taught me anything it was to hold onto happiness with both hands.

Michele's mum had decided to host Christmas dinner this year, inviting Adam, Ben, Mel, their children, and me. I was relieved to receive her invitation, having spent Christmas Day with her and Michele every year since I was twelve, the year my parents had separated. That first year I'd escaped to Michele's parent's house to avoid having to choose which parent to spend it with. After that my dad and his new wife went abroad every Christmas, while my mum visited her boyfriend's family. It suited me as it meant I could spend it with my adopted family, as Michele and I called them. Michele's family seemed perfect to me. They were happy, warm and inviting, even after her dad died. People would drop by for a drink and to exchange gifts and chat. I loved it there. It simply became the norm every year, a present under the tree, a place set for me at the table. I became part of their family, Michele became like a sister to me. When Adam came along it continued, just a change of venue as Michele took it in turns with her mum to host. I was planning on spending Christmas Day with Michele's mum regardless, especially this year, the first one we had to face without Michele. I had been concerned Ben and Mel would want a 'family only' day. It was important we could spend this difficult milestone with Adam too; none of us were looking forward to it but at least we'd have each other.

The familiar sound started, Skype, Max calling. My favourite moment was always when we first connected. Every night his eyes would light up and smile when he first saw me. It was better than any medicine, the way he looked at me, like I was the only woman in the world.

'Hey beautiful.' He always opened with that and it always made my smile widen. 'How's your day been?'

'It was good. Going out for cocktails was fun.'

'Your eyes look drunk,' he said, laughing.

I looked at myself on the screen; they had that shiny glazed look about them.

'Tipsy,' I corrected. 'So what have you done today?'

'Cleaning.' Max rolled his eyes. His parents were arriving on Sunday to spend Christmas in Verona. 'Preparing for my mother's scrutiny. The first thing out of her mouth is always to ask if I'm eating enough, she'll say I look like I'm wasting away.'

I laughed. I could imagine his mum worrying about him, especially after all he'd been through. I'd never met her but from everything he'd told me, I liked her.

'I need to check, move back, let me see?' I teased, brave from the alcohol.

Max moved away from the screen, teasing me, slowly lifting his shirt, uncovering that horizontal line above his waistband I loved, that I could remember tracing with my kisses. The memory awakened feelings inside, filling my stomach with butterflies.

'You look pretty perfect to me.' I couldn't disguise the look on my face or the desire in my voice.

'Why thank you,' he said, smirking as he sat back down, the attraction between us still apparent.

'Is it tomorrow you're taking Adam Christmas shopping?'

'Yep, he's staying at his friend's house tonight, I'm not picking him up until the afternoon, which means I can have a lie in.'

'Which means we can talk late,' Max corrected, grinning.

'That too.' I winked.

My mobile phone rang.

'Is that your phone?'

I was going to ignore it until I saw Adam's name.

'Hang on Max, it's Adam,' I told him as I answered the phone.

'Hey Ad.'

'Is that Alex?' It was a girl's voice.

'Who is this, why have you got Adam's phone?'

'I'm Sarah, there's something wrong with Adam.'

'What? Adam's at Tim's house, are you with them? Can you put Adam on the phone, please.' I was starting to get irritated and anxious.

'Erm, yes we're at Tim's but there was kind of a party. Adam was drinking. A lot. I've never seen him drink before. Please don't be mad. I don't know what to do.' She sounded frightened. I could tell by her voice that this wasn't a joke. I sat up, my mind racing, quickly sobering up.

'How much did he drink?'

'He knocked back a whole bottle of vodka. A big bottle.'

'Where is he? Can I talk to him?'

'He passed out on the chair, we can't wake him. He looks really pale.'

'Has he taken anything, drugs?'

'No, no, nothing.'

'Sarah I want you to shake him and say his name.'

I could hear her following my instructions, along with other voices in the background.

'He won't wake up. We've tried and tried. He's not moving.'

'Okay, put your hand under his nose, can you feel him breathing?'

'A bit, slightly. It's really slow, really faint.' She was starting to panic. So was I.

'Sarah, tell someone there to phone 999, now.' I needed to stay calm.

I heard her shout to Tim and him shout back, panicked, asking what he should say.

'Tell Tim to say you need an ambulance, that Adam is unconscious, he's sixteen, you think it's alcohol poisoning.'

I heard her relay the message. My mind was racing but focused on her voice.

'They're trying to pick him up, they're going to put him under a cold shower, that'll help, won't it.'

'No,' I found myself shouting as hyperthermia popped into my head. Now thankful I had owed my boss a favour and agreed, albeit reluctantly, to become a first aider at work. One of the other trainees on the course had told a story about finding someone in that very state and the instructor had been extremely firm about what *not* to do. 'Sarah, tell them to stop. No cold water. Put Adam on the floor in the recovery position. Do you know what I mean by that?'

'Yes, we did it at school.'

I could hear her instructing the others and Tim shouting instructions from the 999 operator as I waited on the phone, helpless, willing the ambulance to arrive. Minutes felt like hours. Adam was breathing, he wouldn't choke if he was sick in the recovery position. He needed to stay warm.

'Sarah, are there blankets or coats to put over him?'

'Yes.' She shouted at them to cover him up, to keep him warm. 'They're already covering him up.'

'You're doing great. Can you check his breathing again for me?'

I could hear the sirens in the background getting louder.

'They can't feel anything, wait, let me check, I don't know.' She was becoming more distressed. 'The ambulance is here,' Sarah shouted.

'Sarah, stay on the phone with me, okay.' I was praying she was mistaken, that he was still breathing.

Sarah described what the paramedics were doing and repeated what they were saying for me.

'They're laying Adam on his back, talking to him, squeezing his finger, telling him to wake up, to open his eyes. He's not though. They're checking for a pulse… cutting his teeshirt… attaching sticky things to his chest… They said he's hypoxic, I don't know what that means.'

I did, he wasn't getting enough oxygen in his body, to his brain. I closed my eyes, willing this not to be happening as Sarah kept talking.

'They're putting a tube down his throat and squeezing a bag to help him breathe… They said they're getting a good rise and fall from the chest… They're putting him onto a stretcher.'

She put a paramedic on the phone.

'We need to get him to hospital, he's unconscious, in a critical condition. You should make your way to the M.R.I. now.'

The phone went dead as the words filtered into my brain, slowly connecting, catching up. I couldn't breathe. I couldn't move.

'Alex, what's happening?' I looked back at Max, the fear on his face mirroring my own.

'Adam's unconscious, he's not breathing on his own, the paramedic said he's critical, that I should make my way to the hospital now.' I was speaking slowly, trying to catch my breath. My whole body was shaking.

'Alex, it's going to be all right,' Max tried to reassure me.

I looked at him, shaking my head, filled with disbelief. The dam that had been holding back the tears burst and they came flowing out. I was hysterical with fear.

'I can't. I can't do this again. I can't face it. What if I get there and he's…'

I couldn't say the word. The vision of Michele's body lying before me in the morgue slammed into my brain, suddenly replaced by a vision of Adam's body. I closed my eyes, desperately trying to push it away.

'Alex, look at me.' Max was shouting at me. 'You need to calm down, breathe, look at me.'

I looked at Max through my tears and tried to control my breathing. I was still shaking uncontrollably.

'You're going to be okay, you can do this. Adam needs you. Phone a taxi now, say it's an emergency so they send one straight away.'

Taxi? Then I remembered, I'd been drinking, I couldn't drive. I listened to Max's voice, following his instructions, allowing him to think for me as he told me what to do. I phoned a taxi, and they despatched one to me immediately. I put on my coat and shoes and retrieved my phone, purse and keys, stuffing them into my pockets. Then I sat back down on the bed, looking at Max. I couldn't speak, I could barely comprehend what was happening.

'Does Ben know? Give me his number, I'll call him,' Max offered.

I looked down at my hands, clasped together in an attempt to stop them trembling, then back at Max, my eyes overflowing.

'No, I'll call him.' I took a deep breath. I was petrified I was going to arrive at the hospital to find Adam… I couldn't even think the word… the same way I'd arrived at Michele's house that day to find her, gone, forever. 'Max, I'm terrified,' I admitted, holding my head in my hands as I wept.

'Alex, what can I do?' He sounded desperate.

'Hold me.' It was my only answer. I needed to be held, soothed, like he'd done in Verona. I needed to draw strength from him to get me through this.

My phone buzzed with a text. The taxi was outside. I looked at the screen, at Max.

'Email me if you can,' he said.

I nodded and ended the call, running outside to the waiting taxi. Once inside, I called Ben continuously on both his landline and mobile but he didn't answer. I left messages and texts explaining what had happened, instructing him to go to the hospital. I thought about calling Michele's mum but she was still away on her pre-Christmas break.

When I got to A&E I was ushered to a waiting area and told they were still working on Adam. I saw Tim and a young girl sitting there. They both nodded hello to me, both pale and anxious.

'Are you Sarah?' I asked.

She nodded.

'I'm Alex.'

She sat up straight, alert. 'How's Adam, they won't tell us anything?' She was desperate for information.

I sat down with them. 'They're still working on him. What happened?' I asked.

Tim spoke first, looking down at his hands, nervously clasping and unclasping them. 'It was just supposed to be a bit of Xbox after school at my house but it got tweeted about that my parents were away and I was havin' a Christmas party. Most of the year group turned up. Adam was actin' weird.'

Sarah interjected. 'He was sad, you know with it being the first Christmas without his mum.'

'Some lads brought booze and Adam grabbed a full bottle of vodka and started neckin' it.'

'We told him to stop, that it would make him sick but he said it–' Sarah stopped.

'Go on,' I encouraged her.

Sarah and Tim looked at each other then back at me.

'He said it made the pain go away.' She paused. 'You know the pain from missing his mum.'

I nodded. Yes, I knew that pain very well.

'Has he been drinking before tonight?'

They both shook their heads. I could tell they were telling the truth.

'Have you both called your parents?'

'They'd gone to stay with friends for the weekend but they're on their way back now,' Tim said.

'My mum's coming to get me,' Sarah said. 'Did I do the right thing phoning you? The boys said he just needed to sleep it off but he didn't look right.'

'You definitely did the right thing. Thank you,' I said, hugging her. 'Did you call Adam's dad first? How did you know to call me?'

'You're ICE in his phone,' Sarah said and seeing my confused look, explained, 'in case of emergency, we did it at school in September, you put ICE and the person's name and number so if something happens they know who to call.'

I couldn't help but think I had let Adam down somehow, that I wasn't up to the role he had trusted me with. I didn't see him twice a week anymore, since Ben had taken over football, but we still texted several times a week, and he regularly came over for dinner, I'd even taken him to his first gig. He hadn't slipped away as I'd feared. He'd told me about staying at Tim's. I searched my brain, desperately trying to recall exactly what he'd said, whether he'd lied to me about Tim's parents being away. I'd never known Adam to tell a lie.

We sat waiting in agonising silence, jumping each time we heard footsteps in the corridor until a doctor finally approached us, asking to speak to Adam's parent or guardian. I explained the situation and he ushered me into a quiet corner of the room, informing me that Adam was still unconscious in Intensive Care, stable but critical, whatever that meant. They'd pumped his stomach and were rehydrating him. A machine was breathing for him. They were concerned about loss of oxygen to the brain. I was desperately trying to concentrate, to focus on and process every word. The doctor cleared his throat, looking down.

'I need to ask, was this an accident or could it have been an attempted suicide?'

The moment the words left the doctor's lips, my vision blurred and the room began to spin. I felt the doctor grab me, helping me to a chair, apologising but saying he had to ask.

I remembered a few days after Michele had died, Adam screaming at me that he wanted to die too so he could be with her. He was furious back then, just venting, he hadn't meant it. Or had he? Had he been hiding it from us? Deep down inside, did he still feel that way? Michele's death had been devastating. Adam found her, tried to resuscitate her. I thought he was doing okay. His friends said he was in pain, but I drank to numb the pain of losing her, of missing her, it didn't mean I wanted to die.

I focused on the doctor through pools of tears, shaking my head, 'No, it was a stupid accident. He's a teenager, he doesn't understand risk like you and me.' Then the question burst out of my mouth. 'Is he going to die?' I held my breath as the doctor answered.

'The next twenty-four hours are crucial, we'll know more then.' He squeezed my shoulder. 'Do you want to see him?'

I nodded, steadying myself on the wall before slowly following the doctor, copying him as he applied alcohol hand rub from the dispenser. When I went into Intensive Care I didn't recognise Adam. I looked around for him before realising he was right there in front of me. I couldn't see his face, it was hidden behind tubes he was attached to, endless tubes and wires, and surrounded by machines flashing and beeping. The doctor explained what everything was but I couldn't hear him, all I could hear was my heart beating in my ears, like a deafening, ticking bomb about to explode. I needed air.

I sprinted down the corridor, searching for exit signs, running outside into the windy night, and around to the side of the building until I was alone. I stood doubled up, holding onto a wall, retching and trying to catch my breath, unsure if I was going to be sick. Eventually my breathing stilled and I slid down the wall, hugging my knees, watching litter and broken branches being blown around by the angry gusts as though my emotions were controlling the weather. I gazed up at the black sky, a few stars visible between clouds, shaking my head, tears escaping.

'You can't keep him,' I shouted up at the sky, my voice getting swept away, 'you need to send him back. I know he misses you but tell him, he's sixteen, he has his entire life ahead of him. Tell him he has to come back. We love him. We need him. We can't lose him too. Please Michele, send him back.' I didn't think it was possible to feel pain any greater than what I'd felt that day in July when Michele had died. I was wrong. I opened the locket, gazing down at Michele. 'I'm sorry, I've failed you, I didn't stop this happening, I should've done something, done more, I've let you down. I promised I'd take care of him for you. I'm so sorry.'

I held my head in my hands and sobbed, replaying and scrutinising every conversation I could remember having with Adam, searching for some clue I'd missed. Our last conversation had been just that lunchtime, he'd sounded fine, he was looking forward to going shopping for new football boots tomorrow, later today. I knew he was dreading Christmas without her but we all were. I reached for my phone, switching it on, gripping it tight. Ben had texted, he was on his way. I re-read all of Adam's text messages but even with that knowledge, with hindsight, there was nothing to suggest he was struggling enough to end it all.

I saw an email from Max.

To: Alex
Subject: Any news?

I found myself pouring my thoughts out to the one person I could.

To: Max
Subject: Any news?
They're worried about loss of oxygen to his brain, he's in Intensive Care, critical but stable, hooked up to a million machines. I couldn't handle it, I ran outside. I know I

need to go back in, I will, I just need a few minutes. I want to sit with him and hold his hand, I do, but I'm terrified, what if there's permanent damage, what if he dies? Max I can't do this, I know I need to be strong for him but I don't think I've anything left, I just can't do this, not again, I can't lose him too. They asked if he might have done it on purpose, how could I have missed that? It's all my fault, I've let Michele down, I should've protected him. How is this happening?

The screen became a blur through my tears. I managed to press send then switched my phone off and sat staring straight ahead as time seemed to slow. I felt a weight pressing down on my brain, as though I was on the verge of a breakdown. My mind felt like a branch on a tree that could snap at any second and I had the power to let it, to take the easy option, to simply let go and not have to think any longer, it'd all be over, no more struggling, no more pain. I closed my eyes and imagined the peace but all I could see was Adam. I needed the pain to stop but Adam needed me more. It took every ounce of strength I had left, but I pulled myself up, forcing myself to stand, forcing my legs to hold me up as I took a few deep breaths, dried my face and slowly made my way back inside.

As I passed the waiting room I heard shouting. Ben's voice. I went inside to find Ben frantic, shouting at Tim's parents, accusing them of being irresponsible. I automatically leapt between them, facing Ben. He saw me and stopped, his anger turning to tears. He was terrified too. I threw my arms around him and held him as he crumpled to the floor, sobbing. Tim's mum knelt down and held him too as he apologised in between sobs. Sarah's mum appeared.

Everyone started filling her in on what had happened. It was sensory overload. I left Ben being comforted by Tim's parents and walked down the corridor, applying alcohol rub and going back into the room where Adam lay, stopping and catching my breath as I took in all the equipment he was attached to again, following each tube and wire. A different kind of sensory overload.

'I know it looks scary,' a nurse said, trying to reassure me as she led me to the chair beside his bed. I sat down, automatically reaching for Adam's hand but hesitating, stopped by the sight of tubes and chords and the pulse monitor he was attached to. 'Go ahead, it's okay, hold his hand, talk to him, he needs you right now.'

I slowly placed his hand in mine. He felt limp. I was afraid.

'Can he hear me?' I asked the nurse.

'No one knows for sure but I think he can.' She gave me a hopeful smile as she pulled the curtain around, offering us some privacy.

I watched Adam. He looked like he was sleeping, just like Michele had. Tears started to escape, flowing down my cheeks. I followed each tube and wire to the drip or machine it was connected to. Each one fighting to keep Adam alive.

'I need you to fight, Adam. If you can hear me, I need you to wake up.' I was trying to be strong but I couldn't stop the tears escaping. 'You belong here. We love you, we need you. I know you miss your mum, I do too. It hurts like no pain I've ever felt before but that's not a reason to give up, to stop living. You start fighting, you open your eyes. Don't you dare leave me. You remember the odds you beat to be in this world, how determined your mum always said you were to be born, you can conquer anything, remember. Now conquer this.'

I was in pieces, sobbing but trying not to let Adam hear; if he could hear me at all that was. I thought about stroking his hair but that had always helped him sleep, and I needed him to wake up. I lay my head down on the edge of the bed, holding and squeezing Adam's hand as I focused on the howling wind outside that was thrashing up against the windows, like a crazed mother desperately trying to reach her son.

I opened my eyes to Ben calling my name. My hand was still holding Adam's. As I turned to look at Adam, a pain shot up my neck from lying bent over. Adam was still asleep, still unconscious. Ben helped me up and we both stood back as the nurse and doctor walked around the bed, checking and noting figures on machines.

'What time is it?' I asked Ben. My head was pounding, the start of a hangover intensified by all the crying.

'Nearly six.'

'I fell asleep?' I couldn't believe I had dropped off.

'Not for long and anyway it's better than just sitting there.'

'How are you holding up?' I asked him.

Ben shook his head. He was calm now, his anger replaced by disbelief and hopelessness. I felt it too.

'Do you think he'll pull through?' Ben asked through tear-filled eyes.

'He's got to,' I replied, being strong for the both of us. I couldn't face any other reality, I had to make this one my truth.

We returned to Adam's bedside, sitting and staring at the tube breathing for him, at his chest rising and falling. I put my ear to Adam's chest to hear his heart beat. As long as I could hear that, everything was fine. Then I rested my head back on the edge of the bed, holding Adam's hand. Ben did the same on the other side. We stayed that way for hours.

After carrying out further checks, the doctor approached us. We both stood up straight, anxious. She informed us that there was no change, that Adam remained in a stable condition, which was a good sign. She encouraged us to go home and get a few hours' sleep, freshen up, change into comfortable clothes and come back refreshed, that we'd be more use to Adam rested. I noticed her look me up and down when she mentioned changing into comfortable clothes. I looked down at myself, still wearing my dress from last night, appropriate for cocktails but slightly overdressed for the I.C.U. I thought back to meeting Max. I'd been inappropriately dressed that day too, wearing my black funeral dress on that sunny afternoon, then scaling a wall in it.

Neither Ben nor I wanted to be anywhere but by Adam's bedside. I sat back down on the chair next to Adam, holding his hand and squeezing it. I needed to wake him, to talk to him. I stood and walked to the gift shop, buying some paracetamol for my throbbing head, a large bottle of water for my dehydration and an array of newspapers and football magazines, returning to Adam's bedside and reading newspapers the way he did, from the back page in, always football first. We sat for hours working our way through them all in between the nurse's checks. I was determined to fight my heavy, tired eyes and find a story that would pique Adam's interest enough to wake him, until I eventually succumbed to my tiredness, sitting back in the chair and closing my eyes for a few minutes.

I woke to Mel arriving, gently shaking me and insisting I go home at least to shower and change, that I'd feel better for it. I really didn't want to leave Adam but I agreed. The sooner I left, the sooner I'd be back. They promised to call if anything changed.

I leant over the tubes, kissing Adam on the forehead and whispering that he'd better be awake by the time I got back, and that I loved him. I had to say that last part in case it was the last time. The fact that it was even a possibility was unbearable. I didn't want to think it but I couldn't help it.

As I made my way outside to the taxi, the cold air hit me, stinging my face. The temperature had dropped. I sat back in the taxi, shivering and drained, filled with anxiety and hopelessness. I closed my eyes and grasped my locket, feeling completely alone in the world.

15

SATURDAY, 20TH DECEMBER

I got out of the taxi and dragged myself along the path, past broken branches scattered on the ground from last night's storm. I was struggling to keep my eyes open, exhausted and hungover, my head pounding. The world felt fuzzy. I had decided I would shower, lie down and try to sleep for an hour, concede to my exhaustion. When I reached the front door I was startled by a figure in a large coat sitting on the step, looking up at the sound of my approaching footsteps on the gravel. The fuzz cleared as I blinked, my eyes wide. It couldn't be. He stood. Was I dreaming? Was I still at the hospital, asleep by Adam's bedside? He grabbed me, enveloping me in a hug. I prodded myself hard, I could feel the pain, I was definitely awake. I gently pushed him back so I could look at him, could search his face, slowly tracing it with my fingers, captivated by those beautiful deep brown eyes.

'Max. Is it really you?'

He nodded, smiling but concerned. I expected to blink and for him to disappear, an over-tired illusion created by my brain in turmoil. I placed my hands firmly on his coated chest, pressing him. He was real.

'How's Adam?'

'The same,' I answered, closing my eyes and swallowing back the tears as I pictured Adam lying in the hospital, hooked up to machines all fighting to save his life. Max pulled me close, holding me and placing a long kiss on the top of my head.

'You're here, you're really here, how, why? Are you okay?' I was in equal amounts comforted yet concerned in his arms.

Max squeezed me a little tighter as he spoke. 'Last night, I asked what I could do, you said hold me, so here I am holding you.' He made it sound so simple, maybe I should have asked months ago. Max placed his hands on my cheeks, searching my face. 'You look exhausted.'

I was startled by how cold his hands were. 'You're frozen,' I said, taking his cold hands in mine and rubbing them, trying to warm them.

'I've been sitting on your doorstep waiting for you since this morning. Well I sat in a coffee shop down there for a while.' He pointed in the direction of the local shops. 'But I was afraid I'd miss you.'

'But how do you know where I live?' I was so confused.

He reached inside his pocket, pulling out the envelope that had contained the wallet of disposable camera photographs. My mind raced back to the old man in the shop tapping the envelope while repeatedly saying, 'casa casa,' then back to the hotel that last morning when I realised Max had taken some photographs, leaving me the wallet and taking the envelope.

'I didn't notice for weeks but your address is written on the envelope.' Max shivered. He looked as exhausted as I felt.

'Come inside, sorry.' I unlocked the door, ushering him inside and climbing the stairs to my apartment door, Max following. It felt surreal, him being there. Once inside, he put his bag down, we shook off our coats and he sat on the stairs, removing his shoes.

'Bit overdressed for the hospital,' he teased, looking me up and down then pulling me to him, sitting me on his knee. I instinctively wrapped my arms around his neck and nuzzled into him, breathing in his smell as he held me, gently rocking me, instantly calming me. It was exactly what I needed, like a distressed baby being rocked to sleep in its parent's arms. I was dumbfounded that he was in my world, in my apartment, yet being in his arms felt completely natural. We slipped back into it like we'd never spent a day apart. He still knew exactly what I needed and how to calm me. I thought back to Michele's bedroom after I'd smashed the perfume bottle, the infinite number of times I had imagined him holding me since coming back from Verona. Now, when I needed him most, he was here.

He kissed my forehead then tilted my head so he could look at me.

'My turquoise beauty.' He softly stroked my cried-out puffy eyes with his thumb.

I settled back into his embrace, staying there for a few more moments. 'Aren't your parents arriving in Verona tomorrow?' I suddenly remembered.

Max nodded. 'Yes, but I needed to be somewhere.' He caressed my cheek as he looked into my eyes. 'I'll see them in a few days when I get home, they'll understand.'

I tried to push that from my mind, he was here now. Skype didn't offer these senses, touch, smell… taste. I could feel the energy between us. The blood seemed to drain from my head as my heart-rate increased. I wanted to touch his face, to lean in and kiss him but I was suddenly unsure. I didn't want to think about goodbye, of the pain it would stir, not right now. I could feel him shivering. It was December, not a day for sitting outside on cold stone for hours.

'You need a hot shower to warm you up, come on.' I stood, breaking the intensity, distracting myself away from thoughts of intimacy, and led him upstairs to the bathroom. 'I'll make a cup of tea.'

While Max showered I went downstairs, filled the kettle, getting mugs out of the cupboard and adding a teabag to each. I was stunned. Max was here in England. Here in my apartment. My head was filled with endless questions.

I carried the steaming mugs upstairs and found Max in my bedroom, standing beside the bed, towel drying his wet hair, wearing only chequered pyjama bottoms. I leant against the doorframe holding the hot mugs of tea and watched as he pulled a teeshirt out of his bag and began putting it on, taking in his naked chest. His teeshirt fell, highlighting that horizontal line above his waistband I loved. My body tingled. Nothing had changed, I was still incredibly attracted to him.

'You're not going to make me give it back, are you?' he said, tugging at my Damien Rice teeshirt he was wearing.

I quickly moved inside, removing the lustful look from my face and replacing it with a smile, shaking my head as I put the mugs down.

'Is it okay if I take a nap after this?' he asked, holding up the cup of tea. 'It's been a long night. Why don't you take a shower and try to sleep too?'

How could I say no to those eyes filled with concern for me?

I grabbed my phone before heading to the bathroom. I knew Ben and Mel would let me know the instant there was any change, and I could be back at the hospital in twenty minutes. I tied my hair back and let the water fall on my face, not allowing myself to think about anything except the feeling of the water, the bubbles of the soap suds and the smell of coconut from my shower gel. I returned to the bedroom wearing my vest and pyjama bottoms. I felt better for a shower and clean teeth. Max was sitting up in my bed, drinking his tea. He gave me an approving smile as I came into the bedroom and joined him, sitting down next to him, finishing my cup of tea.

'It's strange being here, it's so familiar,' he said, looking around the bedroom, the room where I'd Skyped with him every night for months.

'You've slept there a few times.' I gestured to where he was now sitting in my bed. The very place I had put my iPad or laptop on those nights we'd fallen asleep together. He smiled at me, that wonderful, captivating smile of his. 'Let me ask, you have washed that teeshirt since I left Verona, haven't you?' I teased.

Max nodded, scrunching his nose up. 'Yes, when it started to smell more like me than you.' He leant into me, inhaling me. 'That's the smell I've missed,' he said, tickling my neck with his nose, making me giggle. I'd missed being with him so much.

'I love that you're here,' I said, turning serious, concerned that him returning to England would open old wounds, 'but were you okay, on the flight I mean, I don't want you being here to bring back painful memories. I know you never wanted to come back, you didn't have to, although I'm glad you did.'

'Trust me, it was more painful not being here. Last night, after you went to the hospital, I was pacing my room, I felt helpless. Then when I got your email... I hated that you were afraid and alone and there was nothing I could do. Then I remembered the envelope with your address. I wanted to be here with you so...' He paused, grinning at me. '... I jumped on a fucking plane.' I hid behind my mug, half smiling and half cringing. 'Well two planes actually, there was an early flight via Munich. I was fine, I was so desperate to get here it distracted me from everything else. I didn't know which hospital, but knew you'd have to come home eventually.'

'Thank you,' I said, looking directly into his eyes to emphasise how much I meant it. Max placed our mugs on the bedside table and shuffled down in bed, holding his arms open, moving us into our position, my head back in his nook, our arms wrapped around each other, Max stroking my hair. The way I'd imagined myself sleeping every night since Verona. I closed my eyes and finally exhaled, a breath I felt like I had been holding since Sarah's phone call last night. Last night when Max had been a thousand miles away, a two-dimensional picture on a screen. Now here he was, comforting me in his arms. I slowly absorbed his monumental gesture.

'You stayed awake all night worrying about me, flying to me.' I leant up on one elbow, placing my hand on the side of his face and caressing his cheek with my thumb as I looked deep into his eyes. I loved him so much, that certainly hadn't changed. The way he cared about me. My entire being was urging me to lean in and kiss him, my body ached for him, but I couldn't. My mind was filled with the reality that I'd have to say goodbye again in a few days, which brought with it a deep, sickening ache that struck inside, filling my eyes with tears. I quickly pulled my hand away from caressing his face.

'He'll be all right, he's a teenager, he's just sleeping it off. Remember how much we slept when we were teenagers.' Max wrapped his arms around me, automatically assuming I was thinking about Adam rather than the hopeless dream I had of a future with him. 'Why don't we try to sleep, just for an hour.' He tucked the covers around me, holding me in our position, stroking my hair.

I closed my eyes, listening to Max's heartbeat, thinking back to listening to Adam's heart beating earlier. Adam was alive, that was all that mattered.

* * *

When I woke up snuggled in Max's arms I thought I was still dreaming but as I reached consciousness all of my senses confirmed it wasn't a dream at all, he was really here. I held him tighter, breathing in his scent. My nightmares had lessened since returning from Verona. I still had them but they were more occasional now. Each morning when I woke I remembered Michele was gone but with less anxiety and ferocity. I was, with Max's nightly help, learning to manage it. Waking now however brought with it a new sadness and trepidation. Adam. I carefully turned so as not to wake Max and reached for my phone, concerned I had slept through a text message or call from Ben, but there was nothing. I was supposed to have taken Adam shopping this afternoon for his Christmas present. We would have gone for something to eat, maybe even watched a film at the cinema after. I lay wondering if Adam would get to do any of those things ever again. As if sensing it, Max reached out, putting his arms around me, moving me back to my nook. I glanced up at him, he looked fast asleep still. Did he have a sixth sense when it came to me? I leant up on my elbow and watched him as he slept, remembering doing the exact same thing in Verona, which brought back the dread and sadness I had felt knowing I was leaving, knowing I had to say goodbye, thinking I would never see Max again.

I couldn't fall back to sleep, my mind was filled with thoughts of Adam. I needed to get back to the hospital. I carefully crept out of Max's hold and went to the bathroom, brushing my teeth and splashing my face with cold water, holding pools of it on my swollen eyes, before heading downstairs to make coffee, unsure if I should wake Max or leave him sleeping. As I frothed the milk, Max's arms appeared around my waist, embracing me from behind. He kissed my head and rested his cheek on the side of mine. I rested back into him as I held the frothing milk jug. I could feel the exchange of electricity between us.

'I hope that's a pumpkin spice latte you're making.' He yawned as he spoke, his breath making my neck tingle.

I wanted to turn around and kiss him, remove the teeshirt he was wearing and explore him, rediscover him. It was tempting to let ourselves get lost in each other for a few days but then what? The inevitable goodbye, it wasn't like he was going to stay forever. I thought back to waking alone in the hotel room, to leaving Verona, the pain, the misery of missing him. I couldn't do it to myself, not again. There had been enough pain. The realisation made me stand upright, slightly away from Max as I busied myself pouring the steaming milk into mugs and stirring them. Max sat on the worktop, his head tilted to one side, carefully searching my face, trying to read my thoughts as I handed him his drink. I knew he sensed it. I didn't want to talk about it now though, I needed to get to the hospital. Max insisted I eat something first. It was strange, missing something I didn't have, but having Max there to take care of me, it felt wonderful. On the drive to the hospital he placed his hand on mine on the gear stick but unlike in my fantasies, it filled me with an uneasiness. As incredible as it was having Max there, it was also a painful reminder of what I desperately wanted every day but couldn't have.

As we buzzed the intercom and went into Intensive Care, we were greeted by the beeps and sounds from the equipment surrounding Adam. Sounds that had been foreign to me only a day ago, now familiar. Adam's face was still partially hidden by the equipment breathing for him. Ben and Mel were sitting next to each other on chairs at his bedside. They looked up as we approached, standing and meeting us at the end of the bed.

'Any change,' I immediately asked.

Ben shook his head, looking despondent and exhausted. Mel was looking at Max.

'This is Max, my, friend.'

Ben held out his hand. 'Any friend of Alex's, man.'

Hellos and handshakes were exchanged as I made my way to Adam, leaning over and stroking his hair, kissing his forehead where there was a gap in the equipment.

'I thought I told you to be awake when I got back,' I told him, holding his hand and grabbing my locket. I didn't know why I was willing Michele to somehow intervene, like she was floating around with some magical power, or why I had imaginary conversations with her. I guess it was more comforting than the truth that she was gone forever. I heard my name and turned as Mel asked if Max and I minded if she and Ben went for a walk and to grab some coffee; they needed to stretch their legs but wouldn't be long. I nodded and promised to call if there was any change. A call I felt deep down inside was becoming less and less likely, but I wasn't going to give up hope.

Max joined me and we sat by Adam's bedside, picking up the papers and magazines I'd read to him earlier. The nurse came and greeted us. It was the same nurse who had made me feel comfortable holding Adam's hand, who'd encouraged me to talk to him. I liked her.

'Where are Adam's clothes, his wallet?' I asked her.

She walked back to the desk area and returned holding a large plastic bag.

'Some of his clothing was cut off him,' she started to explain.

'I just need this,' I said, opening his wallet and pulling out the photograph of him and Michele with cake-covered faces, the one he kept with him always, the one that held the power to make him smile. I looked at them both in the photograph, happy, alive. It made the reality seem impossible, how one of those smiling faces was no longer in this world was enough to bear, two was incomprehensible. I steadied myself, swallowing back the tears as I gave the bag back to the nurse, then sat and recounted that day Adam had turned thirteen, encouraging him to just open his eyes and he'd be able to see for himself. He didn't. So I began to read the football stories to him again, the ones I had already read earlier, anything to feel like I was doing something.

After a while, Max put his hand on my arm. I could tell he was concerned about me.

'Let me read for a while.' He took the paper from me.

I sat back, watching Adam intently as Max read, studying his face, hands, body, searching for any slight movement, a blink or twitch, anything to suggest he was still in this world with us, that he could hear our voices, that he knew we were there willing him to wake up, to breathe on his own. To live. Eventually I rested my head back and closed my eyes, allowing Max's voice to soothe me. I put my hand on his arm and left it there, grateful I had him to rely on. Michele had always had my back; even after James left I still had her. Max was now offering me that security of someone looking out for me. I felt stronger by him being there, strength I thought I'd exhausted last night.

Max's movement made me open my eyes; he was standing reaching into his pocket.

'Did I fall asleep?' I asked, yawning. I had a habit of resting my eyes for a few moments and instead falling asleep.

'Yep, your snoring woke some other patients though.' He smiled and winked, teasing me, still knowing how to make me smile.

I looked around but our curtains were pulled across at the sides, separating us from the others. Max carefully leant over Adam, placing the earphones he'd just cleaned in Adam's ears.

'Those newspapers would send me to sleep. What kind of music does he like? Something upbeat,' Max asked.

'Hang on,' I declared, rooting through my bag for my earphones and a splitter I sometimes used at work. I plugged my set in too, placing one in my right ear and handing the other to Max. As he placed it in his left ear I held out my hand for his iPod, scrolling through it and inadvertently hovering over 'Wires' by Athlete, the stirring lyrics appearing in my mind like a soundtrack playing. I scrolled on, settling for 'Time Machine' by Viva Brother. Adam had heard it in my car and loved it, especially the guitars, he'd texted me that night to say he'd downloaded it. I adjusted the volume so it was loud but not ear damaging loud and we both sat, intently watching Adam for any reaction. I shuffled songs by Catfish and the Bottlemen and Royal Blood, two bands I knew he couldn't keep still to, hoping the loud guitars and drums would force him to move. It was a wonderful idea and a much better way to pass the time than reading boring newspaper stories over and over.

Next I chose a song Adam knew from being a few months old. I'd offered to look after him to let Michele sleep. He'd been fussing. I knew he was fed, burped and changed and was unsure what to do so I'd sat on the floor, my knees bent, Adam resting there facing me and played 'Say Something' by James. I'd rocked him from side to side with my legs, singing along like it was a lullaby. It had been a favourite of mine back then, I'd been especially taken with the desperation in the singer's voice as he'd sang about needing a new life. I could still picture Adam as a tiny baby, his eyes widening, his tiny arms flapping to the music as though he were excited by it. Then he'd completely relaxed, stopped fussing and lay, his eyes focused on mine as he listened to this very song. I think that's when we bonded. Now here we were sixteen years later. I sat forward, holding Adam's hand, willing him to wake up, to say something, anything.

I eventually sat back, exhausted. Max put his arm around me and I rested my head on him, closing my eyes, as we listened to Ben Howard's second album, Adam's favourite. Only two weeks earlier I had taken Adam to see him, it was his first concert and I couldn't have asked for a better introduction. I'd made sure to stand relatively close to the stage as where you stand can completely alter your experience, the closer and more immersed the better. They were an exceptional set of musicians and cleverly used stage lights and monitors to create an atmosphere of intimacy. Adam had been mesmerised watching Ben Howard play guitar, live, right there in front of us. I'd excitedly told Max all about it that night on Skype. How I'd watched Adam experience the magic of a gig for the first time. How, like me, Adam couldn't stand still, dancing and moving to every song, the music taking hold. I'd concluded that I'd enjoyed watching Adam's reaction almost as much as the gig itself. I felt like I'd passed the gift of live music onto him. It was also good having something else we could share, an excuse to spend quality time with Adam.

Max nudged me from my thoughts and I opened my eyes to find him wide-eyed, staring at Adam. I followed his gaze to see Adam's eyes... open. Before I could react, they closed again. I shot forward, causing the earphone to pop out of my ear, and grabbed Adam's hand, gesturing at Max to get the nurse.

'Adam, open your eyes again. You're safe, you're fine. It's me Alex, look.' I was willing him to open them again.

The nurse appeared, moving us to the foot of the bed, out of her way as she carried out checks.

'His eyes were open, weren't they?' I needed clarification from Max that I hadn't just imagined it.

'Yes, he opened them for a few seconds, he definitely opened them,' he reassured, placing his arm around my waist and biting the nails on his other hand as we watched the nurse, anxious, afraid of being hopeful in case it was an insignificant reflex that meant nothing. I thought about immediately phoning Ben but didn't want to get his hopes up. The nurse bypassed us, moving to her desk and making a call before returning to Adam. All we could do was stand and watch. A doctor entered, joining the nurse, who updated her on things I couldn't hear clearly and didn't understand. She carried out her own checks, some looked the same as the ones the nurse had already done, I guess she was double checking. She gave the nurse instructions then approached us. I felt my stomach lurch as my insides filled with both hope and fear, desperately willing her to tell us quickly.

'I've assessed Adam's condition and he is now breathing by himself,' she informed us, her words immediately filling me with relief, forcing the tension to leave my body. 'We are lessening the sedation we were giving him to make him comfortable with having the ventilator tube down his windpipe. He should start to become more alert and then we can remove the tube.'

I was repeating her words over in my mind waiting for the 'but,' but there wasn't one. I turned to Max who looked as stunned as I did, still biting his nails.

'It's good news,' the doctor assured us, smiling and placing a hand on each of our arms for emphasis before walking away.

'Thank you,' I shouted after her, a delayed reaction.

Max pulled me in and hugged me. I felt numb, as though I couldn't believe it until I saw it with my own eyes. I was protecting myself, stopping myself getting my hopes up so that they couldn't be dashed. After everything that had happened I was simply too fragile to be any other way.

'I need to call Ben,' I said, releasing our hold and reaching into my back pocket for my switched-off phone.

'I'll do it, you stay here with Adam,' Max offered, taking my phone and leaving the I.C.U.

I stood at the foot of Adam's bed, grasping my locket and thanking Michele.

By the time Adam opened his eyes again Ben and Mel were back. Ben had hugged him, reassured him, kissed him. I smiled, thinking how Adam would be cringing if he wasn't so out of it. The relief I felt when Adam recognised us, that his body worked, that his brain function was normal, that he was going to be fine.

The nurse explained that they were going to remove the breathing tube from his throat as he no longer needed it and put him on an oxygen mask instead. She explained it would be difficult to watch, that he would gag as they removed it but it was completely normal and not to worry. We all stood at the foot of the bed, expectant, terrified, as the nurse explained to Adam what was about to happen. Max had my hand firmly in his. The nurse placed a suction tube inside Adam's mouth, hoovering around. I could see Adam's breathing become more rapid, he was panicking, looking all around, his eyes wide. I knew he was afraid. I grabbed Max's hand tighter. The nurse reassured Adam, talking to him softly and explaining everything she was doing as she began to untie parts of the tube, getting him to turn his head so she could open the strap that was holding it in place, but it was really fiddly and took a while. Adam began biting down on the tube in his mouth, I knew he wanted it out, that he was distressed. As the nurse began suctioning his mouth with the tube, Adam's face turned red, bulging, he was gagging, lifting his head and banging it down on the pillow, thrashing. Another nurse moved to the head of the bed, clasping Adam's head to hold it still. I watched a tear escape and slowly run down his cheek. I released Max's hand and darted over to Adam's bedside, holding his hand tightly and kissing the back of it. I couldn't stand there watching him suffer, feeling helpless. I imagined Michele there. 'I've got him,' I told her in my head.

'Adam, it's all right, look at me, look at me Adam. I know it's impossible but try to relax, it'll all be over soon. Breathe with me.' Adam's eyes focused on mine, just like when he was a baby, and he stopped thrashing. I smiled reassuringly, taking slow, deep breaths, encouraging him to do the same. 'Squeeze my hand as hard as you need to, it's okay,' I reassured him, as the nurse told him to cough, pulling out the tube and immediately suctioning, getting him to bang his lips together. Adam gagged like he was vomiting, clearly distressed, but he didn't take his eyes off mine. Even though I was petrified for him – the tube removal was gruesome – I didn't show it. He was squeezing my hand so tight he surprised me with his strength but I didn't let him know it hurt, I had him, he was okay. I stroked his hair, calming him as the nurse placed the oxygen mask over his nose and mouth and busied herself checking his heart rate, pulse, oxygen levels and so on, telling us they were all good, explaining his throat would be a little sore. I felt his hand relax in mine and saw his face relax.

Adam grabbed the oxygen mask, he wanted to say something but the nurse replaced it, telling him to rest. He slid it down long enough to say 'sorry', his voice breathy, then quickly replaced it.

'You're going to be fine, don't worry. We're all just happy you're all right,' I reassured him.

I knew I needed to find out what had really happened at Tim's. I held his hand in mine and leant down so I was next to his ear, so no one else was privy to what I was about to ask him. 'You remember drinking a bottle of vodka?' Adam looked at me sadly and nodded. 'The doctor asked me if it was possible you were trying to…' I paused, wondering how to word it but I needed to be blunt. '…if you were trying to kill yourself.' Adam's eyes widened and he shook his head frantically, squeezing my hand. I knew from his instant reaction that the thought had never crossed his mind. Relief washed over me. I hated that he'd been the one to find Michele. I couldn't face it destroying him. 'It was just a stupid accident?' I checked. Adam nodded, regret apparent. I kissed him on his forehead, tears of relief forming in my eyes. 'I'm guessing you're done with drinking,' I whispered, giving him a wink. Adam nodded, squeezing my hand.

I reassured Ben and we headed over to the doctor at the desk to confirm it was a stupid, misguided, teenage accident. She informed us that Adam would be transferred to a regular ward soon, that he needed lots of rest but if all went well they would discharge him in a day or so. He would be home in time for Christmas.

16

DECEMBER

We sat on a wall outside the hospital, my head resting on Max's shoulder, his hand on mine. The same way we'd sat on his bench watching the sunset over Verona that first night. Even then, after only spending a few hours with him, I remember feeling a sense of dread at the thought of our time together coming to an end. Now the thought was unbearable. I tried to push it from my mind, breathing in the cold night air, which was refreshing after the stuffy hospital; the silence after the chaos. The doctor had finally convinced us all to go home and let Adam rest, but I needed a moment to gather my thoughts, to try to comprehend all that had happened.

I noticed Max looking at me. He had a grin on his face but I couldn't make out his look.

'What's going on inside that head of yours?' I questioned, smiling.

He looked at me adoringly, the way only Max looked at me.

'You, with Adam, the way you calmed him.' He placed his hand on my cheek, leaning in so his forehead was resting on mine. 'You were incredible.'

I stared into his beautiful, sparkling, once smiling but now serious eyes. The intensity between us made my heartbeat quicken and my breathing shallow. I gazed down at his lips, centimetres from mine. The urge to kiss him consumed me. I'd imagined this moment countless times since coming home but never once in any of my fantasies did Max leave in a few days. It took everything I had but I pulled away, jumping down off the wall and holding out my hand for Max.

'Come on, I need a drink,' I told him, indicating the bar across the road.

As we walked in, we were distracted by the live music coming from upstairs, both stopping at the foot of the old staircase to listen, reading the poster advertising the band, 'Bear's Den,' as their harmonious folk music floated downstairs capturing our attention.

'Fancy it?' Max asked, already knowing my answer.

We joined a room full of people all focused on the stage to our left. I noticed tiered seating to the right, which from a quick glance was full, but I didn't mind, I much preferred being close to the front. I took Max's hand and carefully led him through the crowd, finding a gap. Max stood behind me, slightly to my right as we became transfixed, like the rest of the crowd, on the three musicians before us, giving everything of themselves for our entertainment. The security it bestowed finally allowed me to digest the events of the last twenty-four hours and the sheer quantity of emotions I'd experienced in that short space of time.

Thinking back to last night, to getting the phone call, the panic, the dread, the fear, the helplessness, the memories it stirred. To screaming up at the sky in desperation, lost and alone, on the verge of letting go, realising there was nothing left, that I'd exhausted all of my strength; my limit had been exceeded, never mind reached. The elation I had felt earlier when I'd laid eyes on Max, accompanied by the anguish of knowing I'd once again have to say goodbye to him soon. Finally, the relief that Adam was all right.

The three bearded men stepped to the front of the stage and formed a close semi-circle as they introduced the song, 'Above the Clouds of Pompeii.' The lead singer began to play a tender, soothing melody on his guitar, joined by a second guitar and a banjo. Their ethereal harmonies transported me to another world. I was captivated. The lyrics were clearly personal, anguish visible on the lead singer's face, loss in his voice, his raw emotion commanding the silenced room, briefly connecting every soul watching. I stood in awe. I'd always admired the bravery of songwriters, how they were prepared to relive a painful memory over and over every time they played that song, laying their souls bare for everyone to judge. I hoped they understood how giving so much of themselves helped the takers, those like me, who retreated with their pain, who listened to such inspirational songs and drew strength from them.

As I turned my head to share what a beautiful song it was with Max, our eyes met and his lips were on mine, taking me completely by surprise. Through the shock, my body reacted instinctively, leaning into the passionate kiss, while my head struggled to understand what was happening, screaming at me to pull away, that it would only make saying goodbye harder. My heart was pounding, my brain in turmoil, my senses heightened, all the while being serenaded by this poignant song, as charged with emotion as I was, leaving me powerless to stop Max's kiss.

Our lips eventually parted and we both focused back on the stage, but I couldn't concentrate. My head was swimming with thoughts, confused, trying to process what had just happened, what it meant, fluctuating between elation from our kiss and the sorrow of our reality. I wanted to turn and have him kiss me again. I wanted to rewind to that moment one more time, to savour it, to hit pause and stay there with him listening to those wonderful musicians forever.

Part way through their next song, 'Agape,' tears began to gather in my eyes as the chorus spoke to me, merging with my dread… I didn't want Max to leave, how long did we have? Hours, days, until I was alone again. I didn't want to be without him. Back in Verona I'd naively believed I could come home and slip back into my life and Max would become a wonderful memory. I now faced the reality that a world without both Michele and Max in it was an empty, lonely place. No matter how hard I had tried to get on with living my life, the truth was, it no longer fulfilled me. I had convinced myself that our daily contact was enough, it was certainly better than the month of nothing, but that was when we were a thousand miles apart. That was before Max had dropped everything and flown all night to offer me strength and comfort because he knew I was falling apart. That was before I could feel his breath on my neck and what his touch stirred inside of me, finally forcing me to face my true feelings head on. Why did loving someone always become painful? James, Michele and now Max? Max held my hand, stroking it with his thumb as the chorus built, the passionate harmonies pulsating in my ears. I felt overwhelmed.

I didn't want to lose him, not again, I'd lost enough. My eyes fixated on the door to my right and I found myself bolting through it to the empty roof terrace, my only thought that I needed air.

Max appeared, concern and confusion on his face. He placed his finger under my chin, gently tilting my head so I was forced to look at him. Forced to look into his dejected eyes. I never wanted to hurt him, that was exactly what I was trying to avoid, hurting us both.

'Alex, I don't know what's going on, you've been pulling away from me all day, I thought it was Adam but...'

I needed to be honest with him, I'd been honest with him about everything else in my life. As the words gathered, so did the tears.

'I love you, and I'm miserable without you. I just want...' I broke off, looking down.

'What, you just want what?' His voice was gentle and loving.

I looked at Max through the pools of tears.

'You,' I shrugged. 'Every day. But not on a screen. Time's all we have, remember, spend it with the people we love. But it's not always that simple, is it?'

Max placed his hand on my cheek. 'So let's make it that simple.'

'How? Your life's there, my life's here.' I swallowed hard, shaking my head. 'The thought of saying goodbye to you again.' Saying the words felt like I'd been stabbed inside.

Max wiped away the stray tears that were now escaping, then pulled me close, wrapping his arms around me, holding me tight.

'What if I stay?' he whispered, kissing my head.

'For a few more days? But then we'll be right back here again.' I held him tighter, I didn't want to let go.

'No, I mean what if I stay, here, with you, indefinitely?'

'What?' I pushed back on his chest, out of his embrace so I could see his face, meet his eyes, check I'd heard him correctly.

He shrugged, his eyebrows raised, the corners of his mouth turning into a smile. 'I mean it.' He wrapped his arms around my waist, his flirtatious eyes holding mine. 'I'll stay here in England.' He pulled me closer so our lower bodies were pressed together, that spark within igniting. 'No more pulling away.'

I looked at him suspiciously. 'Are you just saying that to get laid?' I grinned.

'I could play you a Kings of Leon song for that,' he teased, winking as I blushed, before getting serious again. 'What do you say?'

As his words sank in, my head filled with questions.

'But what if you hate England?' I began casting doubts upon his solution.

'I won't. You're here.'

'But all the memories, what if they trigger—?'

'I've never been to Manchester before so there are no memories, nothing here is familiar from back then. Honestly, I'm fine.'

'What if you begin to resent me for making you leave your friends, your life in Verona?'

'You're not making me leave, it's my choice, and I can still visit Verona.'

I hesitated as past insecurities etched their way to the surface.

'But what if you decide you want more?'

Max placed his hand on my cheek, he knew what I was referring to, he could see the fear and hurt in my eyes. 'I won't. I don't see children in my future, I see you, I want to be with you.'

'But what if you change your mind?' I instinctively stepped back as fear bubbled its way to the surface.

'Alex, you need to stop assuming you know what I want better than I do.' He was running his hands through his hair, frustration evident in his eyes. 'You don't get to decide what's best for *us* without giving me a say in it, like you did in Verona. Or tell me I need my friends, my life in Verona more than I need you, or presume children are more important to me than being with you. No. I want you. Why can't you see that? What do I have to do to convince you?'

I swallowed hard, stunned by his passionate outburst.

He took a step towards me and reached for my hand, gently stroking it with his thumb, looking deep into my eyes. I could see the distress in his. As he continued, his words became gentle. 'Alex, I'm not James. I know you're afraid, but you don't need to be. I could never hurt you. If I wasn't certain, if I had any doubts, I wouldn't be here. This might sound corny but when I met you it's like you switched me on, I came alive. I wanted to spend every second with you. Then that month after you left…' He shook his head. 'I was miserable. My days revolve around talking to you but I don't want to talk to you on a screen anymore either. It's all I've been thinking about.' He caressed my cheek. 'This, what we have, it's rare. I was lucky to find it once, but to find it again. Alex, my life is better with you in it. If staying here is what it takes for us to be together, then I'll stay. I don't want to waste any more time missing you when you're right here. Stop pushing me away. We're alive, let's make every day count, let's choose to be happy.' He pulled me closer, resting his forehead on mine, his eyes filled with love. 'In the words of your favourite poet, let me love you.'

I looked into those hypnotic brown eyes, absorbing his words, his honesty, replaying our time together. How he'd shared his favourite place with me because it was what I needed, held me when I needed to be held, tucked an extra blanket around me to ensure I was warm enough, took things slowly and followed my lead, agreed to saying goodbye on my terms, been on the other end of a computer the moment I needed him, dropped everything to be with me when I was in pain. All he had ever done was take care of me, be there for me, make me happy, love me. I didn't believe he was capable of hurting me. I trusted Max most in the world. He'd never given me any reason not to, just the opposite in fact, a million reasons to trust him. When I imagined my future all I could see was Max, he felt like my destiny.

I nodded as a smile escaped across my face, which Max caught, making his eyes sparkle.

'By the way, I love you too,' he whispered, his breath making my smiling lips tingle.

I looked at his mouth, millimetres from mine. My body ached for him. I leant in and kissed him, desperately trying to make up for those lost months. We wrapped our arms around each other, kissing, becoming each other's oxygen, our touch screaming urgency, tears escaping as the reality of the situation sank in. This time tears of happiness. In that moment we could have been anywhere in the world, I didn't care where, I was happy. Max felt like home to me, home wasn't a place, it was being with him. Without him, a part of me was missing. He'd made me not want to be alone anymore, and now I felt lonely without him. He'd become my best friend, my confidante, my lover. In times of happiness, it was him I thought to share it with. When I felt sad and lost or missed Michele, it was him I sought to comfort me. All of my dreams contained him. I held Max tight, I was never going to let him go now I didn't have to.

We made our way home, barely managing to reach the bottom of my stairs before clothes were thrown off and our bodies slammed together, desperate to fulfil months of yearning. I had missed Max's lips on my mouth, my ear, my neck, my breasts. How his body felt pushed up against mine. His smell, I pulled him closer, inhaling him. His strong arms and shoulders. His weight on top of me. The smooth skin on his back, his behind. How my body felt wrapped around him, how it responded to his touch, how he could make my entire body tingle. The intensity we shared as we made love, watching him come undone on top of me then collapse into my arms.

We lay, panting, there on the hallway floor, cushioned by our coats and clothes. Max placed a long kiss on my lips. When our mouths parted, I looked into his beautiful, smiling eyes and ran my fingertip down his nose, tracing his laughter lines, onto his lips, remembering that last night in Verona when I'd been so desperate to memorise every detail of him, afraid of forgetting anything, convinced I would never see him again. I couldn't believe he was here in my arms. Max stroked my cheek as he looked at me the way only he did, I felt adored.

'I love you,' he mouthed.

'I love you too.' We both had huge grins on our faces.

Once wasn't nearly enough to satisfy the craving. Getting a drink of water from the kitchen turned into us making love again. I was powerless to resist Max as he stood naked behind me at the sink, kissing my neck, running his fingertips down my arms and onto my sides, around to my stomach, as one hand caressed upwards to my breast, the other travelled down. I almost dropped the glass in the sink, as his touch resonated throughout my entire body. I'd missed feeling like this, what Max's touch could do to me, heightened by the intensity and love between us. I closed my eyes, leaning back against his chest, my body electrified by his warm skin against mine, his breath on my neck, his expert hands knowing exactly where my body needed to be touched. I reached behind, my fingers in his hair, pulling him into my neck. I slid my other hand up the back of his thigh and onto his behind, pulling him closer so I could feel him pressed up against me, as the pleasure increased until I momentarily lost control of my body, then stilled, my breathing slowing, my body relaxed, my legs weak. Max held me, placing gentle kisses across my cheek, neck, shoulder. He turned me to face him and lifted me so I was sitting on the edge of the worktop, placing himself between my legs. I wrapped them around him and edged forward, our bodies again becoming one. That's how we continued, kissing, caressing, moving together, losing ourselves in each other as we experienced that wonderful feeling of ecstasy.

We finally reached my bed somewhere in the early hours of Sunday morning. We lay in our embrace, both spent from making up for lost time and exhausted from being awake for most of the previous night – me at the hospital and Max flying to be with me – finally falling asleep in each other's arms, completely relaxed, contented and satisfied. For the first time I closed my eyes, and despite missing Michele, I felt a stillness inside.

It was the middle of the afternoon when we woke – I always slept better with Max. After we'd eaten, as I cleared away the pots, Max shouted for me. I walked upstairs to find a bubble bath drawn, surrounded by candles. Romantic and intimate. I lay encased in bubbles, enveloped in Max's arms and legs, listening to the playlist I'd created for us, each song a memory from our time together. Our journey. Max had loved it.

'I know you have plans for Christmas,' Max started.

'We,' I corrected. 'We have plans. Are you sure your parents are okay with you staying here for Christmas? They did just fly to Verona to spend it with you.'

'Yes, they're fine, I promise. I've been thinking though, seeing as we're spending Christmas here, what do you think about spending New Year's week in Verona?' he asked. 'We can go Saturday to Saturday so you're back in time for work.'

I turned to look at him, bubbles sloshing. 'I think that's an excellent idea.'

'I'll book our flights then,' he said, kissing the top of my head.

The prospect of going back to Verona filled me with excitement. I couldn't wait to revisit Max's home, his bar and club, to see those incredible photographs in his office, and our view again, and he could take me to the restaurant with fairy lights.

I lay in Max's arms, watching the flickering candles creating shapes on the tiled wall while listening to our story so far in songs. 'Be Still' by The Fray came on, taking me back to that afternoon after our initial telephone call when I had woken to find that song in my inbox. I remembered how in that moment I'd wanted to leave my life to be with him, yet here he was leaving his life to be with me.

'What will you do for work? What was your job when you lived here?' I'd never thought to ask him before.

'I was two thirds of the way through qualifying to become an architect. It was long hours though, you have to be dedicated, passionate about it. I don't know if I am anymore. I've never even considered going back to it. I guess I've got some thinking to do.'

All the buildings and bridges he'd pointed out, I remember thinking how knowledgeable he was; it made sense now.

'There's no rush though, the bar and club make a decent profit. I can be your house-husband, have dinner waiting when you get home from a hard day at work.' He began tickling me, both of us giggling. I turned to face him. The moment our eyes met, our appetites returned. I'd forgotten that insatiable lust at the start of a relationship. It was fantastic.

* * *

We spent most of Monday and Tuesday in bed, making love, sleeping, talking, laughing, cuddling and listening to music, only dressing to visit Adam in hospital before they discharged him, and for an impromptu trip to the supermarket at three in the morning, which we were forced to make because we were hungry, there was no food in and the takeaways were all closed. Our body clocks being out of sync turned out to be a blessing as we managed to buy everything I had promised to take to Michele's mum's house on Christmas Day while avoiding the crazy Christmas rush of shoppers, long queues and bad moods. We only saw one other shopper the entire time we were there. Max began pretending we'd been locked inside after closing time, discussing what we'd eat first, both choosing things we hadn't eaten in ages. Max craved sugary English cereal, whereas I was caught between the biscuit aisle and jam doughnuts; Max could even make mundane tasks feel exciting.

On Wednesday, I showed Max around my city, his new home. We started at my favourite place, a hidden quadrangle within my old university. He'd shared his favourite place with me, it was only right I shared mine with him. We crossed the normally busy road, relatively quiet with it being Christmas Eve, passing the 1950s grey concrete Student Union building, then the modern glass structure, before reaching the magnificent early 1900s gothic building that stretched the entire length of the road. I led Max through the thick stone archway into the hidden quadrangle. Even though it was only a stone's throw from the bustling street it was like you'd entered another world, offering much needed peace and respite, a place to sit and think. Not only was the architecture stunning, but the building I always sat facing was covered in ivy most of the year, which turned an enchanting deep red in the Autumn; that was my favourite time of the year to visit.

As we sat on one of the black metal benches, drinking our take-away coffees, I thought back to the various times I had sat there alone in a daze over the past five months since Michele's death. I recalled staring at those bare vines clinging to the wall as though they were somehow depicting me clinging to a hopeless dream. I looked across at Max, my dream now a reality. He turned to face me, his bent arm resting on the back of the bench, a confused look on his face.

'What is going on inside that head of yours?' he asked.

I beamed at him, enjoying the feeling of contentment inside and simply told the truth. 'I'm happy.'

We continued the tour, passing the Central Library, the Town Hall, the old banking district, the Royal Exchange theatre and various modern creations, on our way to the shops. I wondered if it would awaken the passion within Max to resume his studies.

After some last minute Christmas shopping we joined friends at my local pub, enjoying glasses of mulled wine around the fire pit in the walled garden. To my friends, Max was a complete stranger, I'd never spoken of him before, yet suddenly there we were, madly in love before them. Max was quiet at first, I knew he was uncomfortable around strangers, but he soon relaxed after a few drinks, especially when the conversation turned to music, then to how we'd met. I enjoyed listening to Max recount our time together, viewing myself through his eyes. I loved the way he saw me.

Although I'd been dreading it, it actually turned out to be a wonderful Christmas Eve. I sat, looking around at my friends laughing, at Max beside me, safe in the knowledge that Adam was healthy and home. The only thing missing was Michele. Nothing would ever be the same without her. I closed my eyes and imagined her there with us, picturing her smile. I could still hear her laugh. I felt that familiar heat hit the backs of my eyes as tears threatened so I looked up at the sky, pretending to look for stars, balancing the tears until they disappeared. I felt Max cover my hand with his, giving it a gentle squeeze. I may have been able to hide my heartache from my friends, but not from Max, he knew exactly who I was thinking about. This time of year made me miss her even more, but then we'd shared twenty years of Christmas times together, it was inevitable.

I woke on Christmas morning a mixture of happiness from being in Max's arms, and sorrow as Michele immediately entered my thoughts, along with Adam and how he must be feeling waking up for the first time in his life without his mum on Christmas Day. I carefully moved so as not to wake Max and reached for my phone, texting Adam,

'I miss her too. We'll get through it together. I'll see you in a few hours. I'm ALWAYS here for you X'

A tear escaped as I wrote it, that void inside more apparent today. I opened the locket and looked at her, which today evoked a smile and tear-filled eyes. I imagined what she'd say to me if she could. 'Look after Adam for me today, hug him for me even if he tries to resist because he's too old, and hug my mum for me, thank her for being the most wonderful mother I could ever have asked for. Remember it's okay to miss me – especially my over-cooked turkey – but focus on being happy, happy's *allowed*. You deserve to be happy.' Tears escaped as her voice appeared in my mind as clearly as if she were on the other end of the phone. I leant up on one elbow, wiping my tears as I watched Max sleep, repeating her words in my head. *Focus on being happy.*

When Max eventually woke, we phoned our parents to wish them a Merry Christmas. My calls were easy but Max had a little explaining to do. It seemed he'd left poor Luca to break the news to his parents when they'd arrived. Fortunately Luca had been singing my praises though and Max hung up smiling, saying his mum was excited to meet me in a few days, suddenly filling me with nerves.

We arrived at Michele's mum's house, exchanging hellos and hugs. I gave Adam his Christmas present, the £250 football boots he'd been obsessed with. The same ones worn by all the best footballers. I had planned to surprise him when we were shopping on Saturday, but instead he'd been lying in a hospital bed.

Adam threw his arms around me. 'Thank you, they're ace.'

He snatched them out of the box to try them on, finding the football shaped odour balls and 'warning smelly boots' hazard sign I'd put underneath. Adam looked at me with a goofy grin, no words were needed, I knew he too was picturing her, holding her nose as she yelled at him to put his stinking boots outside. It had been an ongoing battle between the two of them for years.

I followed Michele's mum into the kitchen, offering help as a pretext to check how she was feeling. She was, as she always had been, utterly organised, she'd always amazed us with how effortless she made it all look. She led me into the dining room where the table was beautifully decorated, and pointed to the sideboard. It was filled with framed photographs of Michele. It seemed she had a photograph of her from every Christmas since she was born, some alone, some with me, with her family, with her dad, with Adam through the years. My eyes filled with tears as they settled on the photograph from this time last year. Only one year ago she had been here in this very room with us, smiling, alive. It made the reality seem impossible. My stomach tensed. Her mum grabbed my hand and gave it a gentle squeeze. A small part of me still imagined Michele walking through the door, or waking up to find it had all been a terrible nightmare.

'I needed her here with us today.' She put her arm around me as we searched the photographs together. She'd included my favourite, me and Michele laughing hysterically as we held up the exact same bracelet we had unknowingly bought each other one Christmas. We had cried with laughter as we opened the exact same present, it was a bracelet of the infinity sign engraved with the words 'best friends are sisters you choose for yourself.' Now I had both of them at home, one of the many things I couldn't bear to part with during the house clearance.

'They're wonderful.' I turned and hugged her. 'She always said you were the most wonderful mum she could ever have wished for,' I told her for Michele.

After dinner, Max and I cleared away the pots and filled the dishwasher while Michele's mum entertained Ben and Mel and their two little ones. They were exactly what she needed today. Happy, giggling children running around was a wonderful distraction for her.

Max pointed out of the window to where he'd spotted Adam. 'Go, I'll finish up here.'

I grabbed my coat and headed outside.

'It's weird, isn't it?' I said sadly, sitting beside Adam on the old swing set.

Adam was looking down, gently rocking back and forth, scraping the soles of his shoes along the ground. 'Yep. At least I'm not expecting her to show up like I used to. It's like I've processed it now, accepted it. For ages I used to think she'd text or call or turn up at Dad's to pick me up.'

'That's how I felt in the restaurant in Verona, I kept expecting to see her.'

Adam stopped rocking and looked at me. 'Did you like Verona?'

I nodded, smiling at the memories of my time there. 'Yes, it's a beautiful place. I can see why your mum fell for it.'

'I like Max by the way, he's nice.'

'I'm glad you like him.'

I thought back to visiting Adam in the hospital on Monday. One of the two times Max and I had managed to get dressed and venture outside. Adam had been moved to a regular ward and

Max and I had struggled to find him at first as Adam had pulled the curtains on either side of his bed for privacy. I greeted him with an enormous hug and he greeted me with the wonderful news that he was being discharged later that day, with strict orders to rest. The doctor had only just made the decision and we were the first visitors, so I left Max with Adam while I phoned Ben. When I returned to the ward, I stopped momentarily as I heard Max and Adam chatting and laughing. I hadn't meant to eavesdrop behind the curtain, I was simply thrilled they were getting on so well.

'That's so cool. I've never met anyone who owns a nightclub before. But if you have all that over there, why move here?' I heard Adam ask.

'Because Alex is here,' Max said.

'But why doesn't she move there with you? She loves music. You own a nightclub and a bar. Seems like a no-brainer to me.'

'It's not that simple. Her life's here, her work, her friends, her apartment, her family, you, she adores you, she'd never leave you.'

As I'd stood eavesdropping behind the curtain, I realised Max was doing it again, putting me first. His life, his work, his home, Luca and his friends were all in Verona, yet he was prepared to give everything up so that I didn't have to.

'Can I ask you something?' Adam said, pulling me from my thoughts.

'Anything,' I replied, slowly swinging back and forth.

'If it was just you and Max, no ties, no job, no apartment, no me. Where would you want to live, here or in Verona?'

I stopped swinging and looked at Adam. 'I don't know, I haven't considered it.'

I hadn't, not seriously. I'd thought about it when I was emotional and desperately missing Max, fantasising about a fresh start, but I'd never considered it as a plausible option.

'Well you should.' Adam looked at me earnestly. 'I know I'm only sixteen, but I've known you all my life. I saw what you went through when James left and the operation. I know you tried to hide it from me, pretend you were fine, but I've got eyes and ears. I've never seen you this happy and you deserve to be happy, it's what Mum'd want. Max told me about his life over there and it sounds great, it sounds like you. I don't want you to stay here because of me, 'cause I'm going to university in a couple of years so I won't be here. I need you to know that if you want to go to Verona it's okay, I'm okay, you won't be leaving me or abandoning me. I know you'll always be there for me, no matter where you live.'

I was stunned and extremely moved. I was no longer talking to a child. No, Adam was now a young man.

'Plus,' he added with a smirk, 'I can come over in the holidays and hang out in the bar and meet cute Italian girls.' We both laughed. He looked directly at me, 'Just think about it like you're free, 'cause you are.'

I nodded, looking into Adam's eyes. 'Wow, you have your mum's wisdom.' It was like I was looking into Michele's eyes, like I was talking with her. That was exactly the type of thing she would have said to me.

Just then, Max appeared carrying two mugs. 'Aren't you two freezing? Here, hot chocolate to warm you up.' He handed us both a mug topped with fresh cream and mini marshmallows, giving me a wink, checking I was all right. As I looked into his eyes I could feel my love for him, it was like the blood pulsating through my veins, I could physically feel it inside of me, it was that strong.

Adam stood to leave us alone, holding out his mug for me to clink. 'Promise.'

'Promise,' I agreed, smiling at him and clinking his mug.

Max sat down on the swing next to me. 'What was that about?'

'Nothing,' I reassured him, turning my attention to Adam, who had reached the kitchen door. 'Adam, will you bring me my handbag please,' I shouted.

He nodded as he went inside, reappearing a few moments later with it, then going back inside.

I placed the mug on the ground and pulled out of my bag a hand-sized box wrapped in silver paper with a large bow, handing it to a confused looking Max.

'Confession time,' I grinned. His eyes were glued to mine. 'You know yesterday when I went wandering off in the bookshop and left you reading on the sofa for ages.'

'For ages, yes.' He nodded, his eyebrows raised, a hint of sarcasm in his voice.

'I wasn't actually in the bookshop. I snuck away to get you this.'

'So early in our relationship and already you're lying to me,' he teased, shaking his head, smiling. 'Wait, I thought we agreed no presents yesterday, you wouldn't let me get you anything.'

'You're paying for my return flight to Verona, that's already enough,' I insisted.

I watched Max intently as he unwrapped the paper. It reminded me of how he'd watched me by the river that day when he'd given me the locket. I held it between my fingers as Max opened the box to reveal a watch. I knew the second I saw it in the window it was the one. Of course it had to be a designer watch with a price tag to match, but it was perfect. It was different, all black, the bracelet and the dial. I liked the way it caught the light and glistened, it reminded me of his eyes. What had caused me to be ages was waiting while I had the back engraved.

'There's an inscription,' I told him.

He turned it over and read the back. It was a lyric from the Josh Record song, 'Bones,' that we both loved, telling him that he'd never be cold again now he had my love to keep him warm. Max looked at me inquisitively, searching my face for a moment; it was that look he got when he was up to something.

'What?'

He shook my question off, smiling as he put the watch on and stood, holding out his hand for me to join him, grinning as he reached inside his jeans pocket for his iPod, placing one earphone in my ear and the other in his, pressing play on 'Bones,' the choral-like harmonies filling my ear.

'I love it, I really love it, thank you,' he said as he swayed us both in time to the music, his eyes still grinning. Then he kissed me, a long, slow, passionate kiss as Josh Record sang to us about loving someone and rebuilding their broken heart.

We were interrupted by cold specks hitting our faces and looked up to see snow falling from the blackness above. I still didn't know why I had such thoughts, I knew they were irrational, but in that beautiful moment, Michele seemed so close. I felt the soft flakes land on my face, my lips, my eyelashes, my tears. 'Merry Christmas, I miss you, Adam's fine, your mum's fine, they miss you too,' I told the sky, in case she could somehow hear or see me. I snuggled back into Max's loving hold, my eyes closed, dancing in the snow to the end of the song.

17

DECEMBER

We slept most of Friday, Boxing Day, exhausted from what had turned out to be a very late night at Michele's mum's house. After surprising Max with my gift of a watch, we'd gone inside to play board games, then when the snow had become heavier, we'd all ended up outside having snowball fights, creating snow angels and building snowmen. It had been heartwarming to see everyone smiling and laughing. I'd hoped somehow Michele could see it too, could see Adam and her mum laughing hysterically as Adam put snow down Ben's back, making him scream and jump around as he tried to shake it out. Catching them in the moment, happy like that, enjoying life again, had been the perfect Christmas present. I'd stood watching them, my hand in Max's, and for the first time I'd had a real sense that everything was going to be all right.

Despite the early hour, I'd arrived at the airport for our Saturday morning flight filled with excitement rather than tiredness. Max had created a playlist with the theme of flying, starting with a band called People in Planes. I'd deviated from our usual genre to share 'The Last Day of Our Acquaintance' by Sinead O'Connor. It contained one simple lyric I'd always believed could read the state of any relationship, about holding hands when the plane took off. Max was relieved he'd passed my test, holding my hand tightly throughout take-off.

Arriving back at Max's house didn't disappoint. In fact, it gave me a feeling of coming home, a comfort like I belonged. I never thought I'd set eyes on it again, not in real life, anyway. We had the house to ourselves as everyone was staying with Luca's parents for Christmas. As Max took my case to the bedroom, I stopped in front of the photographs of colourful blobs and graffiti that I'd previously been unable to identify. Now, with my inside knowledge that Max had taken them in the tunnel at Casa di Giulietta, I found these remnants of people's declarations of love beautiful. I wondered how many had survived the test of time.

When I went into the bedroom, Max had already started to make room in his chest of drawers and closet for my things. I took my toiletries into the bathroom and noticed a spare toothbrush head in the holder. I picked it up, running my thumb along the bristles, recognising it as the one I'd used all those months ago. I remembered how placing it there that morning had made me wish living with Max was my reality, our toothbrushes together, our lives together. How much I'd desperately wanted to stay.

Max appeared behind me, placing his arms around my waist and resting his chin on my shoulder. 'I couldn't bring myself to throw it away. I liked seeing it there next to mine. It reminded me that you were once really here. I thought maybe if I left it there you'd come back.'

I turned around to meet his sparkling eyes, throwing my arms around his neck. 'It worked.' I smiled. 'I came back.'

After unpacking, I suddenly had an urge to see everything again. 'I want to see your bar, your office, walk around, see the amphitheatre, go to our view, can we?'

Max looked bombarded. 'We've got all week, you know.'

'I know, I just want to see it all again. I never thought I would.'

We wrapped up in warm coats and set off, gloved hand in gloved hand, iPod on, sharing earphones as Max played music to accompany our stroll around Verona, making everything even more magical. We crossed Piazza Bra, now deserted, the Christmas markets gone, taking with them the tourists, allowing me to experience the city out of tourist season. We stopped to take in the huge metal shooting star sculpture that stretched from inside the amphitheatre out into the main pedestrianised square where we were standing. It was certainly striking. Max pulled me close, swaying me as R.E.M. began singing 'You Are the Everything' to us, both of us grinning as we looked into each other's eyes, remembering the last time we'd listened to the song, when I'd imagined staying in Verona and being Max's everything. We danced, surrounded by Christmas lights. Verona was even more beautiful than I remembered.

Next, we headed to Max's club, quiet and empty, the complete opposite to that night I was there, which strangely felt like last week rather than months ago. It was closed over Christmas, opening again on New Year's Eve to allow his staff time to visit family and friends. Max viewed time as a far superior currency to money.

'Have you ever held gigs here?' I asked, standing on the dance floor, taking it all in.

'In the club?'

I nodded.

'No, just small acoustic stuff upstairs. Why?'

'It would make a great venue, don't you think?' I was looking around, picturing it, comparing it to venues in Manchester.

'I guess, I've never thought about it.'

'Where do bands play in Verona if they're not big enough to fill the amphitheatre?'

'They don't. You have to go to Milan or Padova.'

'There's no smaller venue here?' I was amazed. Manchester was filled with gig venues, every band played Manchester.

'Well, Villafranca's only a thirty minute drive from here, there's an outdoor venue there,' he added.

'This would be perfect,' I said, walking around, studying the space. 'You'd have the stage there, a raised stage too, so everyone could see the band, I hate venues where you can't see. It'd take a while to get it on the map but imagine bands stopping off and playing here on their European tour, all aspiring to come back one day to play the amphitheatre.'

Max grabbed me, pulling me close like he had the last time we were on that very dance floor. His eyes were smiling. He was looking at me the way only he did, like I was the only other person in the universe. 'Before you get carried away, may I remind you we're going to be living in England.' As he said it, I saw a flash of sadness in his eyes. 'Although it's a bloody good idea. Why didn't I think of it?' He smiled, then placed a long kiss on my head. I noticed the smile didn't reach his eyes.

Upstairs, I headed straight to the office to see his incredible creation in person. I stood before the six framed photographs of the bridge, our view, the beach, the sunflower field, the river, and the wall of love, swept away in memories. This time though the memories filled me with happiness, because for the first time they were the beginning of us, rather than the end. I thought back to leaving this very office that night. I'd felt like I was leaving a piece of my heart behind. I turned to Max, who was now sitting on the sofa staring straight ahead at the wall of album covers, lost in thought. I walked over, sitting beside him.

'Tell me what you're thinking,' I said, holding his hand.

He exhaled, shaking his head, his eyes wide. 'When I should tell Luca and Aria, and my parents, Dante, everyone.' He looked overwhelmed.

'Can they spend a few days getting to know me first?' I asked. 'The woman who's stealing you away.'

Max met my eyes and nodded in agreement, putting his arm around me as I rested my head on him.

'I'm going to miss it,' he said, looking around his office. His gaze fell on me and he began to smile. 'But not as much as I missed you.' He began tickling me until we found ourselves lying down, him on top of me. He stopped tickling me and began to kiss me, which led to us making love right there on his office couch. Something I'd fantasised about many times after our Skype chats, secretly wishing I'd been there in his office with him rather than one thousand miles away. Now I was, and my fantasy had become a reality.

We eventually headed back to Max's house, falling straight into bed, our early morning flight finally catching up with us. As we lay embraced in our position, my mind was doing that thing it did when you were exhausted but couldn't switch it off, thoughts bubbling to the surface. I suddenly began firing questions at Max as rapidly as they entered my mind.

'Where's the local shop? And chemist? And post office?'

'Do you need something?'

'No, I'm just wondering.'

'A five minute walk, and there are a few in town. The local shop nearby sells pretty much everything though.' He began yawning.

'Do you have supermarkets, like in England?'

'Yes, several. There's a huge one a ten minute drive away.' He paused, tilting his head to look at me. 'It's not some third world country you know,' he laughed.

'What about a doctor or dentist?'

'Mine are nearby, Luca has one in town.'

'But how do you understand them, if it's medical terms and in Italian?' I quizzed.

'My doctor and dentist both speak English.'

'Is there anything you don't have, anything you miss that you had in England?' I asked, propping myself up on my elbow and looking at him.

Max shook his head. 'No. The opposite in fact. The pace of life's slower. The food's better, there's a cafe down the road that bakes delicious fresh pastries every morning, and there's my favourite restaurant, I doubt you can get Italian food that good anywhere else. And there's *our* view.' He looked confused. 'Why all the questions?'

'No reason,' I answered, yawning and settling back into our position.

The following morning I woke with a plan, which I shared with Max over coffee in bed.

'You've got stuff to catch up on at the office.' I knew this because he'd told me when we were there yesterday. 'So why don't I go for a walk and meet you later for lunch?'

Max looked shocked. 'I can come with you.'

'No, you go and do your thing,' I insisted. 'I promise I won't get lost.'

I knew the route into town now, my surroundings were familiar and I'd started to remember landmarks. It reminded me of secondary school, how I'd initially got lost as I'd tried to navigate the vast building with endless corridors but after a while the familiarity had made it shrink somehow, along with my increasing sense of belonging after I'd met Michele. That was how I was starting to feel about Verona, like I belonged. I wanted to spend a few hours alone to imagine what it would be like if I actually lived there, give myself time to think. I hadn't told Max because I wanted to see how it felt being back. Assess it as my home. Fully weigh up my options, but I was seriously considering relocating my life to Verona. Every time I pictured our future together it wasn't in England, it was always in Verona. Max was fully prepared to move his life to be with me, but I recognised the sacrifice he was making. I could see the sadness in his eyes. Whereas I found myself craving that fresh start I had always dreamed of, beginning again in a foreign land, away from all the memories of James and Michele. Not that I wanted to forget Michele, but home wasn't the same without her, she was constantly missing, I felt it every day. The emptiness seemed to be pushing me to seek something new. I had spent Friday and yesterday doing what I'd promised Adam on the swing set, thinking about it like I was free.

I decided to sort through my thoughts the old-fashioned way, with pen and paper, as I sat in a coffee shop I'd stumbled upon.

- *Adam – Skype, phone, text. Can fly back in a matter of hours if needed, easily (as Max did). Can regularly visit. Adam can come here in the school holidays. Chase Italian girls. Can keep in touch with Michele's mum. Would be lovely having her over to stay, an excuse to spend quality time together.*
- *Mum – busy living her own life, mostly stay in touch with phone calls now anyway. Max has a landline! Could visit each other. The flight would be shorter than the drive!!! Besides, sun might do her good.*
- *Dad – busy living his own life, mostly text, odd phone call. Can visit each other. Give him somewhere new to go on holiday.*
- *Friends: Would I miss them? Yes, but not enough to stay. Skype etc, plus catch up when I visit.*
- *If I want to go to a gig/dancing/hiking/for coffee – Max.*
- *If I need to talk – Max.*
- *If I need to talk about Max – when have I ever told anyone anything personal about myself?!!! Besides Michele (and Max)!*
- *Work – Take a sabbatical, can always go back to it. Try something new? NEED to learn Italian!!! Help Max develop the club into a live music venue??? I'd enjoy that!*
- *Apartment – downstairs just sold for £220,000 so I'd make £60,000 profit = financial independence while I figure work out.*

I folded my thoughts away in my pocket and wandered around peaceful Verona until I reached Michele's bridge. I rested my gloved hands on the stone ledge and looked out at the view that had captured my friend's heart, where we'd scattered her ashes. I thought back to that day and the person I had been back then, broken. Not even aware of the damage I'd been carrying around until Max had unearthed it. I'd been living in darkness and Max had switched a light on, causing me to face my demons and finally move on. I still didn't know what it was about him, but it felt as though everything up to that point had been a dress rehearsal, filling time until our paths crossed. Max felt like home. Not like other places I'd lived, I mean the way you felt about your childhood home, that nostalgic tug, that eternal fondness. I knew my life with Max would be rich with happiness. The values he held, the way he lived his life, the things he held dear. His view of the world fitted perfectly with mine, we both understood the value of time and the need to spend it wisely. Max complemented me. He completed me.

I closed my eyes and pictured Michele, wishing I could somehow share my happiness with her. She felt close, there on her favourite bridge. I'd been desperately searching for somewhere since I could no longer visit her house and there it was, right in front of me, the very place where I'd said my final goodbye to her, where I'd met Max. I could feel her presence as though she were stood next to me, leaning on the bridge and looking out at the view too, her voice clear in my mind. 'Do you want to go? So go then, forget everyone else, do it for yourself, don't have regrets.' The advice she'd given me all those years ago about that summer in America.

As I looked down at the water, I felt the heavy invisible shackles that had been bearing down on me crumble away. I stood up straight, feeling lighter, filled with clarity. I had nothing to lose; if I found I was desperately unhappy in Verona, Max would move to England, he was already prepared to. He was always putting me first, but now it was my turn to put him first.

For the first time in years I felt certain of what my future held. I knew exactly what I wanted. I had made my decision.

I met Max at our pre-arranged meeting point, the coffee shop around the corner from the hotel where I'd stayed. He looked relieved to find me there, impressed I knew my way around so quickly. After enjoying a mug of hot chocolate to warm me up, Max drove us to our view, insisting it was too cold to walk. We parked on the road before running through the gardens to the far wall and climbing over. I was for once wearing appropriate clothing for scaling walls, jeans and boots. Even with the leaves gone and the trees bare it was still beautiful, allowing me to see even more of the view that had been previously hidden by foliage, including the road far below where Max had first discovered his place of solitude six years ago. I could see the sadness in his eyes as I watched him look out at the view, taking in the city where he'd rebuilt his life. As overwhelmed and honoured as I was that he would leave it all behind for me, I couldn't let him. I rested my head on his shoulder as I collected the words in my mind, about to tell him of my decision when Max placed a small box in my hand causing me to sit up and look at him.

'Open it,' he gently ordered.

I removed my gloves and slowly opened the lid to reveal a slim platinum band set with small black diamonds all around. It was simple, elegant, stunning.

'It's a commitment ring, it symbolises never-ending love.' He picked it up, the diamonds sparkling like his eyes as they met mine. 'You don't have to wear it on that finger if you don't want to but if you ever feel afraid or have doubts, look at it and know I'm not going anywhere, I love you, unconditionally. I know it's only been a few months, but I can't imagine my life without you. I choose to wake up with you every day.'

His words made me smile, it was my version of commitment that I'd shared with him at the beach all those months ago. Another example of him putting what I wanted first. I held out my left ring finger; I knew it would make Max happy. It wasn't about marriage or God or anyone else, it was a symbol of Max's commitment to me, and I was proud to wear it for the world to see. He placed it on my finger – the one he'd looked at in the water to check my relationship status – then kissed it, not once taking his eyes off mine. I wrapped my arms around him, hugging him tight, about to tell him thank you when he spoke first.

'I know you think I've been having doubts, all your questions and giving me space today but I want to be with you. I'm moving to England.' Max released our embrace and faced me.

'But I don't want you to,' I told him.

As he absorbed my words, I saw confusion then panic then hurt hit him. I needed to tell him quickly.

'Because I'm moving to Verona, if that's alright.'

Max was staring at me with a confused look on his face.

'All those questions was me getting my head around it. Me wanting to be alone this morning was me trying on the city, seeing if it fit.' I was smiling, but Max looked stunned.

'What about Adam?'

'You know when you brought us hot chocolate in the garden on Christmas Day and heard us promise something?' Max nodded. 'Adam was making me promise I'd think seriously about where *I* want to live. If I had no ties, what *I* would want to do. He thinks I'll be happy here, so I've been considering it and I think Adam's right.'

'Are you sure?' Max's face was full of concern.

'Max, where would you rather we live, Manchester or Verona? Tell me the truth.'

'If I'm honest, Verona.' He looked hesitant.

'Decision made, Verona it is.' I giggled as I massaged away the worry lines on Max's forehead. 'But I'm going to need another drawer and definitely more closet space. Will Luca and Aria be all right with me moving in? And if Adam comes to stay from time to time?'

'Of course they will.' A smile spread across his face and I saw relief wash over him. I hadn't appreciated the burden he was carrying until I saw it fall away.

He grabbed my hands in his, looking at me intently. 'Alex, are you sure?'

I nodded as I looked into his smiling eyes, the sparkle had returned. 'I wouldn't be saying it if I wasn't certain. I picture our future here. I want to move here. I don't feel like I'm giving anything up. If I hate it then we'll reconsider, but I want to try. We'll still have to go to England next weekend and stay for a few months while I work my notice and sell my apartment and car, and furniture, and change my address, and pack. There's so much to do, I'm going to need your help. And you need to start teaching me Italian and help me apply for a residence permit so I can stay longer than three months. It's completely overwhelming, but I'm excited.'

'You've been looking into a residence permit?' Max looked stunned.

I winked, smiling. 'I've done my research.'

'So you didn't think I was having doubts?'

I shook my head. 'Not for a second.' Max placed his hand on my cold cheek, pulling me towards him to kiss me. 'Wait.' I pulled back. 'You're not going to return my ring are you,' I teased, 'because I really love it?'

He shook his head, laughing, then kissed me, passionately. If it wasn't so cold it would definitely have turned into another Kings of Leon moment but that would have to wait until we got home.

Home. I liked the way that sounded.

Max put on some music when we entered the bedroom, taking my hand in his and softly placing a kiss on it before twirling me under his arm and pulling me close. I recognised the singer's raspy voice, Paolo Nutini, singing 'One Day.' Such a sexy song. It had an old feel, like it was being played on an old gramophone. Max tightened his grip so our bodies were pressed together, slowly moving in time to the music as his eyes intensely held mine. I listened to the lyrics and imagined us old and grey, looking back at those photographs we'd taken with the disposable camera of the time we fell in love. Max began twirling me around and around until I was dizzy, before pulling me in close again. Electricity was surging through my body where it connected with Max's. From the look in his eyes, he felt it too. I rested my cheek on his chest, closing my eyes and enjoying the feeling. Thankful that lyrics about leaving and crying no longer spoke about my life and I could simply focus on the passion of the music. Max caressed my cheek and I opened my eyes to look at him. His eyes were focused on my lips, then his mouth was on mine, our kiss becoming hungry, passionate, our caress urgent as Max removed his jumper, then mine, our bare chests together, then more clothes removed as we found the bed. Max momentarily stopped to tell me I had just made him the happiest man alive, meaning the Verona move, but being with him… it was the happiest I had ever been.

The following morning brought with it fear and dread as I was due to meet Max's parents and Luca's parents, along with, thankfully, Luca and Aria. If anyone could allay my nerves, it was Luca. Max had booked his favourite restaurant in Verona, the one he'd told me about with a ceiling of ivy and fairy lights in the walled garden. Unfortunately, the garden was too cold to eat in this time of year – I'd just have to wait until the Spring to enjoy it.

Everyone was already there when we arrived.

'Are we late?' I whispered to Max, gripping his hand tightly as we walked towards the table. It was important to me that Max's parents liked me, accepted me.

'No, bang on time. Relax,' he reassured.

Luca jumped up, greeting me with his wonderful customary bear hug as he whispered in my ear, 'I knew I'd see you again. Didn't I tell you, you put the sparkle back in his eyes,' giving me a wink as he released me. I gave Aria a hug then Max introduced me to Luca's parents, who each greeted me with a double-sided kiss. Max's dad shook my hand; I could clearly see the resemblance, same cheek bones, but when I turned to greet his mum it was as if I was looking at Max, those sparkling eyes looking back at me. The familiarity of her eyes instantly put me at ease. As I held out my hand for her to shake, she grabbed me, embracing me in a hug. Then she took my hand and led me out into the garden for what she called 'girl talk.' I could tell Max wanted to intervene, but was helpless to do anything.

We sat, me thankful I hadn't had time to take my coat off yet. She was tall like Max and very attractive, her hair in a neat bob, an oversized pashmina wrapped around her.

'I'm sorry to steal you away. Please don't be nervous.' She spoke gently, her words carrying kindness. 'I've just been so desperate to meet you, the woman who's captured my son's heart.'

I felt myself blushing.

'I couldn't believe it when Luca told us how Max had dropped everything and flown to England to be with you. He wouldn't have done that if it wasn't serious.' She gave me a knowing smile as she glanced down at the ring Max had given me yesterday, that I was wearing on 'that' finger. 'Not even me, his own mother, could get him to return to England.'

I began to explain the exceptional circumstances but she stopped me. Concern spreading across her face.

'How is Adam?' She genuinely seemed to care.

'He's doing better, thank you.'

'And what about you? It's a lot, to lose someone.'

I took a moment to assess how I felt in that moment. 'I'm doing okay. Although, that's mainly down to Max, he's really helped me through it.'

As she smiled, her eyes smiled too, just like Max's.

'He told me about you, after you left. Well, after I interrogated him. We Skyped one day and he looked so down, I was worried about him. I never for one second imagined it was because he'd met someone. I knew even before he told me when you were back in touch, I could see it in his eyes, how happy he was.'

Yes, those eyes that gave away his every emotion.

She reached across and placed her hand on mine, giving it a gentle squeeze. 'Thank you.' She looked deep into my eyes as she said it. 'Seeing him happy like he is.' Her eyes filled with tears. 'Well, let's just say, it's been a long time since I've seen him–' Her voice caught in her throat and I gave her hand a gentle squeeze back.

'It's been a long time since I've been this happy too.'

We both smiled.

She stood, clearing her throat and running her palms down

the soft fabric of her pashmina, composing herself. 'Right, we had better get back before Max sends out a search party.'

As we sat down at the table, Max moved closer. 'I'm sorry, I didn't expect her to kidnap you, not before the starter anyway,' he whispered, giving my hand a gentle squeeze. I smiled as I looked down at my hand in his. Now I knew who he got it from.

*　*　*

Max covered my eyes as he led me into the bar, with Luca and Aria following. It looked magical, fairy lights strewn across the ceiling, candles on the tables. I knew it was going to be a wonderful New Year's Eve. Max had just broken the news to Luca and Aria before we'd left home. Luca had been visibly excited and relieved at the same time. He'd been afraid he was going to lose Max to England. It was obvious to anyone that they were more like siblings than best friends and I knew better than anyone how much it hurt to lose that.

As I sat next to Max, my hand in his, time seemed to slow, the busy bar in the background, Max chatting and laughing with Luca and Aria. I felt such contentment, my life had somehow and very unexpectedly fallen into place. Serendipity.

Dante took to the stage, playing a few songs to the already full bar, before announcing the special guest. Max looked at me. He had that look on his face, the look he got when he was up to something, as Dante asked everyone to welcome... Josh Record. I thought I'd misheard Dante at first because of his Italian pronunciation. Then I saw Josh Record take to the stage.

I looked at Max wide eyed. 'How?'

Max was grinning, looking extremely pleased with himself.

'I emailed him, he said yes, I blew the budget getting him over here. I couldn't afford R.E.M. but I thought there's no way you could say no to spending New Year's Eve with me if I had Josh Record playing in my bar. I know how you like to fly around the world to gigs.' He laughed.

'Wait. So you had this planned all along? Before Adam and everything?' I was stunned by his plan.

'Since the start of November. I needed to see you again, properly, not just on a screen, and thought maybe we could work something out. Find a way to be together. I was going to surprise you when we Skyped on Christmas Day and email you a return plane ticket, but turns out I was with you on Christmas Day and you gave me this,' he pointed to his watch with the Josh Record lyric engraved on the back. 'I thought you were psychic. Again,' he laughed.

I remembered the look on his face when he'd read the inscription, like he was up to something.

'So when you asked me if I fancied New Year's in Verona, when we were in the bath?'

Max was nodding and smiling. 'I'd already bought your ticket.'

The love I felt for him. I wrapped my arms around him and placed a long, savouring kiss on his lips before resting my head on his shoulder and watching in awe as Josh Record sang his beautiful song 'Bones' to the captivated audience, Max's watch holding my engraved declaration of love taken from this very song. This song that we'd danced to in the snow.

I thought back to when I'd gone to see Josh on that disastrous date. Then glanced over at Max, who was equally mesmerised by the talent before him. I smiled. We were such similar souls, we truly did belong together.

As Josh began to play 'For Your Love,' Max took my hand and led me to the space in front of the stage, creating a makeshift dance floor. Luca and Aria joined us, followed by others, putting me at ease, people to blend in with. Max placed a kiss on my left ring finger where I wore his beautiful promise to me, a daily reminder of his unconditional love. Then he pulled me close, our arms wrapped around each other, slow dancing as Max sang along to a love song it felt like he himself had written, his declaration of love to me. Our stories now becoming each other's. Here we were at the beginning, our entire lives ahead of us, the possibilities endless. No one knew what the future held but we were seizing the day, living in the moment, choosing happiness. I stared into his beautiful eyes, filled with love and contentment, mirroring my own, as everyone else in the bar, in the world, seemed to disappear. All I could see was Max. All I could feel was happiness.

BEHIND THE MUSIC

Regardless of the reader's taste in music, they will appreciate how *The Bridge* explores the cathartic and uplifting power of music, with music acting as a central theme throughout.

Music was a huge inspiration to the author when writing *The Bridge,* naturally accompanying scenes while she wrote, or inspiring the next part of the story to play out in her mind.

For those familiar with the songs, these well-curated musical moments will add to the narrative of the story and complement certain scenes, as the lyrics and arrangements of music convey what the characters are experiencing in the moment; creating a soundtrack that will resonate with the reader. Especially when Alex and Max begin exchanging songs as love letters.

Which song would you send?

If you would like to listen to Alex and Max's journey in songs, head to Spotify and search 'The Bridge' playlist.

ABOUT THE AUTHOR

SM Tovey has always had stories running around her mind, she remembers being told off at school for living in a fantasy world, but this story was different, it forced her to start writing, pouring out of her, her fingers often struggling to keep up with her brain. Then the real work began, working with a professional editor to develop her writing skills further.

The Bridge was shelved for several years as she became busy with other projects, but she revisited it during the lockdown of 2020, gave it one final edit with fresh eyes, and with encouragement, finally took the leap to share it beyond friends and local book clubs. *The Bridge* is her debut novel.

Follow *thebridge_book* on Instagram or *@The_Bridge_Book* on Twitter #TheBridgeBook

ACKNOWLEDGEMENTS

My greatest thanks goes to Amy, for being on this six-year journey with me, without you there wouldn't be a book. For your unwavering encouragement and support, from day one when you read those first few paragraphs and demanded more. When I reached 12,000 words and we googled 'How long is a novel?' LOL For finding time in your busy life to read and critique, despite living in different time-zones. And for always believing that this story, that fell out of my head, should be a book. That these characters deserved to exist in the wider world. Love you girl, always.

Thank you to Kathryn Hughes, for taking time out from writing her second novel to meet me for a coffee and chat, when this book was in its infancy and I had no idea what to do next. And for recommending my wonderful editor, Tony Fyles. Thank you, Tony, for teaching and pushing me to be a better writer. For your honesty, insight, and entertaining comments. Working with you was challenging and fun, and has been invaluable in my development over the years.

Thank you to Martin Orme, the most incredibly talented digital illustrator, for bringing my vision to life and creating my beautiful book cover. I love it.

Thanks to Trish, for endless memories and inspiration, and Clare, for your continued support, time and giving me that final push to go for it and get it out there.

Thank you to musicians and artists, that entire industry, who continue to create and put themselves out there for our enjoyment, and for the power and connection of live music. Please know how valued you are. Special thanks to the musicians who provided sparks of inspiration throughout my writing. And to Damien Rice, I'd hit a wall and then you released My Favourite Faded Fantasy. I'll never forget lying on my lounge carpet listening to it for the first time as Part Two began to form in my mind. Thank you for inspiring me.

Finally, thank you Scott, for loving travel and music as much as I do, for putting up with me disappearing for hours and hours when I'd lose all track of time as the story poured out of me, and for the endless love, lattes and cups of tea. X

 Matador

For exclusive discounts on Matador titles,
sign up to our occasional newsletter at
troubador.co.uk/bookshop